SHATTERED LIFE

AN AJ CONTI NOVEL

SHATTERED LIFE

James A. Bacca

LUMINARE PRESS

WWW.LUMINAREPRESS.COM

Printed in the United States of America

Cover Design: Melissa K. Thomas

Luminare Press
442 Charnelton St.
Eugene, OR 97401
www.luminarepress.com

LCCN: 2019910754
ISBN: 978-1-64388-208-6

To my wife, Kristina, for being my guiding light through it all. Her love of the original idea for this novel fueled my desire to bring it forth.

ACKNOWLEDGEMENTS

MANY THANKS TO THE PEOPLE WHO HAVE READ, edited and advised, especially Jean Young and Stuart Horwitz, who I have grown to admire beyond editing.

Many thanks to our dear friend Beth Woods for all of her encouragement over the years.

CHAPTER ONE

Turlock Police Detective AJ Conti drove north on Geer Road to follow up on his homicide investigation. With his window down he enjoyed the crisp central California morning air while singing along to his streamed music.

The police radio squawked and a dispatcher advised a patrol sergeant of a man acting wildly in his driveway... armed with a rifle and machete. AJ knew dayshift meant there were less available units and being five blocks away he decided to back up the sergeant. He knew if it turned nasty detectives would be called out anyway.

The residential area looked relatively new with manicured lawns, front yard trees per city ordinance, all less than ten feet tall, and no broken down cars parked in the road or up on blocks in the driveway.

The patrol sergeant arrived seconds before AJ and both could see the man in the driveway wearing only jeans and holding weapons. The sergeant parked on the opposite side of the street while AJ parked on the driveway side. If the man decided to lower the rifle, AJ wanted to make sure he and the sergeant were not in the same line of fire. The sergeant approached until he stood on the sidewalk directly across from the man.

AJ stayed on his side and walked slowly until he made it to the front of the house. He stepped behind a Ford Ranger in front of the house for cover, and his Glock remained trained on the man while the sergeant spoke. AJ could hear the man complaining of his wife trying to leave him after he got fired for using drugs. Far more important than the man's words were the non-verbal factors which the sergeant seemed oblivious to or he would have had his weapon out also.

In the man's left hand he held what appeared to be an older single shot .22 rifle. AJ felt he had to be right handed when he saw him holding the rifle mid-barrel nowhere near the trigger. In the other hand, the man waved a Kukri Machete around wildly and pointed it at the sergeant when yelling. A few feet to the right of the man AJ saw a puddle of fluid and it seemed pretty clear it wasn't motor oil. Not to mention the blood covering the guy's chest had to come from somewhere.

AJ's gut told him the guy's wife had to be inside the house, probably cut up all to hell. He couldn't let the sergeant continue to baby the situation if they had any chance of getting inside and possibly save the woman.

"You're wife's in the house, isn't she?" AJ said.

"Who the fuck are you?" the man yelled, pointing the machete in AJ's direction.

"I'm the detective who's going into your house to check on her."

AJ took two steps toward the driveway, his Glock locked on the man's chest. AJ ignored the fact he had moved under the twenty-one foot distance rule they were warned about in academy training with knife attacks. But in situations like this, AJ felt those rules were more like *suggestions*. He had to make a move…the chances of a machete not causing serious harm to the woman and her bleeding out were slim.

Not everything needs a standoff and a negotiator, he thought.

"Why'd you do it?" AJ asked, employing the element of surprise while the guy tried to figure out what to do.

"She slept with my best friend. I wasn't gonna stand by and let it happen a second time."

"She was going to leave you anyway, you getting fired only made it easy." Another statement to keep his mind occupied. He'd either fold or get pissed off. Either one would work for AJ.

"Now, put down the weapons…I need to check on her."

The man remained quiet for a second until he realized what AJ said.

"Fuck you, man. You ain't going in there without going through me first." He dropped the rifle at the same time he raised the machete.

AJ took two more steps, whispering loud enough for him to hear, "Have it your way."

The man's eyes broadened, visibly caught off guard by the comment. When his eyes squinted with anger, AJ knew it would be over soon, one way or the other.

The man barely took one step closer when AJ put two rounds in his chest and one in his head. AJ looked at the sergeant, motioning for him to cover the man, before he raced into the house.

AJ wasn't sure what other parts of the house may have been attack spots but the living room had blood spatter all over the place. He spotted a woman's foot in the kitchen sticking out past the cupboard and seeing the huge swath of blood on the carpet she had clearly crawled there.

As he started toward her he saw her other leg in the middle of the living room. A knife in her hand, the woman somehow had the strength to arm herself with a knife from the kitchen counter before she passed out. AJ felt for a pulse, astonished when he felt a faint one.

"Sarge, get an ambulance here. Quick," AJ roared.

He leaned over, inches from her ear and whispered.

"You're amazing. Hang in there, we're going to get you help."

CHAPTER TWO

Todd sat in his house on Rose Avenue in Turlock, California, thinking about how far he had come. Lying on his couch with Streak, his cat, Todd's mind drifted back to a dozen years before.

Keeping things private or personal in a foster home was difficult, but he worked hard to keep his name and feelings locked away. He chose to use his middle name, vowing never to use his first name once he set foot in the first foster hellhole, a far cry from being a home. His name would be private, something no one could take from him. As far as he was concerned, his first name died when the rest of his family had been taken from him, and his new life would never resemble his past one.

He had been dealt three blows in a row; his family being erased, being placed in a foster home where he received regular beatings, followed by a foster home where the man preyed on the younger ones with his wife indifferent to his action.

Todd knew, even back then, the person responsible for sending him to the abyss of foster care would pay for it. His goal to live in his mind only lasted until he got revenge… beyond reaching his objective he did not care.

His struggle centered on hearing things his parents told him about how to treat people with respect and kindness.

Doing as they taught him came easy. Watching out for weaker kids in foster care, helping co-workers out during the holidays, and treating patients at the hospital where he worked with tenderness made him feel good.

Experiencing the system letting people down, along with seeing those who not only allowed it but did nothing to change it, led to a growing anger within him. He believed if any of those people experienced what he went through they would not be so willing to cover or protect those who do wrong, especially to children.

I'm sorry Mom, Dad, he thought. *Some people don't deserve respect and kindness.*

TODD'S THOUGHTS SHIFTED TO SAMARITAN HOUSE, a group home for boys. It was a beautiful two-story Victorian home with six bedrooms, a large dining and living room, enlarged kitchen to accommodate the boys, and three bathrooms. Upstairs were four bedrooms, along with two bathrooms. One downstairs bedroom belonged to the counselors, with the second used as a *privilege*, which had to be earned. Todd earned the benefit of having the room to himself, but instead, he shared it with Peanut, a younger boy aptly named for his size. Thanks to Todd nobody messed with Peanut.

When he first arrived, Todd recalled taking inventory of the eight other boys. He learned from previous foster homes an unofficial ranking always existed…toughest to weakest. The weak ones were regularly used for chores, often being ordered around almost slave-like. At some of the homes, the weaker ones were used for sex and not only by other foster kids. He pledged never to be a weak one, although he got tested in each home. Protecting himself from several foster "dads" led to Todd being moved around more than most.

He was sent to a group home after an incident with his last foster father sodomizing one of the younger boys. Todd had a sock full of rolled quarters hidden in case he needed to protect himself. He raced to his room, grabbed the sock, and sprinted to the young boy's room. The man, still on top of the boy, never saw Todd. He struck the man above his ear, splitting his head open. While the man lay on the floor, pants down around his knees, bleeding severely from his wound, Todd ran to the kitchen and grabbed a knife, prepared to remove the man's genitals. The man's wife stopped him by covering her husband with her body, begging Todd not to kill him. Todd was never charged since the couple couldn't tell the truth about what really happened. The male foster care social worker refused to listen to him, telling Todd he was incorrigible, followed by transferring him within hours.

AT THE SAMARITAN HOUSE TODD INSTANTLY RECOGnized the leader, a tough looking white boy who the others called "Taz", short for Tasmanian Devil. Although Caucasian, Taz liked to dress and talk like the Mexican gangbangers dominating the area. Taz was sixteen, fairly muscular, with a shaved head except for the six-inch ponytail growing out of the middle of the back of his head, held together with two hair ties.

When Taz first walked into the room he stopped, staring at the new arrival. Leaning to the side he jutted his chin back and forth as if to say, "You'll be mine."

"Hola, carnan," Todd said.

"I ain't your fucking brother," Taz snarled, his fists curling by his sides at the same time he stuck his chest out.

Todd returned the stare, holding it until one of the counselors stepped in between and directed Todd to his new room.

He remembered thinking he would have to act soon or the ritual Taz would exact would be long and arduous. When given time to roam the house to get acquainted with it Todd began gathering his tools. He found a pair of six-inch beard scissors in one of the counselor's shaving kits. In the kitchen he located the flatware drawer, deciding he'd get one of the forks when he volunteered to do dinner dishes. Once he figured out where Taz slept his recon was complete.

At thirty minutes past midnight Todd decided he had waited long enough. Having checked the doors earlier he knew they would not squeak…he slid out of his room. He opened the door to Taz's room waiting to make sure Taz and his roommate were asleep. He placed the scissors in his underwear, and put the fork in his left hand. He was acutely aware the first steps of surprise and control were crucial to his success. He moved closer to the bed, ready to abandon the plan if Taz displayed even a hint of alertness. Standing over the relaxed snoring body face down on the bed, he recognized his future was at stake.

Todd knew taking care of Taz would change not only the living conditions the rest of his time at The Samaritan House, it would also change his self-confidence about his capabilities to handle any situation.

In one swift motion Todd's left knee hit the back of Taz' neck at the base of his skull at the same time he pushed the fork prongs into his left carotid artery. Taz' ponytail had been perfectly off to the side as if it had been scripted, making it easy for Todd to position his scissors at the perfect angle. Taz went from a dead sleep to totally at the mercy of someone he couldn't even see. Todd held his position long enough to make Taz realize he no longer had control. He bent close to Taz' ear while giving one more tug on the ponytail.

Todd whispered, "I'm not a threat to your kingdom, but you fuck with me, I'll cut your head off and shit down the hole."

The next morning Todd got up before any of the others had stirred so he could replace his tools. At the breakfast table the other boys were whispering until Taz got up and stormed out the front door, his ponytail reduced to a stub. Taz' roommate looked at the other boys, smiled and pointed at Todd saying, "He's Da Man!" For the next four years only the counselors, and Taz, called him Todd, the others saluted him as *Da Man.*

CHAPTER THREE

D ani Larson sat in the dark in her home in northwest Turlock, California, taking a mental break from trial preparation. Holding a soda, she stared at the constant flow of lights moving across the flat screen...the volume on zero. The room seemed still, the only sound coming from the aquarium filter, while every detail of that long ago warm summer evening stayed locked in her memory.

THE GAME WAS IN MADERA. HER TWIN BROTHER DAVID played shortstop for the Turlock North All-Stars. Dani loved watching him play because of his love for the game and though they squabbled, the two were best friends.

Men were always telling her father how good David played, especially for only being ten. The youngest boy on the team, David was smaller than the other boys, except for when he played the game.

Dani could see his face. His smile stood out, his blondish hair and blue eyes made it even brighter. Unlike Dani, he took very little seriously. David enjoyed life, and everybody loved him.

The game had been close the entire time and with one out, and a runner on third, David came to the plate. Dani fidgeted, chewing on her fingernails. Before stepping into the batter's box David looked in the stands to find Dani. He smiled as if to tell her it would be okay. Dani softly put her hand on her mother's leg.

"David's going to score the runner," she said matter-of-factly.

"How do you know?" her father asked.

"He told me," she said. Her parents looked at each other, both questioning exactly how strong their children's bond really was. They often said what the other had on their mind, amazing their parents when they never corrected each other.

David stepped in the box looking as relaxed as always. On the first pitch David pivoted, slid his right hand up the bat executing a perfect suicide squeeze to score the runner, putting his team ahead for the first time. Jogging back to the dugout David winked when he looked at Dani.

"I told you," Dani said, without looking at her parents.

In the bottom of the seventh inning with two outs, runners on second and third, David made a diving catch to end the game. The victory meant the Turlock North All-Stars would be traveling to Fresno in three days, playing in the Sectional Championship game against the Fresno East All-Stars.

THE NIGHTMARE OFTEN RETURNED, THE DETAILS OF THAT fateful day generally the same.

She could see her family car driving north on Highway 99, and David talking nonstop. Despite being well past their bedtime, she and David were wide-awake. Passing the signal light at Delhi, a few miles south of Turlock, they were getting close to home.

Their mother, turned to face them, her arm on the top of the seat, her head resting on her arm. She had such a warm smile on her face, and not saying a word, instead listening intently to them talking.

Dani reached over touching David's arm when the thick patch of Eucalyptus trees next to the railroad tracks appeared.

"We're getting close to Hobo Junction," she said.

"Maybe we might get lucky," David said.

They loved "Hobo Junction," especially in the daytime when they could see it better. Even though they had never actually seen a hobo, they still got excited every time.

Their father had told them stories about how the hobos would always stay in the grove of Eucalyptus trees, which provided shade from the heat in the summer along with shelter from the cold misty layer of tulle fog in the winter. The Eucalyptus grove supplied the only protection near the tracks for miles in either direction.

David scooted to the middle of the seat so he could lean next to his mother. He said he could see the green street sign for Bradbury Road, the old country road crossing Highway 99 near "Hobo Junction." Dani could not see anything when she tried to look around the right side of her mother's head. She stayed in her seat looking out her window.

Dani heard the fear in her father's voice as he bellowed "Oh my God." Before she could move her eyes, Dani heard her mother scream.

Everything began moving in slow motion as light filled up the car all around her. Dani looked to her left. No longer on the seat next to her, David began to drift over the front seat, floating in the air like when the magician did it on TV.

Dani felt the seatbelt begin to push on her stomach as her body slowly bent in half. Thrusting backward after the belt had stopped her, she no longer saw David. Her head struck the window frame behind her ear causing her to black out.

Dani woke with a young man dressed like a hobo standing over her. The stench in the air made her sick as she looked around trying to figure out where they were. Her mind could not register what the man kept saying, but the realization of the accident began to become clearer.

The pickup truck smashed the front of their car into the front seat causing thick, black smoke to billow from the vehicles. The car on fire in the middle of the road a few hundred feet away no longer looked like her parent's car.

Dani's head started to spin when she realized her family had not gotten out of the car. Tears began flowing as she wrapped her arms around her drawn up legs, rocking back and forth in the road.

"No, no, no ..."

DANI BOLTED FOR THE BATHROOM, VOMITING FROM THE smell embedded into her memory. She rinsed her mouth out several times before wiping her face with a damp washcloth. Knowing she wouldn't sleep, she shuffled across the carpet to the living room letting her mind wander...for a brief second settling on the hobo.

I wonder where he ended up, she thought.

At the accident, Dani had lost track of the hobo. The paramedics tried telling Dani only emergency personnel were there and no one saw a hobo. They also told her flying through the window saved her life. Despite Dani trying for a long time to convince people a hobo had unlatched her seatbelt and pulled her from the burning car, nobody ever believed her.

The morning after the accident her belief was confirmed. The nursing staff had stepped out leaving Dani alone, her head propped up with her eyes closed. She did not hear anything, but she opened her eyes when she felt his presence. She had no idea how long he had been there.

Although they had never spoken to each other and she did not know him beyond him saving her, his presence did not scare her. Neither knew what to say as their eyes filled with tears. The hobo seemed to be as uncomfortable visiting her as she felt not knowing what to say.

She remembered he had laid Raggedy Ann and Andy dolls beside her, softly rubbing the hair from her forehead and squeezing her hand as if to reassure her.

She recalled he looked young, like a teenager, although she couldn't remember much of what he looked like other than his dark eyes. She could see hurt and compassion went deep into his soul.

Dani recalled staring at each other for a few seconds, thinking there really were hobos in "Hobo Junction." Instinctively she wanted to tell her father, followed by reality returning. Dani remembered crying after he left, repeatedly asking herself the same question, "Why did he have to save me?"

Although she no longer asked herself the question, she often wondered why her whole family had to be taken in such a way. Despite the fact it had been nearly twenty years Dani could close her eyes and picture her family as if they were still there. The family who adopted her had been wonderful, and she loved them dearly. Dani promised herself never to forget her real family and spent countless hours trying to remember the details of her early life.

The little dimples on her mom's cheeks when she would smile, and the beautiful long blond hair softly draped over her shoulders were embedded in Dani's memory. She could recall the unique smells of her mother's favorite body splash and shampoo, comforting Dani when she needed to be held as a little girl. She could hear her mother laughing as she had so often.

Dani could feel her father's gentle strength as if he were hugging her once again. She could always pick up the hint of his cologne under his short beard. His strictness came in his look. With it he could tell her of his disappointment, while at the same time telling her he understood. She could picture it easily.

Even as a child Dani knew her parents loved her, but it wasn't until several years later before she realized how wonderful they really were.

Missing her parents did not compare to her harrowing feeling of loneliness from not having David with her. Dani felt half of her died that night. David had been born a few minutes before Dani and seemed to watch over her naturally from the time they could walk. They knew how each other thought, could feel what the other felt, and could sense each other's feelings. The tie went beyond the beautiful friendship they had; their souls were like one.

She never got to see David again. People at the hospital were nervous around Dani, and no one explained to her what actually happened.

Dani recalled asking one of her nurses about David. The look on her nurse's face, followed by the speed the staff left the room, told her David had died, too. She cried until she could cry no more.

Strangely, David's soul somehow seemed to be with her, she could feel him like she used to before the accident. Dani felt lonely—not alone.

CHAPTER FOUR

Suzi Anderson sat in her Madera, California, apartment, and reflected on how she could never have guessed her life would change so dramatically. Only months before Bethany Walker had saved her from the hell she experienced living with her boyfriend. Now she had a secretarial job she absolutely loved, working for the social workers at Madera Children's Hospital. The only negative was Bethany, her favorite social worker who became like an older sister, had left a month ago.

Suzi remembered the first time they met like it was yesterday.

"I'VE BEEN WATCHING YOU," BETHANY SAID. "YOU'RE walking around aimlessly. Let me help you?"

"How can you help me?"

"I'm a social worker at a hospital. I know a lot of people who could provide care and assistance for you. You would have to trust me though. Please, let me help you?"

Suzi had become bitter knowing a lot of people back home in Georgia would have helped someone on the streets like her.

"Not a soul here has stopped or offered me the least bit

of help…until you," said Suzi.

"At least sit in my car, try to warm up for a few minutes. I promise you can get out whenever you want."

"It would be nice to warm up. I never realized how cold this fog can be," Suzi shared, her arms tightly hugging her chest while walking with Bethany to the car.

"If you don't mind, how did you end up on the streets?"

"Two years ago my mom passed away from breast cancer," Suzi said. "I lost my best friend…I never felt so alone in my life."

Bethany listened with compassion.

Suzi described meeting a boy shortly after the funeral and he seemed kind, even understanding at first, so she never saw it coming. Not once had the boy laid a hand on her back home. But, things changed in California and the beatings became regular.

"I really believed he would kill me someday."

Bethany took Suzi in, paid for her attorney, and helped her get a restraining order. Suzi lived with her for nearly three months. Bethany seemed to know everyone who could help Suzi regain control of her self-esteem and her life, including the secretarial job at the hospital. Bethany restored Suzi's faith in people.

By the time Suzi moved into her own apartment she had joined the choir at church, and began volunteering at the shelter for battered women. Suzi now loved life and like Bethany, providing care for others had become her new mission.

IN THE PARKING LOT OF MADERA CHILDREN'S HOSPITAL

a balanced mix of excitement and sadness filled Todd's body as he sat in his car.

Before a long stay at a hospital years before, Todd's life seemed wonderful. His parents were kind and gentle, always showing him their love and telling him how proud they were of him. His sister had been the kinder of the two of them. She cared about him and his accolades more than he cared about hers…he knew she made him a better person. He missed them all wondering how different life might have been if they were still together.

Todd's young age at the time, and the trauma he suffered, led to his not remembering what hospital he had been taken to. Making matters worse the ambulance companies in the area where his trauma occurred had closed long ago, increasing his difficulty in figuring everything out.

Thus, his excitement at being back at the place where it all started caused goosebumps on his body. The hospital represented the beginning of pursuing his goal of making *her* pay for sending him to the dives in Fresno known as foster homes, where exploitation of funds not used for their intended purpose and sexual exploitation of the foster children were common. With his plan in place, he could finally move forward.

He found the perfect suit and tie at Goodwill and along with thick black-rimmed glasses he had an educated look. He had achieved his desired look to carry out his plan.

The signs inside the hospital were a little confusing, but a young volunteer turned out to be helpful and her directions led him to the auxiliary offices. Two women discussing lunch walked out of the door labeled Social Workers.

He entered and heard the lone office assistant talking on the phone. He checked her nametag before scanning the business cards on the far left counter. Something was wrong.

Though he had scoured the employee parking lot he never saw the car or license plate he had been seeking. And now, no business card.

I paid that bloodhound to confirm she still worked here, he thought. *If the lame fuck ripped me off he's gonna pay.*

His first inclination was to act like he walked into the wrong office and leave before she hung up. Before he could turn and leave, she replaced the phone in the receiver.

"Can I help you?"

I've got to do something and quick.

"Hi Suzi, I'm Michael," he lied. "You have a beautiful accent. Let me guess, somewhere in the south?"

Her dimples appeared. "Georgia. About an hour outside of Atlanta."

"Really…what the heck brought you here?"

"Followed a boy," she said with pure disgust.

"I know, pretty stupid."

There's my shot, she's gullible following a guy all the way out here, he thought

"Ah, don't be hard on yourself," he said. "How are you supposed to know if you don't give it a try? You can always go back."

Looking straight into her eyes he shrugged his shoulders.

"Not everyone is bad you know. Besides, as pretty as you are you've probably already replaced him."

Blushing, she said, "Not yet."

Bingo.

"Would you…maybe like to have lunch with me?" he asked, lowering his head, hoping to appear more modest than coy.

The possibility of being with someone so nice, and the bonus of his being cuter than the last one, instantly made her want to say yes.

"I...I don't even know you," she said, fighting her impulse to say yes.

"You're right, I'm really sorry," he said, looking down and backing away. "I didn't mean to make you uncomfortable." He turned toward the door, thankful he had not exposed his reason for being there.

She smiled, "I can't believe I'm about to say this. I can't go until twelve-thirty. I have to wait for at least one of the social workers to get back."

He turned to see her smiling, her knuckles white from her hands rubbing together, and her shoulders shrugged.

"I might as well have a nice lunch since I came all the way down here," he shared. "How about sandwiches, maybe over at Woodward Regional Park, it's close by. I saw a little deli not far from here. We could at least have a little time to talk. What do you say?"

The nervousness in his voice and his fidgeting gave her a good feeling. His smile is what made her give in. Familiar with the sandwich shop Suzi gave him her favorite order.

He's a gentleman, too, she thought when he refused to take her money.

He turned to leave.

"Wait, Michael. What is it you needed?"

"Oh yeah," he said, rolling his eyes. "Between you and your accent I forgot all about it."

Suzi lowered her head, looking up at him with smiling eyes.

He hesitated, knowing if he answered her she would be a witness. He felt perspiration building and hoped she did not see it on his forehead. But, his need to know won out.

"I came here looking for Bethany Walker, but I didn't see her business card. She used to be my social worker when I was here as a kid. I owe my life to her." He started to pull out an envelope with a card in it from his inside jacket pocket, making sure she saw it.

"You're so sweet," Suzi said in her slow, melodious southern tilt.

"I know exactly what you mean, she's the one who helped me get away from the jerk I followed out here. She's wonderful. It's not very often these ladies get to hear those kinds of special things. I'm sorry though, she left about a month or so ago."

"Ahhh, man, I really wanted to leave this for her today. It took me a while, but I wrote her this special note." He looked at the card, lowering his head and slumping his shoulders.

"I think I can help," Suzy said, calling him closer with her right index finger. Looking around first, she whispered,

"Bethany recently sent us a card letting us know how she's doing. She works at Emanuel Medical Center in Turlock now. I'll get her address and bring it with me." Sitting back in her chair with a huge smile, she said, "Now, get outta here and go get those sandwiches. I'm starvin."

CHAPTER FIVE

A s they finished their lunch, Michael shared, "It's too bad you have to go back to work. It's been great talking with you and getting to know you a little. I've really enjoyed myself."

"I have, too." Suzi softly placed her hand on top of his. He smiled.

"You relax. I'm going to throw all this away." He looked around the park on his way to the trashcan. Walking back he had yet to see anybody else in the area. Moving behind her he gently put his hands on her shoulders.

Smiling, she laid her head back, looking into his eyes.

"This has been wonderful."

With a fake smile he winked at her. She rolled her head forward as his fingers massaged the back of her neck and he scanned the park one last time.

In less than three seconds he buried the blade of his Bowie knife up to the indent at the base of Suzi's skull, the forty-five degree angle taking out her brain stem.

His eyes darted back and forth, sweeping the park for any movement. Feeling at ease, he took a deep breath. He laid Suzi's lifeless body across the table, her head positioned sideways on her arms as if she were taking a nap.

He wiped his blade clean on her skirt before reaching

into her purse to retrieve the paper with the address. He looked at it, then at her.

"Thank you, Suzi." He softly brushed her hair one time, a twinge of sadness overcoming him. Knowing he could not leave a witness who could identify him did not always make the kill easy. *I kind of wished she would have let me go*, he thought. *I liked her.* He stroked her hair one more time.

Todd was overtaken by the juxtaposition of having to kill Suzi, while feeling he needed to make sure nobody violated her or disturbed her in any way. She was at peace and he needed to make sure she stayed that way.

Walking to his car he surveyed the park again and got in when he felt pretty certain there were no onlookers. He slowly drove away. Well away from the park he made a U-turn; creeping back into the area he pulled to the curb so he could ensure she was protected.

Sliding on a pair of latex gloves he wrote Bethany's name and address on an envelope while he checked the park every few seconds. He opened a drugstore card with a picture of a stick figure next to a basic square house like a child would draw. The fact there were no words made it a perfect choice.

Bethany Walker,

The kid on the front has a better house to live in than what I did.
You could have done more.

From Your Past,
S

From his car window he looked at Suzi and saw a homeless man walking toward her. He knew from experience where you see one, there are more nearby. He set the card on the passenger seat, and got out of the car, drawing the Buck General Bowie knife from its sheath once again.

Staying behind trees as he approached, he kept an eye on the homeless man. At the same time the man reached for Suzi's purse Todd came up from behind. Pulling back on the man's forehead with his left hand, he put the knife to his throat, pausing for effect.

"I can identify with you better than I can with her. So, I'll give you one chance to live. I *will* kill you if you screw it up. You understand?"

The homeless man, stiff from fear, managed to nod.

"You're going to leave her exactly like she is. Nothing moved or taken. Make sure you tell all the other trolls the same thing. I'll kill you all if I have to. You'll go back to whatever hole you crawled out from under like I never existed. You look at me…I'll kill you. Now…how many of you live over there?"

"Four," the man said, his voice shaking. "Me, my old lady, Baggy, an old guy we kind of help out, and Shrewd, Baggy's friend. He can make something out of nothing."

He had been around these kinds of people enough to know they stayed in tight knit groups, except for the occasional loner. He would have to take the homeless man at his word.

He let go of the man's forehead and reached into his pocket. Pulling out his wallet he shook his hand to unfold the flap, then put it in front of the man's face.

"Take the cash. Don't touch anything else. There's enough to help all of you more than what you would've got off of her."

His options limited, the homeless man's two fingers shook as he reached in to take out the cash. Seeing some fifties and twenties his fear turned to excitement.

Pulling the wallet back around and putting it in his pocket, he said, "It's for all four of you. You get greedy—you get dead. Share nothing with the police. *Nothing*, got it?"

The homeless man nodded without taking his eyes off the cash. His mind locked onto one thought…a decent meal.

"Now, get out of here. Remember, *do not* look back."

The man took off in his best rendition of a run. True to his word the guy never looked back.

Todd made sure Suzi remained as he left her, secure in his mind she would not be abused, then he returned to his car. Before leaving he put the card in the glove box in case he needed it as a ruse another time. After he took off the latex gloves he wrapped the blue pen in one of the gloves. He already knew which mailbox he planned to drop Bethany's stick figure card in, along with what trashcan the other items were going to.

CHAPTER SIX

D r. Papadopoulus had been a psychologist for close to two decades. In his fifth year of having his own practice the local police asked him to evaluate an officer on leave after a shooting. He knew something must have happened given he knew the area psychologists most often used by police agencies. He later found out two of them gave opposing opinions.

After that occasion he knew he wanted to be part of the psychology community to evaluate police officers and others who experienced critical incidents. He set out to learn all he could.

After becoming one of the psychologists regularly used by police agencies, he met AJ and admired him for being straightforward, almost to a fault. The industry would have frowned on Doc contacting AJ and having lunch with him after professionally evaluating him, but in AJ he saw an opportunity to learn and understand police officers better. Something told him to be honest with AJ about his personal risk as a psychologist, along with his motive for requesting to meet with AJ away from the office if he wanted AJ to agree to do it.

Their lunch meeting led not only to a professional friendship, never crossing into their personal lives beyond the polite questions anyone would ask, but also to Doc being the closest thing to a Forensic Psychologist Stanislaus County had.

AJ HAD BEEN PUT ON ADMINISTRATIVE LEAVE AFTER killing the man with the Kukri machete. Standard operating procedure was to send anyone involved in a critical incident to the police psychologist, Dr. Papadopoulus. Without the doctor's clearance no officer could return to work. The litigious environment in California forced everyone's hand under the basic philosophy doing so ensured the officer would be safe when returning to duty, thereby ensuring safety to the citizens.

Taking his seat in the waiting room, AJ marveled at the department sending him to see Dr. P., as law enforcement personnel throughout the county affectionately referred to him. Not because AJ expected to circumvent the rules or avoid an evaluation before returning to work. Rather, the two had long been professional friends and his direct supervisors knew AJ and Dr. P. often met for lunch. They had connected after a couple of AJ's first shootings years before, yet the department kept sending him to Dr. P. every time he had to be cleared.

"AJ, the doctor will see you now," said Dr. P's secretary. She'd been with the doctor since AJ met him, and stopped calling him Detective Conti a decade ago.

"You know the way," she mumbled, not missing a beat typing on the keyboard as AJ made his way through the door leading to the back.

"Hey, bud. Be with you in a second," Doc said. When he

finished writing he closed the file, and stood.

AJ always preferred to sit in one of the two accent chairs instead of on the couch. He put his cell on silent and Doc walked towards him with two cups of coffee, sitting in the chair opposite AJ and placing the coffee on the table between them.

"Good to see you, AJ."

"Thanks, Doc. You know how much I like my coffee, although it seems like we could have done this at one of our regular coffee spots."

Doc shook his head and grinned, knowing no response would make AJ happy.

"Doc, I shot the poor bastard two days ago. I got to get back to work."

"Geez, AJ. Maybe you could pause for a second, you know, have an ounce of compassion for the dead."

"I do have compassion, not for him though ... I have it for his mother .... that part always bothers me. He's still her son."

"Comforting words to hear, at least you're not robotic."

"Of course not," AJ said, shaking his head in disappointment at Doc for even making the comment.

"Lest we not forget, I saved the woman. If it were up to the patrol sergeant or administration we would still be talking the guy down, meanwhile she'd be rotting inside the house."

"Thanks for the visual AJ. Right before lunch."

"No problem. Thought it might help move the process along."

"Asshole. Why do you do this to me? I thought we were friends."

AJ laughed, bringing a grin to Doc's face.

Over the next ninety minutes Doc did the mandatory evaluation, made up mostly of drinking coffee while they talked about AJ's homicide cases. In case any administrator might question him, Doc could say he completed a thorough review while he looked them square in the face. They both knew only one of the administrators had ever fired his weapon in the line of duty, only wounding the suspect. No administrator wanted to acknowledge what people like Doc knew, those like AJ who had been in multiple shootings don't carry the emotional baggage first-timers do.

Doc made sure he assessed AJ in his own way, looking for any signs AJ crossed the line to the point he enjoyed hurting or killing people. In his opinion he hadn't. AJ simply displayed an unwillingness to let foolish administrators and their rules prevent him from doing what was necessary to help others.

Doc knew AJ really did not care for all the new tactics like tasers, rubber bullets, or shooting someone with a beanbag. In AJ's experience those only worked on people lacking the internal fortitude to do whatever it took to accomplish their goal. The repeat offenders facing life in prison, the hard-assed criminals, or those pumped up on drugs would fight right through them.

"I don't understand the rush to get back? You know half of the department doesn't approve of the way you go about things. You in a hurry to be ridiculed?"

"Look, I need to get back to help my victims who were murdered, they need someone to find their killer. You know as well as I do time is critical in homicide investigations. I don't really care what those people in the department think." AJ paused, took the final drink of his second cup of coffee, and set the cup on the table. He slid to the front of his chair clasping his hands in front, resting his elbows on his thighs. "I try to keep it pretty simple, Doc," AJ said, his voice almost monotone. "I got to go home, Sarge got to go home without having to be the bad guy by actually shooting someone, God forbid, and most importantly the woman got to go to the hospital instead of the morgue. Like I said, who the hell cares what they think."

"I know, I know. You always say, 'right is right, wrong is wrong, and there's very little grey in between.'" Doc paused, only for a second.

"Wipe the silly grin off your face."

"I'm glad to see you understand, Doc…you know… when I went to the hospital yesterday the woman thanked me for saving her life. Her appreciation's good enough for me."

THE CHIEF OF POLICE WANTED TO FIRE A.J. IRONICALLY, he had no choice but to applaud AJ's conduct to the public once several battered women's organizations lauded the department for taking action to save a woman's life. It appeared the organizations thought like AJ did…the woman deserved to live. AJ returned to his homicide investigations two days later.

CHAPTER SEVEN

D ani had been with the Stanislaus County District
Attorney's office for nearly three years before being
assigned to prosecute her first felony drunk driving case
where the victim died. No trial before affected her so deeply.
Other than the holidays, it took a heart-wrenching moment
to cause her to replay the worst day of her life.

Dani's nightmares began when she first attended the
autopsy eight months earlier. Seeing the mangled body of
the once beautiful sixteen-year-old school girl, lying on the
cold stainless steel table, the onslaught began. The impending trial caused Dani to gradually lose ever-increasing
amounts of sleep.

*Just make it through the closing arguments, then you
can rest*, she thought. Dani knew she could not endure it
much longer.

"Perfect," Dani said, standing in front of her full-length
mirror in her navy suit and white blouse. Her closing argument outfit. Looking in the mirror as if it were a jury Dani
extended her arm.

"Nathan Price had a blood alcohol of point one nine,
over twice the legal limit."

Dani had nailed the closing in her mind at least a dozen
times in the last twenty-four hours. Despite her practice the

butterflies stirred in the dark pit of her stomach, building strength with each passing hour.

This case affected Dani more than most, more for personal reasons than professional. Nathan deserved to go to prison, not a short local jail sentence followed by a long probation. His incarceration seemed like the least she could do for the victim and her family.

Dani had been unable to look at Nathan for any length of time throughout the trial. Every drunk driver was the same to her, taking on the face of the man who killed her family. The technicality they were not the same did not matter. The fact they all caused the same affliction in the same manner seemed to be enough. Dani's goal not to let any other family suffer as she had provided her strength. To reach her goal she pictured the face of the man who killed her family.

In actuality the two had very little in common. Nathan Price was fifteen years younger, much more athletic, good looking, and he had no previous drunk driving arrests. Her family's killer had been arrested nine times for drunk driving, with two previous accidents causing injuries. A thirty-six-year-old construction worker who missed more days of work than he showed up for, he looked like a bum when he hadn't been cleaned up for a jury.

Dani's experience prosecuting drunk drivers taught her they had one thing in common; they all lacked compassion for anyone else, focusing only on what would happen to them. Nathan had done nothing throughout the trial to make her alter her opinion.

CHAPTER EIGHT

———⊱✦⊰———

Todd had been patient over the years as he gained the experience he would ultimately need to reach his two-pronged goal: one of making one woman suffer like he had, and the other woman pay for what she had done to his life. Once he located Bethany Walker he started the ball rolling with the first card he mailed her. Six months before he found Bethany he discovered Dani Larson worked at the Stanislaus County District Attorney's office. He had attended a number of her trials, and resigned to wait for the right case with the right outcome, then he could make her begin to suffer.

Todd first discovered Nathan Price through the media. When Dani drew the case as prosecutor Todd could not have been happier. Todd's contact had given him enough information about the Price family, Nathan in particular, to conclude he was a snobby rich kid. He had seen before what money could buy.

Despite working graveyard shift as a nursing assistant at a Modesto hospital, Todd made every effort to be in the courtroom for every motion, continuance, and even jury selection. The more Todd attended the more he felt Nathan would play right into his plan. To be set he really needed Nathan's parent's money to work its magic by way of the defense attorney for whom they paid handsomely.

Todd understood the outcome of the trial would have a huge impact on whether his plan would kick into full gear or he would have to wait.

I need his defense attorney to do his thing and go win this case, he thought.

NATHAN'S PARENTS HAD NO PROBLEM WITH ATTORNEY Tom Sullivan's fees, especially with his stature of being a seasoned defense attorney with many favorable verdicts for his clients. Tom also had a reputation for spending the money necessary to dig up the one witness who could shed a positive ray of light for his client. Putting a crack in the armor of the prosecution's case meant the jury would have to entertain a reasonable doubt theory, hopefully one of them grasping it and not letting go.

The police never gave Nathan's claim of an earlier fight before the accident any credence. As far as they were concerned the marks on his face, along with his swollen eye, had to have come from the accident.

The defense started questioning, "Now Officer McNabb, you testified earlier the defendant had some injuries to his face when you arrived on the scene, correct?" Sullivan asked.

"Yes."

"Was anybody with the defendant at the scene?"

"No, other than the firemen who responded for medical assistance."

"Is it your opinion the injuries to the defendant's face came from the accident?"

"Yes."

"Can you tell me if you did any follow up investigation regarding the defendant's claim about the injuries coming from an earlier fight?"

"No, I didn't."

"Did the defendant ever make any comments to you or your partner about him being the driver of the blue Camaro?"

"As far as I can recall, he never said."

"You assumed he had to be the driver, correct?"

"I didn't assume anything," McNabb said, a little muffed Sullivan would suggest such a thing. "He was the driver."

"Really? Did you ever see my client in the driver's seat?"

"No, I didn't," McNabb said.

"Do you have any witnesses to the accident who place my client in the driver's seat," Sullivan asked.

"Other than the dead girl, no," McNabb said, staring at Sullivan.

"Your Honor?" Sullivan asked, looking for help.

"Officer McNabb, answer yes or no. You know that," the judge said, before striking the answer.

"I'm sorry, Your Honor," McNabb said.

You're about to be, Sullivan thought.

"Besides fire personnel, paramedics, etcetera, you only had the girl, the defendant and two vehicles, correct?"

"Correct. She drove the red Honda, he drove the Camaro." McNabb said.

Knowing he could object on speculation, Sullivan decided to ignore it given he had been leading the officer right where he wanted him to go.

"Didn't the defendant tell you during questioning Mike was the one driving the Camaro?"

"Yes, he also said he didn't know the guy's last name or

where he lived. Besides, the car is registered to the defendant."

"You testified earlier about the blood on the inside of the Camaro?" Sullivan continued.

"Yes. On the steering wheel and in the area of the driver's seat," McNabb said.

"Didn't the defendant tell you the blood on him and his clothing came from the fight he had been in earlier?"

"Yes, although the injuries to the defendant's face along with the blood on his clothing, as well as the car, they appeared to be consistent with each other."

Sullivan paused for effect.

"Just to be clear, you sent samples of the blood to the lab for testing, correct?"

"No. Like I said, the injuries matched those of someone who would have hit the steering wheel in an accident, the car belongs to the defendant, and he happened to be the only other person there."

Sullivan chose not to object to McNabb answering beyond the directed questions; Sullivan was setting the final stage. Before he finished Tom Sullivan would make a six-year veteran of the California Highway Patrol look like he had just come out of the academy.

Dani could do nothing beyond watching the officer dismiss Nathan's facial injuries as though he had been lying. She always tried to keep an eye on the jury, noticing two jurors took great interest in the direction Sullivan led the officer. One, a thirty-three year old man who currently worked at the Modesto Irrigation District, seemed bought into Sullivan's inferences. The second, a female in her early twenties whose brother had a run in with the police, looked happy to watch Sullivan making an officer look foolish. Despite Dani not liking her, she seemed at the time to be the lesser of two evils as Dani came down to her last peremptory challenge when picking the jury. Dani found herself wishing she had taken the other person.

Tom Sullivan's private investigator had located three people who testified Nathan had been in a fight with two guys after he bumped into one of them in Jerry's Club, a little hold-in-the-wall bar directly on Main Street in Turlock.

The bartender, a twenty-two year veteran with the last ten at Jerry's Club, proved to be the most damaging. He had been sober for thirteen years, garnering a well-deserved respect by the police for being a no-nonsense bartender not afraid to cut off people's drinking. The bartender said Nathan seemed to be having a good time, admitting Nathan had started to become obnoxious.

He testified two men jumped Nathan so fast he didn't have time to defend himself. The bartender broke up the fight, ordering the two men to leave out the back door leading to a large parking lot and five minutes later he told Nathan to leave out the front door. He looked directly at the jury when he said he was positive about the consistency between Nathan's booking photo and the injuries Nathan had when he left the bar.

One of the witnesses to the fight testified he had seen Nathan come into Jerry's with another guy. He saw Nathan walk outside alone after the bartender told him to leave, recalling the guy who came with Nathan left within three to four minutes of when they first arrived. Nobody could recall seeing Nathan drive away.

The defense rested.

CHAPTER NINE

⸻ ◈ ⸻

B ased on Officer McNabb's testimony Dani had to alter her closing. Although she prepared for the general defense theories often used in DUI cases, she had no way to prepare for a seasoned officer becoming long-winded, playing right into the defense attorney's hand.

Dani calmly thanked the jury for their time and patience. She explained the law to make sure they had a clear grasp, then expertly walked them through the facts. Dani showed the jury a photo of the girl put into the yearbook as a remembrance. She took small, deliberate steps to move over next to Nathan Price, pointed at him, then told them about Nathan's blood alcohol level like she had rehearsed.

"Nathan went to Jerry's Club, got drunk, became obnoxious which led to him getting jumped," Dani said. "Their witness, the bartender, who never forgets a name, by the way, could not say who Nathan arrived with, yet he wants you to believe he's positive Nathan left alone."

Dani told them the accident occurred on the exact path Nathan drove to go home every day. She ended by telling the jury to stick with the facts; Nathan was the only other person at the accident scene, standing by his car, with injuries consistent to being in an accident, concluding with the fact the defense never produced Mike, the other guy in the car.

Dani had a great deal of respect for Tom Sullivan. She had watched his closing arguments on several occasions when she knew he was in trial. Now she could not watch him through the eyes of an admirer, but was forced to look at him as her adversary. Listening to him lay down a path even the most uneducated juror could follow as to what possibly could have happened and Dani began to feel the anger inside her rise. She sensed Nathan would walk free.

Dani's anger centered on the incompetence of the officers for not doing a few follow up steps to their investigation like she requested to lock Nathan into the driver's seat. So caught up with her anger, Dani did not notice Tom finished his closing argument and she was unprepared for her rebuttal. Flustered, she chose not to give one.

The judge ran a fast paced courtroom. He had previously dealt with all motions by prosecution and defense, along with having gone over jury instructions with the two attorneys the night before. He read through all of the instructions before sending the jury off to their chambers at three o'clock to pick a foreperson.

At ten minutes after four the attorneys got surprising phone calls from the bailiff telling them the jury had a verdict. Both of them dropped what they were doing, hurrying to the courtroom knowing the judge would not wait long before losing his patience. They settled into their seats as the jury filed in. Within minutes the court clerk received the verdict, reading it to the court—not guilty on all charges.

Stunned, Dani could hardly breathe. She felt the color fade from her face, and her stomach began to tighten as though she would wretch. Excitement was everywhere around her and Dani wanted to run out of the courtroom to get away from it. Instead she felt locked into her chair.

After hugging his parents, Nathan shook Tom Sullivan's hand before he slipped away. He walked over to Dani as she was beginning to put her papers into her briefcase.

"Nice try," he said arrogantly, with a smug smile. "Maybe next time."

Dani sat at the table and could hear the girl's parents crying behind her. She turned around to tell them she was sorry, but she wasn't surprised when they never responded.

A glimpse of movement with an almost imperceptible sensation made her feel she was being watched. She looked up from the parents in time to see a man walking through the doors toward the hallway, but the parent's cries brought her back to the moment. She knew she had let them down.

TODD SHOULD HAVE BEEN EASY TO NOTICE WITH SO FEW people inside the courtroom throughout the trial, yet no one knew he had been there.

Witnesses to the case were not allowed in the courtroom during the trial. The two sets of parents sat on opposite sides behind the attorney representing their interests. Four girls who appeared to be the same age as the victim sat directly behind her parents. The three remaining people watching the trial seemingly went unnoticed.

Todd thought there might have been one time prior to the judge entering the courtroom when DDA Dani Larson looked around as if she were looking for someone. He pulled his newspaper up in front of his face as she began her scan. Todd always sat next to the door with his back against the wall. He wanted to be able to exit quickly if he felt his presence being questioned.

Nathan Price had a grin on his face after whispering something to DDA Larson. To Todd, Nathan's body language displayed his being superior to Dani, arrogantly standing over her when he finished. His entire demeanor ired Todd, making his decision easy.

Nathan walked toward the back of the courtroom with a cocky smile on his face, Todd staring at him until their eyes met. The corners of Nathan's mouth drooped, his gait slowed ever so slightly. Todd's head did not turn to follow Nathan as he walked past through the doors.

Instead, he turned his eyes to Dani, still seated at the table, her briefcase on her lap. Todd saw her turn to look at the girl's parents behind her, holding each other, crying. He saw Dani's lips mouth, "I'm so sorry." The young woman's parents never acknowledged her. Standing, he took one last look at DDA Larson, then pushed the doors open.

CHAPTER TEN

Two of Dani's coworkers were not about to let her say she did not want to go for drinks, hounding her until she gave in. The three started at the District Attorney's office within two weeks of each other, unofficially taking it upon themselves to cheer one another up when necessary.

"You know, it's not your fault when you can't convince the CHP officer to come in to meet with you before the trial, then makes an ass out of himself on the stand," Tenisha said.

"Although, you should have sent him the follow up request a second time," Gerard said. Whack.

Tenisha backhanded Gerard's shoulder, giving him her best *I can't believe you* look.

Dani grinned. "Seeing Gerard's face after you smacked him is the best thing that's happened all day."

Tenisha bobbed her head like she had done something important.

"Gerard's right though, I learned a valuable lesson," Dani said. "Costly, but valuable."

Gerard looked at Tenisha, putting his two fingers to his lips. Tenisha nodded. After she grabbed her cigarettes from her purse the two headed outside together.

TODD WATCHED HER WITH HER DISTRICT ATTORNEY buddies. This was one of his favorite parts...the quiet stealthy pursuit. Long ago when first perfecting the hunt he realized how much he enjoyed it, so much so he nicknamed himself *Stalker*.

Sitting alone at the north end of the bar he could see across the room to Dani's table. He could see she was drinking water like she always did while her friends were relaxing from another stressful day of keeping the wheels of justice moving.

The Resting Place seemed to be the favorite of the three hangouts they frequented. He stayed a good two hundred feet behind when they walked from the basement exit of the Stanislaus County Courthouse. Fifty yards away, across K Street on the opposite corner sat their watering hole, a bar with a restaurant. He never understood why they would go to a place where they could look out the large plate glass windows only to see the very building from which they were trying to unwind.

Stalker had been watching them for close to an hour and a half when Dani's coworkers stood. He reached for the glove in his jacket pocket, sliding it on his hand as he watched the table. He thought they were going to leave until he saw the woman taking cigarettes from her purse.

Shortly after the two went outside to smoke, Dani stood. She grabbed her purse, and weaved through the tables of indulging attorneys before going out of sight to the bathrooms. Stalker laid a twenty-dollar bill on the bar.

He walked toward the empty table, keeping one eye on the two outside with the other one on the entrance to the hallway. Walking next to the table he slightly kicked the chair leg enough to cause a distraction as his gloved hand reached for the empty glass. In one quick movement he snatched the glass from the table, placing it in the side pocket of his cargo pants. Loud attorneys trying to out-drink and out-talk each other made the heist easy. He exited the west door onto Eleventh Street before Dani came out of the bathroom.

CHAPTER ELEVEN

Bethany had spent the majority of her adult life focused on helping others as a hospital social worker. In her twenties and early thirties she dated, although she never let anything get serious. Her love remained her work.

Seeing her parents' divorce and her mom being lost with no profession or skills to fall back on affected her, more than she liked to admit. Early in her career she helped her mother financially since her sisters were much younger than her. She never discouraged them from relationships, instead she encouraged them not to be reliant on another person, most especially a man.

Bethany's two sisters were married and had children who she loved spending time with on vacations and holidays. Somewhere in her late thirties her thoughts about priorities began to change.

Taking a job at Emanuel Medical Center in Turlock provided the needed impetus to stave off burnout. Meeting AJ provided an infusion into her love life, and more importantly, a glimpse into having a life beyond the hospital.

She recognized she moved faster in the relationship than AJ, falling in love with him months before. She could tell by the way he looked at her he cared for her deeply. She even believed he loved her, he just didn't know it.

Spending nights at AJ's house happened more frequently than at hers. She didn't mind, especially since she had gradually filled up important areas like the bathroom and the closet with her things. She struggled at first with AJ getting called by the dispatcher in the middle of the night, although even when he didn't have to leave he often got up at three or four to run or to go to the office early.

Knowing AJ would be itching to get back to work having been authorized by Doc to return to full duty she mumbled she loved him but did not even move when he kissed her on the forehead at 5 a.m. when he left.

AJ SAT IN SERGEANT BOYKIN'S OFFICE WAITING FOR HIM, perusing one of the reports he had dictated before "Kukri Man," as some of the officers were calling him, decided to whack off his wife's leg. Boykin had supervised the Detective Bureau for nearly four years and the time had come for Boykin to rotate back to patrol, although he really did not want to go. AJ liked him for his directness, his honesty, and more importantly, Boykin would back his personnel if he felt they were right.

"AJ, for God's sake, it's six-forty-five in the morning. Can't I get to my office to enjoy a peaceful cup of coffee before you arrive?"

"Sorry, Sarge. I woke up at four. Got in a good run, went out for breakfast...nothing else to do so I came to work."

"Four o'clock. My God, you're insane."

"You know what I always say—"

"Yeah, yeah, *sleep's a commodity*. Can I at least have ten minutes to enjoy my first cup of coffee before we talk about the Chief being pissed at you, again, as if something's new."

"Sure. Take all the time you need." AJ headed for his desk.

"Get your ass back in here. I'll make another fresh cup when we're done. Then I'll close my door until I drink it."

AJ laughed, knowing this would probably be the first of a dozen cups of coffee to get cold because everyone knew Boykin only threatened to shut his door.

"Look," Boykin said after AJ sat back down, "you're good on this one. With the women's organizations backing you, there's nothing the Chief or his cronies can do to you. Still, you gotta know they think you're old-timer ways of doing things is long gone."

"They head hunting?"

"Hell, you've been here so long you would really have to screw up bigtime before they could fire you. What I'm hearing is they're trying to convince the city to give you a golden handshake."

"What the hell's a golden handshake?"

"You know, offer to tack on a few extra years of service to get you over twenty years of service and then you might think about retiring. Something to benefit you enough so you'll agree to walk away."

"Whatever …" AJ sat forward, arms on his knees, fingers interlocked, and palms rubbing together.

"Do you believe I was right?"

Boykin sat back in his chair, both hands on his coffee cup. "Yes, AJ, I do. Hell, you saved the woman's life."

"I sense there's more …"

"Yeah, well, nowadays Chiefs everywhere want their officers to coddle everyone, including the bad asses. Cops like us don't think we should."

"You think I ought to take their golden handshake?"

"Lord knows I don't want you to, AJ. At the same time

I don't want you always looking over your shoulder, your mind elsewhere, to where you can't do your job effectively. These robberies, assaults with deadly weapons, homicides… they need to be solved. That's you."

Boykin winced when he took a sip of his coffee. No longer hot.

"In the meantime, start prepping Seth to take on more responsibility. If your time on admin leave taught me anything it was I need to be prepared if you are gone."

AJ stood, nodded, and shook Boykin's hand.

It's hard to dislike a straight shooter, he thought, as he looked at the clock behind Boykin.

"You still have time for a fresh cup. The others don't start straggling in for another twenty minutes."

Boykin grinned as AJ turned to leave.

CHAPTER TWELVE

D ani cried for young Cass, hating the case from the instant she started reading the police reports. The six-year-old had been beaten black and blue by his stepfather after Cass wet his pants on the couch during his nap. His mother, Azar, frantically tried to clean it up before her husband got home.

Cyrus Warda walked through the door when Azar was on her knees cleaning the cushion. Without a word he grabbed the child by his hair, hurtling him across the room. Before Cass could get up Cyrus removed his thick leather belt and started pummeling Cass with the buckle.

Azar silently wept as her son screamed every time the buckle struck his back, knowing what would happen if she tried to intervene. Later, after Cyrus fell asleep, Azar slid out the back door with Cass to take him to the emergency room. She had no idea of the legal obligation for the staff to call the police.

The first day of the trial had been December 6. Dani felt comfortable with the eight women, four men jury. The process had taken the majority of the first day only leaving the two attorneys enough time to give their opening statements before the judge rested for the day.

The second day would not be so kind.

STALKER FELT INTRIGUED WATCHING DANI IN THE courtroom. She seemed to care about the victims in her cases, wanting to help them in whatever way she could. His goal of making her suffer remained the same, though watching her in court provided him a better understanding of her.

Stalker had the day off work and knew Dani had a trial. He showed up at the courthouse early to determine which courtroom she would be in. He took a different seat this time in the middle row, sitting all the way to the wall on the left side behind the prosecution table. He turned as much as he could in the chair to rest his back against the wall while he read his paperback novel, or at least appeared to.

Walking through the large doors into the courtroom a little boy stopped in mid-sentence when he saw the defendant, Cyrus Warda. The boy grabbed the right leg of the woman with him, one of the Child Advocates from the DA's office, holding on tight while hiding his head behind her leg. Stalker looked at the boy, then at Cyrus who stared right at the child. Cyrus grinned, his eyes showing a malicious pleasure when the boy cowed.

Stalker could feel his jaw tightening. Up to then he knew nothing of the exact charges, but what he did know was the look on Cyrus' face. A look he had seen many times before he finally made his way out of the hellhole system masquerading as foster homes and into The Samaritan House. Stalker told himself to stay calm and keep his wits about him. He needed to make sure he looked like any other bystander in the courthouse.

The advocate put her hand on the boy's shoulder when one of the doors flew open and a woman walked through. He could not believe what he saw. The woman walked to the first row of seats directly behind Cyrus, and passed the boy without a glance. He could tell by the way Cyrus looked at her she was likely his wife or girlfriend. His gut told him she was probably the boy's mother, no different than the wives at the foster homes who covered for their husbands. Stalker saw Dani become visibly weak when Cyrus told the woman, "This is almost over—I'll be home soon."

After the judge took her place behind the bench the bailiff brought the jury in. Dani stood to call her first witness. All eyes in the courtroom, including Stalker's, watched her as she turned to look at the woman escorting the boy. The woman's face lacked confidence as her shoulders slightly rolled up. She escorted the boy to the stand. The boy sat in a chair on the witness stand by himself with the Child Advocate in a chair directly behind him.

Dani started by trying to get the boy to tell the court his name. When the boy finally picked his head up to look at her, Cyrus cleared his throat. The noise made the boy look directly at Cyrus causing tears to begin flowing down his cheeks. He turned in his chair, almost leaping into the advocate's lap. She carried the crying boy out of the courtroom without him uttering one word on the record.

Stalker's attention no longer centered on Dani. His sights were squarely on Cyrus. Dani called the woman who earlier ignored the boy as she walked up behind Cyrus... Azar Warda, his wife. Azar testified she took her son to the Emergency Room after he fell out of a tree in their backyard earlier in the day landing on his back on a metal wrought iron gate. Stalker could see the shock on Dani's face as she stood silent. He knew Azar lied for Cyrus.

His anger inside nearly made him leave the room, but he convinced himself to listen to Dani's evidence, believing she would outline the evil within Cyrus. He already knew Cyrus hurt the boy, and he wanted to know how. He heard the lead investigator describe what he saw on the boy the night in the ER along with what he had been told.

Dani focused on the evidence the detective recovered at the residence. Stalker sat forward, putting his elbows on his legs, his prayer hands directly in front of his lips. Dani showed the jury the bloody shirt found on the floor of the boy's bedroom, along with his soiled pants. She also showed them the stained cushion cover from the couch, which the lab confirmed was urine. The last thing she showed the jury before they were released was the two-inch wide, thick leather belt with the large solid brass buckle.

Stalker got up and walked toward the aisle to leave as the judge released the investigator. He felt the redness in his face, and the anger building inside. He had a plan to set in motion and needed to be able to focus. Before walking toward the doors his eyes burned the image of Cyrus Warda into his brain.

You and I have unfinished business, he thought.

CHAPTER THIRTEEN

Several weeks after Nathan's acquittal for killing the girl while driving drunk, Stalker knew he could find him in one of the small bars in downtown Turlock. Nathan was predictable, learning nothing from his past experience and he regularly gloated about his victory while he took his drinking to a new level. Stalker had enjoyed very few of his other kills as most were done for the purpose of gaining experience, building confidence, or to eliminate a witness like Suzi. But, this one he would enjoy. Nathan would serve dual purposes.

After finding Nathan in the Caboose Lounge, a quaint little bar and restaurant, Stalker waited for the right hooker. He had spotted Cherie three weeks before when doing surveillance on Nathan. Stalker had slipped one of her johns a twenty to get her name.

Cherie walked along the row of small shops sharing the parking lot with the Caboose. She walked with more class than her competition and her clothes were seductive, not sleazy.

She paced at the end of the shops, waiting for the right guy and Stalker could tell she wouldn't wait long.

Cherie preferred the kind of guys who exited the Caboose since they were usually higher quality customers.

The reason boiled down to basic street life economics; she could get her fix and still have money left over. Time kept slipping away forcing Cherie to look through the fence to the lower class bars across the railroad tracks. Stalker could tell by her fidgeting her ever increasing need for a fix started making her think about going over there.

Stalker slid out from the darkness to approach her and Cherie jumped. But she calmed when she saw his nice black slacks, black turtleneck and dark leather jacket.

Stalker eased his hands from his pockets when he got within fifteen feet. He could see Cherie's eyes light up when she saw the wad of bills in one, and baggie of white powder in the other.

He provided Cherie with a small taste of the meth and promised her all of the money along with the rest of the powder when she was finished with what he needed her to do.

Nobody offers that kind of cash and drugs without wanting sex, she thought.

She looked at the wad of cash and meth, her heart racing as her weight shifted from leg to leg. The job he wanted looked to be simple, but it also seemed to be freakish for the kind of payout she would get.

He's offering too much for me not to take the chance.

Nodding her head in agreement, Cherie walked toward the Caboose, entering through the double doors. Her gait slowed while looking for the good-looking, young man Stalker had described.

Sauntering toward the bar she spotted him, exactly like the man outside had said. The guy sat at the bar somewhat slouched over as if running out of steam wearing a green sweater with light colored Dockers exactly how he had been described to her.

She hesitated, the risk of it ending badly because the request by the man in black was so strange it gave her the creeps.

You need this money. How hard can it be? she told herself as she walked toward him.

The stool to his left was not taken and she lightly rubbed his arm as she sat.

Cherie ordered a Bud Light and reached to her right, her right breast rubbing his left arm as she grabbed the bowl of popcorn. The young man smiled as he looked at her and his droopy eyes told her he had a lot to drink.

His smile changed. Taking its place was an, *I'm about to get some* grin she had seen so many times. She shivered, not knowing what the man would really get…but lucky wasn't it.

"Sorry, I didn't mean to bother you, I only wanted a little popcorn," Cherie said with a smile.

"It's okay. No harm done," Nathan slurred. "How about we go get something to eat instead of popcorn."

"A little forward, aren't you?"

"I think you'll find I'm worth it," he claimed, placing his palm on her shoulder.

His arrogance turned her off, so she reminded herself her part would be over shortly.

NATHAN LET CHERIE DRIVE HIS NEW JEEP, TELLING HER his parents bought it for him a couple of months ago after he wrecked his car. When Nathan wanted her to stop for beer she convinced him not to worry…there'd be beer at the motel room later on. She drove west on Main Street and turned into the parking lot of the twenty-four hour restaurant next to Highway 99, the motel directly behind it.

"Is this it, Baby?" Nathan slurred, laying his left hand on her inner thigh. "Let the party begin."

Cherie drove past the restaurant to the motel, looking for the room. The man at the Caboose told her to go to room 121, second building, bottom floor, right corner. She parked in front of the room, turned off the ignition and removed Nathan's hand. Pulling the room key from her clutch, Cherie made sure the numbers matched.

She walked into the room with Nathan stumbling behind her. All the lights were indicating the man in black had already been there. A cold chill covered her, feeling like they were being watched. Nathan put his arms around her waist and began to kiss her on the neck.

"You're gonna make a lot of money for all the fun I plan to have with you," Nathan said.

"Whoa, what's the rush," Cherie said as she pried his hands from her. *No way you can pay me what he's going to*, she thought.

Stepping away she said, "See, there's a cooler with beer, like I promised," pointing to the Styrofoam ice chest against the wall.

Cherie took the top off the ice chest and grabbed the sole cold beer standing upright. Reaching for the pop-top a small bubble seeped out of the pinhole at the opening of the can. *This ain't good. I gotta get out of here* she thought.

"Have a beer, kick back on the bed. I'm going to take a quick shower for you." She finished opening the beer then reached toward him.

Nathan took the beer, guzzling a quarter of it.

I can't believe my luck, he thought, settling on the bed with a smile.

His mind played through all the possibilities and he planned on making sure he felt good. Given the fact he would never see her again, he didn't care how she felt.

Cherie turned on the cold water in the shower and let it run. Fifteen minutes seemed like an eternity so she closed the toilet lid to sit on instead of sitting on the seat and pulled out her phone to play a card game while she waited. Lost in the game, a knock on the door startled her. She jumped, shut off the water, and locked her phone.

She closed her eyes for a second, and took a deep breath before slowly opening the door. The black clothing caught her eye first, followed by the sunglasses.

With his left hand he reached out to give her what he promised her. When she started to grab the money he grasped her throat.

Stalker lifted her by the throat, tightly squeezing enough to cut off Cherie's breathing, her life balancing in his hand. Her eyes bulged, her face went pale, and she dropped her phone as her hands instinctively went to his. The smell of her urine on the cheap carpet filled the air.

Leaning forward, his cheek touched hers. "You say one word to anyone, I'll hunt you down," he whispered menacingly. "Get out of town for a while."

Releasing her throat, Stalker let Cherie pickup her phone before guiding her to the door.

Nathan's intoxication helped the Valium laced beer take effect quickly. Stalker pulled duct tape from the bag he set on the bed. Even though Nathan looked unconscious, Stalker learned from previous mistakes not to take chances.

He rolled Nathan on his stomach, taping his hands together within seconds. Flipping him onto his back, Stalker taped Nathan's legs together in case he woke up.

He slowed his pace, ready to enjoy his task. If Nathan woke up it would be even more exciting. Stalker sat on the bed closest to the door and slowly took the remaining items out of the satchel. He tore open the bag with the sterile gloves, putting them on as he had done many times before. Working as a hospital nursing assistant provided him the opportunity to get supplies necessary for his other work. He opened the package with the Nasogastric tube which he had watched nurses put down the nose of dozens of patients. He opened the final package with a 60cc syringe, laying it on the table between the beds next to the phone.

Stalker took one of the bottles of Jack Daniels out of the bag. He thought it would be fitting for Nathan to be filled with the exact same alcohol he had the night he snatched the young woman's life from her as she was driving home. Stalker set the bottle on the Bible left by the Gideon's, then grabbed the NG tube.

He stood over Nathan thinking, *Your time has come. He who lives by the sword dies by the sword.*

He was surprised how easy the tube slid into place, especially without any lubricant. With the stolen stethoscope he checked to make sure it was in place. He listened to Nathan's stomach as he pushed air into the end of the tube as he had seen the nurses do.

Nathan's eyes began to focus through the fog of beer and Valium, so Stalker slapped a piece of duct tape over his mouth. Nathan tried to free himself, quickly realizing he wasn't going to be able to. Stalker smiled enjoying the fear in Nathan's eyes.

Nathan stared intently, his wide eyes filled with terror. Stalker reached into his bag, brought out one drinking glass and a paper bag with something in it. Nathan stared at the bag as Stalker pulled out a second glass. Nathan's eyes started darting, unable to remember where he had seen the man before.

Nathan's eyes shot toward the bathroom, then to Stalker, before going back to the bathroom. He closed his eyes and lightly shook his head. Stalker grinned, realizing Nathan must have thought he killed Cherie first—an unexpected bonus.

"Oh, now you care about her. An hour ago you looked at her like chattel; property you figured you could do whatever you wanted with."

Stalker treated the glass taken from the paper bag as though it were highly valued. He held it up to the light fixture between the two beds ensuring the lipstick around the edges and the fingerprints were still there. He gently placed it on the table, and opened the Jack Daniels pouring one finger worth, enough for a toast, in the bottom of both glasses.

"You're just like the men at the foster homes against which I had to defend myself. It's all about your personal pleasure, regardless of the cost to someone."

Stalker grabbed the Jack Daniels bottle and poured three fingers worth in Nathan's NG tube.

"You, Nathan, you killed that young girl, not Mike. Then you have the audacity to rub your freedom in the DA's face?"

Nathan's eyes were glued to Stalker's face, the reality of his words assaulting Nathan's memory.

"You didn't pay in court for killing her, but today…today is judgment day."

Stalker held up the bottle to show Nathan.

"You love this stuff, don't' you?" Stalker asked, thrusting the bottle toward Nathan's eyes.

"Tonight, you get to have all of this, and more, because it's more important to you than the people you hurt."

Grabbing the end of the tube he poured another three fingers in.

"Those men in the foster homes used the weak ones, over and over. You've done the same thing with women. You've even used your parents and their money, all for your pleasures. It's always about you."

Nathan squirmed, trying to release himself from the tight grasp of duct tape. The evil smile on Stalker's face told him his efforts were futile.

Taking hold of the NG tube, Stalker poured the remainder of the bottle into the tube. Reaching into his bag he pulled out a second bottle, slowly breaking the seal in front of Nathan's eyes before pouring half into the tube.

"Here's to you and the prosecutor," Stalker said. "Two people whose lives crossed paths thanks to our good friend Jack Daniels. The demise of both of you is fair…it's deserved, neither of you could look beyond yourselves to others in need, the forgotten ones."

Stalker emptied the second bottle down Nathan's tube, grabbed the clean glass and took a drink.

CHAPTER FOURTEEN

Turlock was a relatively moderate-sized city along the Highway 99 corridor in the far southern end of Stanislaus County. The agriculture in the county fooled many into thinking the area was slower paced with minimal crime. But, major gang issues existed in Turlock, Ceres, and Modesto along with each city having more than their share of violent crimes and homicides. The central valley of California had long been known by all major law enforcement agencies to be one of the highest methamphetamine areas in the nation.

The door to room 121 stood opened wide with the lights on. The body of a fully clothed man lay on the double bed farthest from the door.

"I wouldn't go in there if I were you," said Knox, one of the senior crime scene evidence technicians assigned to the Detective Bureau. "You know AJ likes to get a look at the scene as undisturbed as possible."

"I know, I know," said Willie, the newest detective in the Bureau because he supposedly possessed tech-wizard skills.

"All I want is to look around. I don't plan on disturbing anything." Willie reached for the yellow barrier tape.

"You go in there before he gets here, he'll know. When he figures it out, you won't be on another homicide scene for months." Knox took a long drag on his cigarette, and blew out several circles of smoke. He didn't care how long it took AJ to get there, he was on overtime and Christmas was less than two weeks away.

Willie didn't believe there would be any way AJ would know he had been inside. He took a cigarette out, and went over to steal a light off the embers of Knox's butt.

AJ WAS FAMILIAR WITH THE MOTEL LAYOUT. A STANDARD cheap motel next to a highway with what used to be a brand name restaurant within walking distance. The motel could be found anywhere in America…the kind that within three to five years of opening went from running a legitimate business to being mostly filled by truckers, prostitutes and drug dealers.

It had almost been two years since AJ worked a triple homicide at this motel. Four drug dealers shot it out. The lone survivor's blood trail led to the open field behind the motel. Officers found him unconscious, his arm across a brown paper bag with three pounds of pure methamphetamine.

AJ pulled up in his '69 Mustang Convertible, letting the strong, elegant engine rumble. He could see the questioning look on their faces; *why would he drive his Mustang on a cold December night when he has a perfectly good city car in his driveway? They would never understand,* he smiled to himself.

AJ shut off the engine and grabbed his folder. Stepping from the car he took a deep breath of the cool night air, letting its crispness fill his lungs. Walking away the car alarm chirped at the same time his mindset began to change.

"Alessandro 'AJ' Conti, nice to see you could finally make it," Knox said sarcastically with a grin. They had known each other nearly twenty years, having been paramedics together before they ended up at the police department. Knox was one of the few who could talk to AJ in such a manner without him returning verbal fire. Something AJ happened to be good at, although not necessarily proud of.

"No problem, Knoxy," AJ said. "Thought I might grab a quick shower before I graced you with my presence since I was on the treadmill when dispatch called. You couldn't have put up with my pungent odor for the next twenty-four hours if I hadn't. Guess my wonderful display of kindness means you buy the first round of Java."

Knox bowed. "Thank you, Oh-Mighty-Great-Smelling-One. And, not only no, hell no. The rook has to pay his dues." Knox winked at AJ as he pointed at Willie.

Willie looked at them like they were both crazy. He hadn't been in the unit long enough to know the Department had an arrangement with one of the local fast food joints for anything they needed when they were out on a homicide scene, with the bill being sent directly to the Financial Director.

"All right rook, you know how I like mine," AJ said. "Fresh…I mean fresh this time, as hot as they'll get it for you." Knox half-smiled when he looked at AJ. Until Willie had enough sense to figure it out he would keep paying for coffee.

AJ went to get the initial briefing from the first officer on the scene. The officer told him Dispatch received a call on the emergency line from a male caller who refused to identify himself. The dispatcher sent part of the caller's message to the officer's mobile data terminal.

They went to the patrol car, the fluorescent green from the MDT screen lighting up the inside. AJ sat in the driver's seat to get a closer look. The caller said – "Nathan took the life of another and she could not let it go."

AJ used the car microphone to let dispatch know he had arrived, then asked if they could pull a copy of the phone call and the radio traffic up to his arrival on scene.

"It's already taken care of," she responded with a disgusted tone.

AJ winced when he heard the familiar voice of a dispatcher who hated him, wishing he had first asked the officer if he had a clue who the dispatcher might be.

She never forgave AJ for not going home with her the night of the Christmas party two years ago. And never understood him not wanting to make the same mistake with someone from work he had made early in his career.

Up until six months ago AJ never wanted a serious relationship. He felt if he wanted to make a real difference being a detective, it would mean not seeing his family because of the long hours. Despite his numerous efforts toward building a friendship with her, she kept her stoic posture whenever AJ was around. After months of trying he gave up.

CHAPTER FIFTEEN

A J waited for Seth to arrive before breaching the outer perimeter of the crime scene. Seth was on his third year in the Detective Bureau, and due to rotate back to patrol in a year. His nasty reputation as being cocky and abrasive at times seemed well deserved. Then again, Seth never lacked confidence. Nearly everyone agreed Seth possessed high intelligence, several levels beyond the average cop. Beyond wanting his best friend to stay in the bureau, AJ needed Seth on his team.

AJ had a trim muscular build to go along with his six-three frame. His olive skin was darker than Seth's but his hair was not quite as dark. Fortunately AJ felt comfortable in his own skin, even with the five inch scar on his left cheek left from the knife of a homicide suspect a couple of years before, because Seth possessed the perfect looks—a sleek build set on a six-five frame with jet black hair. More often than not the eyes were on Seth when they were together.

Years before they became friends AJ sensed Seth possessed a great deal more than the reputation gave him credit for. In Patrol his reports were thorough, and he always wanted to finish his own cases instead of sending them to Detectives like most of the other cops. AJ also found the majority of rookies who got past Seth as one of their Training Officers turned out to be good. AJ started campaigning to Sergeant Boykin to give Seth a shot in the Bureau, so after several months he got offered a one-year training position—nearly three years ago.

"Willie, go to the restaurant, and start interviewing everyone in there," AJ said. "It's all windows, maybe somebody in there saw something useful. Everyone, got it?"

Willie shook his head, mumbling something about never getting to use the skills he had been brought in for as he moped off.

"When you're done get back over here to help Knox process the scene. Oh, by the way, thanks for the coffee." AJ smiled and tipped the cup, followed by the back of Willie's hand popping up for a brief second.

At least he used all of his fingers, AJ thought.

Knox loved the delicate work of looking for the minute pieces of evidence. He stood behind the detectives, his gear beside him, ready to go to work.

"Even from the doorway this one seems strange," AJ said.

"Process this thing from top to bottom, we're in no hurry." General directions meant AJ trusted him, something Knox appreciated; then AJ stayed out of his domain.

"You feeling it again?" Knox asked, his head canted like he hoped AJ would say no.

AJ nodded.

"Damn, I could tell," Knox said. "Wish I understood how you are so accurate with it."

AJ went into the crime scene with a belief; so long as he relaxed, the scene, and more specifically the dead person, would talk to him. Nobody had ever been privy to his belief, with one exception, Seth. Knox only knew AJ would sometimes get a funny feeling.

After Knox finished taking video, they stepped into the room.

"Whoa, smells like a distillery," Seth said, almost pulling his head back from the doorway.

They carefully scanned everything, making sure not to disturb any possible evidence.

"This place seems bare. The bed," AJ said, pointing to the one by the window, "it's perfect, not a single wrinkle in the crappy yellow cover."

"Yeah well, nothing else seems disturbed either…the hangers, the bathroom linen, nothing on the table…the remote's still sitting on the HBO guide," Seth said.

"A little too perfect."

The picture on the wall above the beds displayed a peaceful ocean setting with a lighthouse proudly reaching into the sky, sitting on the edge of a grassy bank jutting out toward the water. With the exception of the dead guy, the room felt tranquil—almost staged.

"One glass of liquor, sitting almost dead center on the bible on the nightstand," AJ said. He shined his Maglite making it easy to see the slight rings of lipstick around the edge.

"I'd almost guarantee its Jack Daniels in the glass," Knox said. The other two nodded as though it were obvious to them, too, even though neither of them had any clue.

Three-inch-wide, gray duct tape bound the dead man's hands behind his back and his legs together, along with covering his mouth.

"You see the crease on it," AJ said, pointing at the man's mouth.

"Yeah, so what," Seth responded.

"Look at the tape on his wrists and legs. Almost perfect,

no major creases. I'd bet he was bound while he was oblivious to the world. His mouth looks like an afterthought."

"Like the guy started to wake up maybe, ready to scream," Seth said.

"Maybe. Whatever it was, it's pretty rare to see such a smooth tape job to restrain somebody. Whoever did this seems a little anal."

WILLIE, RELEGATED TO CHECKING POSSIBLE WITNESS statements, walked into the restaurant. *This is bullshit, man, ain't nobody in this fucking place gonna say they saw anything,* Willie thought to himself as he opened the door to The Diner. When he had been in there while working patrol people didn't pay much attention to what went on outside.

Willie counted only five customers, none of them at the tables to the north side closest to the motel. He shook his head, a vertical furrow forming between his eyebrows as his jaws tensed.

One of the booths had two teenagers sitting on the same side of the table lost in each other's eyes, unaware of anyone else in the restaurant. One middle-aged man sitting at the counter looked like a trucker in his flannel shirt, Levi's, work boots, and coffee thermos next to his plate. A few seats down from the trucker sat a neatly dressed drunk man wearing a richly colored sweater with dark blue slacks, leaning against the wall with his eyes closed.

Besides those customers and waitresses, Willie only saw one other person, a young man dressed in all black clothing sitting alone in the southwest corner booth reading the paper while he drank coffee.

"Hey, aren't you gonna come say hello?" the waitress said. Willie looked over and recognized her, standing with her hand on her hip and head tilted.

Willie turned his head to look at the man in the corner, and back at her. He decided he would get back to interview the man in a second.

"How you doing, Good Looking," Willie said, strolling over to her.

Within a couple minutes she took a break and they ended up in a booth down by the sleeping drunk.

STALKER RECOGNIZED THE DETECTIVE ENTERING THE restaurant. He had watched him for nearly an hour pacing around outside of the motel room, smoking cigarettes, and trying to look into the room without going past the yellow tape—until the other guy smoking with him walked to the restaurant to use the bathroom.

Stalker knew this wasn't the main investigator because this guy never made it inside the room with the other detectives, plus he got sent off to cover the basics…interviews usually leading to nothing.

Sizing up the situation Stalker decided he did not have to leave. With the detective focused on flirting with the waitress Stalker relaxed. He continued watching the motel while he sipped his coffee.

CHAPTER SIXTEEN

"We're getting close to Christmas so we're short on people," AJ said, looking at Seth. "We're going to have to split up."

Another team of detectives were working a homicide from the night before and between the two homicides the one AJ caught would clearly be the harder one to solve, which suited him fine.

"As soon as we get the deputy coroner in here I'm going to need you to deal with anything she needs, then go check the registration desk," AJ said. "We can split going door-to-door. I'll take this side, you can do the north side after you take care of the registration desk. I doubt if anyone back there saw anything, much less would tell you if they did. Willie is checking for witnesses at Lyons Restaurant, or whatever its new name is, before he's supposed to help Knox."

"It's The Diner."

"What?"

"The restaurant. It's The Diner."

"Right. Whatever."

Seth grinned, and looked at AJ inquisitively who picked up on his non-verbal question.

"I want to get the guy's address from his driver's license, go check it out, see if I can find out anything after I'm done with the door-to-doors on this side," AJ said.

Sandy, the Stanislaus County Deputy Coroner, walked in as AJ finished his comment. She wore navy blue slacks with a conservative button up white blouse. She took off her jacket and without a word, using her index finger to point at the bed closest to the door, asked if she could lay it there. AJ nodded.

As a Deputy Coroner she seldom had to wear the Sheriff's Office tan and green uniform. Sandy stood five feet six inches; she had auburn hair flowing to the middle of her back, bright green eyes, a slender waist and slightly larger than average chest making her one of the favorite coroners amongst all of the homicide detectives in the county.

"AJ, Seth, two of my favorites," she said, smiling. "I missed you guys last night."

"Sorry we couldn't be there for you," Seth said. "You knew we couldn't stay away from you for long though." He flashed her a smile.

She grinned, her head bobbing side to side. She enjoyed the game as much as the detectives did.

"Sandy, could I get you to get me the guy's wallet so I can look for I.D.," AJ asked. "Knox has already taken photos of the body in place."

"You're gonna contact the family, aren't you? Dammit, AJ, you know my boss prefers we notify them." Tension between her eyebrows and pouty lips took the place of the grin.

"Look Sandy, I don't have anything on this kid," AJ said. "He's too nicely dressed to be in this place, especially since the Jeep outside comes back to a county address. If it's the same address, I'll say I got it from the registration."

"Why do I do this?" she said, shaking her head before reaching for the wallet in the victim's pants pocket. Pulling out the black tri-fold wallet she could tell it was full. Opening both folds they saw a large amount of cash, and several hundred-dollar bills. She looked away while holding the wallet open in front of her, AJ presumed for her own mental well-being…or plausible denial. He played along by reading the driver's license while looking over her shoulder.

"Nathan Price, twenty-two. According to this he lives in the thirteen thousand block of West Keyes Road," AJ said loud enough for her to hear. He smiled when she turned and glared at him.

"Same as the Jeep. Thanks, Sandy," AJ said heading for the door.

AJ started the door-to-door with the first room east of 121. Nobody recalled seeing or hearing anything out of the ordinary until he worked his way back toward the crime scene from the west. Then he knocked on room 125.

"I wondered if you were going to knock on doors," the middle aged white man said, standing in the doorway in his boxers and white V-neck undershirt.

"What do you mean?" AJ asked while he held out his ID.

"Well, I can't be the only one who saw the pale white prostitute with the drunk guy get out of the Jeep. They went into the room you guys are in," the man said.

AJ asked him for some ID.

Adam Riley lived in San Diego and was travelling to Redding to see his sister who had taken ill. He said his car started overheating after he passed the rest stop south of Turlock and he stopped at Tommy's Auto Repair after he spotted it from the highway.

"What time did you get here?" asked AJ.

Riley said he walked over from the shop around six thirty, ate at The Diner, then stayed and read the paper.

"I got to my room at about eight forty."

"Did you see anything out of the ordinary?"

"I was about to deadbolt the door when lights hit my window, like a car pulling into a stall and I looked out the window. The young lady definitely caught my attention."

AJ waited, quietly taking notes.

"I'm telling you, she's pretty pale. Maybe the dark colored dress with a slit up the side made her legs look whiter, who knows. Cute young thing, though. Got out of the drivers' side of the Jeep. Some guy got out of the passenger side, but I didn't pay much attention to him."

No surprise, AJ thought.

"I really couldn't tell you much more. Never saw her face, I got caught up in looking at her awesome legs."

"Could you identify her if you saw her again?" AJ asked, knowing the answer would be no since he only remembered her legs.

"I doubt it. Like I said, I wasn't paying much attention to her face. I will say, as she stepped out of the Jeep, before I saw those legs, I did sense she didn't want to be here, or she was mad at the guy. I don't know. She...she didn't look relaxed."

AJ gave him a business card, and commented he hoped Riley's sister got better soon.

"Thank you," Riley said. When AJ turned to leave Riley said, "One more thing. You know, you might think this is strange..."

"What is it?" AJ asked as he turned around.

"Look...I can't say for sure she's a prostitute. I don't know, if she hadn't gotten out of the driver's seat, I would have thought for sure...well, you know what I mean, right?"

AJ thanked him again and slid his pen in his jacket

pocket while he walked across the parking lot toward his Mustang. He began thinking about the location of Nathan's house and what he would say when he got there. Reaching for the door handle something stopped him.

AJ learned long ago to trust his gut about being watched by dangerous people. He had nearly been killed several years earlier in a fast food restaurant when he was attacked by a Norteño gang member he had put in prison. His bad gut feeling, confirmed by the cashier's wide eyes, helped AJ turn in time to deflect the knife and kill the guy before AJ got stabbed.

Now, AJ could feel the eyes of wickedness bearing down on him. The ambient light from the motel and the large windows of the restaurant helped assure him he wasn't about to be attacked...at least up close and personal. Still, he knew someone lurked out there...watching. The tingling on the back of his neck and the knot forming in his stomach confirmed to him evil was watching his every move.

CHAPTER SEVENTEEN

S talker noticed the detective he thought was in charge walk out of the hotel room and start going door-to-door. He timed the detective each time someone on the south-side facing the restaurant answered the door. From his surveillance Stalker knew how many rooms were occupied and with the detective contacting five occupants Stalker believed none of them had seen anything based on each contact lasting less than four minutes.

Stalker presumed the detective would go around to start checking the opposite side and calculated it should take less than thirty minutes.

The detective surprised him when he didn't go to the back, instead he walked along the south side to the corner room past the crime scene. Several minutes later he knocked on the door to room 125 and Stalker sat up straight when the room door opened. During his surveillance, there were no lights on in 125. When he walked out of the room no cars were parked in front of any rooms west of Nathan's Jeep.

Realizing he had forgotten to start timing the contact Stalker became angry for missing how many minutes went by. Roughly ten minutes later the detective left the room… over double the time he spent in other rooms.

When he finished the interview, the lead detective did not go back to Nathan's room. Stalker watched him walk across the parking lot to his Mustang. He saw the detective reach for the door handle, stop, straighten up, and take one step back. The detective's right hand settled on his weapon as he slowly turned all the way around, like he was looking for someone.

Stalker smiled to himself, thinking it could be fun. *The detective knows he's being watched*, he thought. *He's like me, he knows how to trust his instincts.*

After the detective drove off Stalker got up, threw a ten-dollar bill on the table for his coffee, and walked toward the door. Glancing to his left, the young detective never looked at him because he was more involved with impressing the waitress. Once outside a plan started formulating in Stalker's mind.

EXCHANGING SMALL TALK, ALONG WITH AN OCCASIONAL nervous glance from the deputy coroner, Sandy, Seth helped load Nathan's body into the black canvas body bag. She pulled it closed causing a ridge to form by the zipper, the waves of extra canvas going all directions.

One size fits all, Seth thought as they lifted Nathan onto the gurney.

"The autopsy will probably be tomorrow around one o'clock. Will I see you then?" she asked, laying the data for her report in the back of her shiny metal report holder.

"I'm not sure, it depends on what AJ wants," Seth said. *You're going to get yourself in trouble here*, he thought.

"Something tells me you could convince him to let you

tag along if you really want to," she said, accented with dimples and a wink.

Before Seth could reply she turned to walk outside, steering the gurney into the back of the van. Despite his desire to follow her so they could continue talking, Seth forced himself to focus on the investigation. He took a deep breath before he began checking on how far Knox got with the evidence collection.

With the crime scene under control, Seth grabbed his leather satchel and walked toward the office. Looking to his right he could see into The Diner. Low lighting in the portion of the restaurant closest to him provided a good look at the mannerisms of the man talking to the waitress.

"Fucking rookie," Seth whispered to himself. His ire rose with each step he took toward the restaurant, but he stopped, his strong fairness characteristic kicking in. There was no way Seth could say anything to Willie for flirting instead of doing his job after what took place with him and the deputy coroner.

Seth's feet rotated on the pavement and headed toward the motel office. His mind on flirting, he reflected on its dual meaning. His and the rookie's flirting with women also meant they were flirting with danger…Seth from his wife, the rookie from AJ.

Nearing the office Seth could see a young Oriental woman with a slight build behind the counter. He pulled on the door meeting resistance from being locked. The woman looked up, smiled, rapidly pointing her finger toward the bank teller type window on her left. Noticing the stucco around the window had not been painted to match the rest of the motel did not surprise Seth.

Lord knows a little paint might eat into their profits, he thought.

Seth did not recognize the hotel clerk so he laid his wallet with badge and I.D. in the tray used for passing bills. The woman's cheeks lowered at the same time the corners of her lips flattened out. She obviously had worked there long enough to know of the several recent arrests of parolees using the rooms to sell crank. She grabbed the wallet, taking her time while she looked at the picture on the I.D., then at him. Satisfied, she passed it through the tray.

After getting her name for his report Seth asked, "Can you tell me who rented room 121 tonight?"

Without a word the young woman turned, plodding over to the far right side of the counter. She pulled a small 3x5 card out of the dull gray, metal, time card rack leaning up against the wall. Above each of the slots a faded white number from using white-out appeared on blue painters tape stuck to the metal. She shuffled back and slid the card through to him.

Seth immediately noticed the name of Nathan Price in very neat handwriting. Not surprisingly, no address or personal information had been listed. Whoever wrote it printed the word Jeep, followed by 3DCA462. Seth recognized it as the license plate number on Nathan's Jeep.

"Were you the one who rented out this room?"

She methodically nodded her head twice, without blinking.

"So, you actually dealt with the person?" he asked.

She cocked her head, her mouth twisting into a scowl before she finally nodded.

Seth pulled the Polaroid Knox had taken of Nathan's driver's license from his satchel. Holding it against the glass, he asked, "Could you tell me if the guy in this picture was the same man who rented the room?"

"It wasn't him," she said with perfect English.

"Could you tell me what he looked like?"

"Not much to tell. A white guy, all black clothes, not quite as tall as you. Definitely not the guy in the picture. We done, I'm pretty busy," she said, obviously disgusted with Seth being there.

"Yeah. Thanks. You've been a ton of help," he said sarcastically.

She cocked her head to the side again giving him her best *Fuck You* look.

CHAPTER EIGHTEEN

⸻

AJ drove west on Keyes Road past several orchards and fields. He slowed near the 12000 block, noticing an array of lights ahead of him refracting off the low ceiling of fog.

Passing a small run-down house on his right the aura of wealth gradually came into view—the Price residence. The large, white, wooden rail fence adorned with blue icicle lighting let everyone know the home made up only a small part of the property owned.

AJ turned in toward the house, multicolored Christmas lights lining both sides of the long asphalt driveway. A large mound surrounded by brick had the appearance of the foundation to a shrine, temporarily being useful as the base to a nearly twenty-foot-high Douglas fir, the most beautifully decorated outdoor tree he had ever seen.

Following the circular drive he came to a massive stone-faced three-story residence. Icicle lights from the house illuminated the entire yard, complete with a Nativity scene on one end, life-sized reindeer and a sleigh on the other. AJ parked in front of the brick walkway leading to two twelve foot solid wooden doors.

Getting out of his Mustang AJ took a deep breath of the cool misty air, psyching himself up. Death notifications were never easy, although he believed honesty and compassion were the keys.

Shortly after he rang the bell the left door creaked open. The Hispanic women in front of him looked to be in her late forties, wearing an all-white work dress and a colorful apron with a Christmas snowman scene.

After AJ showed her his badge and ID she said, "Mr. and Mrs. Price no esta aqui. In Hawaii, tres mas días."

"Who is it?" the female voice somewhere in the house asked.

"Policía, señorita," the woman answered.

The door drifted open for AJ to see her in a purple robe standing at the top of the stairs. He caught himself staring at her natural beauty.

She's got to be in her early twenties, although she carries herself much more maturely, he thought. *Nathan's sister maybe?*

She glided down the long staircase, his eyes drawn to her long blonde hair and elegant facial features.

"I'll talk with him, Dear. Thank you." The Hispanic woman nodded and left.

AJ handed the young woman his badge and ID.

"Sorry to bother you so early in the morning Ma'am. I'm Detective Conti from Turlock Police."

"It's all right, Detective," she said as she briefly glanced at his identification. "What did my brother do now?"

"Your brother Ma'am? You are ...?"

"I'm sorry. My name is Nicole Price," she said as she handed back his credentials while extending her right hand.

The softness of her hand wrapped around his, and her beautiful eyes staring at him made AJ wonder why he wanted to do the death notification.

I should've listened to Sandy, he thought.

"I assumed you were here for something my brother Nathan must have done. He went out last night and never came home. Is he in jail? Did he do something wrong?"

"May I come in?" AJ asked, slowly withdrawing his hand.

"Yes, yes. Forgive me. Please come in," Nicole said. She stepped back, directing him to the study on her right.

"Thank you, Miss Price," he said.

"Please, call me Nicole. Have a seat, anywhere is fine."

The masculine décor caught his attention and the only item in the room with a soft appearance was the large family portrait perfectly centered on the wall above the couch.

Nicole took a seat on the sofa next to him.

"Are your parents really in Hawaii?"

"Yes, for a few more days. Is something wrong?"

His stomach began to tighten.

"You mentioned Nathan went out last night. Do you have any idea where he was going?"

"No, I'm sorry. I don't have a clue. We are very different people. He's twenty-four, with no college education and no direction. I'm twenty-two, will graduate from Princeton this spring, then on to law school. Nathan parties, I prefer a good book by the fire."

"Did Nathan leave here with anybody last night?"

"He left around five thirty, right before dinner. For sure nobody left with him, but I don't know if he picked up a friend or not."

"You know of any drugs Nathan is into using?"

"No idea. My mom told me last month when I called Nathan had been drinking even more than usual after the accident."

"What accident?" AJ asked, acting surprised.

"Nathan and a friend of his, some guy named Mike. I've never met him and got the impression neither had my parents, but they'd been drinking at Jerry's Club in Turlock. On the way home they ran a stop sign, and killed a high school girl. Instantly, I hope, so she did not suffer. Mike fled the scene. Nathan kind of became introverted afterward, he's been drinking more since then."

"I think I remember hearing about it," AJ said. "Wasn't there a trial?"

"Yes. The jury acquitted my brother," Nicole said, lowering her head, her eyes looking down.

"You seem…like you're not okay with it," AJ said, gently pressing for more.

Nicole kept looking at her lap. "I would never tell my parents this, and I'll deny it if you say anything to them…I believe Nathan was the driver…he's been in a depression ever since. Our parents paid for the best lawyer in the area to get him off. The part troubling me is he's never said to any of us he wasn't the driver."

Nicole broke the long silence when she raised her head and looked directly into his eyes. Tears fell down her cheeks.

"I know something terrible has happened, Detective Conti," she said, her voicing cracking.

AJ waited, sensing more would come without his needing to ask.

"I've been expecting this for years. In high school he started resenting our father spending all of his time at work and none of it with us. My father has been trying to buy back his relationship with Nathan, when Nathan only wanted a normal father-son relationship. My mother took my father to Hawaii to relax because he and Nathan have really been going at each other lately."

Nicole paused, wiping tears from her cheeks with the backs of her hands.

"My father feels Nathan is wasting his life away. Every time they argue Nathan gets drunk out of spite. I can't recall the last time I saw Nathan happy. I told my father once he should make Nathan get a job…then Dad got angry at me and wouldn't talk to me for six months. We're a pretty messed up family, aren't we?" she asked, the tears flowing.

AJ grabbed tissues from a box on one of the bookshelves, giving them to Nicole. She covered her face and fell against AJ's shoulder. Despite never having any children, AJ felt as though he were comforting his daughter who recently had her heart broken.

"He's…dead, isn't he?" she asked between gasping breaths.

AJ wanted so badly not to have to tell her. Holding her close, he managed to say, "I'm so sorry."

Nicole jumped up, no longer in control of her emotions and ran to the staircase, ascending without a word.

AJ stood feeling terrible. He took his business card and laid it on the foyer table, taking a last look at the residence interior before seeing himself out.

The Beatles were right, he thought, *money can't buy you love.*

CHAPTER NINETEEN

Stalker drove home and took a walk, giving him time to think about the plan. He returned to The Diner shortly after seven making sure the day-shift waitresses had started before settling into one of the booths along the west wall. He needed a clear view of room 125. He had changed clothes to a more casual look, adding clear-lens glasses to change his appearance. Even though the odds were low someone would recognize he had been in the restaurant a few hours before, he had to take the chance so he could keep an eye on the room. Killing time in the restaurant would not be out of place.

AT 7:17 A.M. ADAM RILEY WALKED OUT OF HIS MOTEL room, figured he'd grab a quick breakfast and make it over to the car repair shop shortly after it opened. Walking across the parking lot he prayed for his sister, thankful for the news she seemed to be stable.

Stalker had watched Adam walk across the parking lot and pass next to his window. He opened the paper wide appearing to read the inner pages and shifted in his seat putting his back against the wall, and the window behind him.

He stared as Adam scanned the room and pulled his paper up a little higher. When he lowered the paper, Adam's eyes were back looking right at him.

Fuck! Don't panic. Nod, hold the stare, he'll look away.

Adam turned and took his table, while Stalker wondered why he didn't have a car in front of the motel room. Stalker knew he'd be in for a long day of trying to follow him without being seen.

He watched Adam eat his breakfast like it might have been the first meal he had had in a while. He looked in a hurry to get somewhere even though he didn't have a car.

When Adam stood to leave Stalker decided to play it cool and hold his position as long as he could and laid a ten-dollar bill on the table.

Adam exited and glanced toward the restaurant one last time. Stalker reasoned he was in the clear because the guy had no reason to suspect anything beyond a casual meeting of the eyes. Stalker stood, grabbed his black leather jacket, glanced around the room to make sure nobody else was paying any particular attention to him, and headed for the door.

He watched Adam cross the highway and saw a small auto repair shop and determined the man must be headed there. He hurried across the street to get closer.

Stalker caught Adam's soft touch of the maroon Toyota Camry, like only an owner would do, parked in the first stall of the lot before going into the shop office. He weighed his options of having to make a move versus trying to get information to be able to track Adam down later. He had to be careful not to allow Adam to see him. About to hide in Adam's car, Stalker heard the mechanic talking in the open bay.

"Where is it you said you were headed?" the mechanic asked.

"I'm going up to Redding."

"I remember now. Didn't you say you needed to get up there in a hurry?"

"Yes. My sister had to have emergency surgery yesterday so I'm trying to get up there to be with her and my mother."

Stalker formulated a new plan in his head and decided to memorize the license plate of the Camry in case his plan didn't work. He turned walking back toward the highway.

CHAPTER TWENTY

A dam folded the receipt, took Tommy's shop tag off the key ring and walked toward his car. He tossed the tag under the Chevy parked next to him, unlocked the trunk, threw his gym bag inside, and pulled out the black CD holder.

Adam listened to the car hum while he took the California map out of the glove box, preferring the old fashion-kind over his cell phone. He wanted to get to Interstate 5 since it had more lanes and the speed limit was faster. Once he knew the route he tried folding the map but realized he had done it incorrectly. Instead of trying to refold it, he threw it in the back.

Adam put the car in reverse and backed up, cracking the driver's window slightly for some fresh air.

"Good luck. Hope your sister gets better," the mechanic yelled, waiving from inside the last bay.

"Thanks. I appreciate it," Adam said, putting the car in drive.

He pulled onto Walnut Road and turned right onto Main Street where he came to a stop under the highway. Waiting for a turn arrow he saw someone on the right shoulder of the onramp trying to hitch a ride. Adam realized it was the man from The Diner.

It's got to be a sign, right? he thought. *I mean, there I was lacking self-confidence and now I have a chance to work on it...with the same guy.* He paused. *I don't normally pick up hitchhikers though...what do I do? Ah heck, he's not like someone I've never seen before, right? Besides, it is pretty darn cold out in the fog, and I could use the company.*

Pulling over to the shoulder he pushed the buttons to unlock the doors and roll down the window, coming to a stop next to the man standing on the shoulder.

"Come on, get in," he said.

Stalker smiled as if he appreciated the gesture, but the smile was personal for the good fortune he felt.

"Thanks," Stalker said as he opened the door and slid onto the seat. "Todd Stevens," he partially lied as he extended his hand.

"Adam. Adam Riley," he replied as they shook.

"Man, you're really helping me out," Stalker said. "I didn't realize how cold it is out there. Damp fog kinda eats right through the clothes."

"Yeah, I had to walk from the restaurant to the repair shop over there," Adam said, pointing back over his left shoulder with his thumb.

"It surprised me how cold I got in such a short distance," Adam said.

"Nice ride. Can't believe you had trouble with this thing, it seems brand new."

"Thanks," Adam said proudly, sitting up a little straighter.

"The engine light came on so I decided to stop. Ended up being nothing. So, where you headed?" Adam asked as he started to pull back onto the onramp.

"I only need a ride to Modesto, about fifteen miles up the road. I've got to get to court and the trial starts at nine thirty. This is gonna work out great."

"No problem, glad I could help. You in some kind of trouble?" Adam asked with an obvious tone of nervousness.

Stalker decided using the angle of supporting his sister might go over well.

"Nah, nah," he said, shaking his head. "It's my sister, she had to end up suing someone who sold her some shoddy stuff. I said I'd try and get up there, lend some moral support, you know. I wanted to be there in case she needed anything."

Stalker could tell the explanation worked when Adam nodded a couple times.

Adam tensely gripped the steering wheel while driving in the center lane. He had driven in fog before in San Diego, but never in such thick fog where he could barely see a couple cars in front of him. After ten miles Adam saw the lights from the Highway Patrol car flashing in front of him. He saw the patrol car drifting side to side across the lanes of traffic going about thirty miles per hour. Cars were gradually stacking up in all three lanes. The fog seemed thicker than Adam had ever seen it.

"Sorry I'm not talking much, this fog is much worse than I'm used to. I live about five minutes away from work so I stay off the freeways if I can, especially when it's foggy."

"Don't worry about it," Stalker said. "I understand. Like I said, I'm happier than heck to get a ride."

Stalker undid his seat belt and leaned forward to take off his jacket. Coming close to where he wanted Adam to stop, Stalker laid his jacket across his lap, sliding his hands underneath. Pulling off his leather gloves, he took the pair of latex gloves he kept in his inside jacket pocket. Stalker put the leather gloves in the jacket pocket and slid the latex gloves into his left hand.

Checking once more, Adam appeared glued to the cars in front of him, not paying any attention to Stalker. He slowly reached around to his right hip, ready to abandon the idea if he needed. When he started to pull up his shirt it stuck on the sheath of the knife. He moved his hand down to unhook the shirt and slid the shirt up as his hand felt for the handle of the knife. With his eyes focused on Adam he withdrew the six-inch shiny blade from its protective cover and moved the knife down his side and laid it on the seat hidden by his leg.

Passing the Ninth Street exit Stalker felt his plan coming together. His exit would be coming up soon so he told Adam he needed to get over into the right lane. Adam did not say a word; he nodded and turned on his signal while checking his mirrors. Stalker eased his right hand under the jacket, quickly sliding on the latex gloves.

They started under the Crows Landing overpass when Stalker brought his right hand out from under the jacket, placing it around the handle of the knife.

"Pull over right up here, before the bridge."

"Are you sure?" Adam asked. "I can take you to the court house." Adam said without looking at Stalker.

"No, this is fine. It's not far. I can walk. Right up there," Stalker said, pointing to his right with his chin.

The car came to a gradual stop and Adam instinctively shifted his right hand to the gearshift lever. He put the car in park, then he let out a deep sigh as he relaxed back into his seat.

"Man, I hope it's not like this the whole way," Adam said, as he started reaching to shake hands. His eyes blinked while turning his head to make eye contact.

Wham. Adam felt the yank of his hair and his head

striking the headrest. He let out a guttural moan from the surprising pain as the knife pierced his neck. His larynx caved in from the force while the blade reached up and penetrated his brain stem. In the blink of an eye Adam's lights were out.

CHAPTER TWENTY-ONE

Stalker wiped his knife on Adam's pant leg, replaced the knife in its sheath, put on his jacket and waited for a short break in traffic. When he couldn't see headlights rounding the bend under the overpass Stalker hastily exited the car, slammed the door behind him and jumped down the embankment between two large oleander bushes.

He crouched in the tall grass pausing long enough to take off his cowboy boots and slightly roll up his pant legs. Wanting to leave a trail for the K-9 he knew the police would use to track him he completely dried his boots with napkins from Adam's car so he could cleanly walk away after the trail abruptly stopped. Carrying his boots he began shuffling his feet down the small hillside in the thick grass between the highway and a four-foot wide asphalt drainage canal running between the hillside and a trailer park.

Stalker turned south at the canal, continuing to shuffle his feet in the grass. He went about fifty yards and crossed the canal, shuffling again through the tall grass on the opposite side.

He leaned against a fence leading to a junkyard south of a trailer park before going back to the canal in the same disturbed grass he came in. Stalker wiped the bottom of his boots off with his red checkered handkerchief from his back pocket, put his boots back on, and then straddled the asphalt where his stocking feet had touched.

Walking north through the water in the canal he came to the dead end of a small two lane road paralleling the south bank of the Tuolumne River. He climbed up the fence, gauged the distance to land on the pavement instead of disturbing the dirt bordering the fence, and pushed hard, sticking the landing right where he wanted.

"I got rid of the witness, and in a different jurisdiction. This worked out much better than I thought," he said to himself, pleased with his efforts.

Thinking of Adam in the car, a smile crossed his face as he began to hum the tune from Wizard of Oz, *If I Only had a Brain*. Then he stopped, feeling bad for the guy who was only trying to be a good brother and visit his sister in the hospital.

AN OLD, TAN, CLOTH COVERED COUCH SAT EMPTY IN THE tall grass of the widened shoulder on the north side of Zeff Road. Stalker wondered how many homeless people living around the river had carnal knowledge on the couch before slipping back into the brush and their homemade lean-tos.

He could see two bridges ahead, the first for Seventh Street. The grace of the craftsmanship on the splendid old stone supports made the bridge beautiful. It reminded Stalker of something Norman Rockwell would paint in one of his classic depictions of a life gone by.

The plain bridge forty feet beyond it to the east had basic metal support beams holding up the old railroad tracks. At some magical point in between those bridges the name of the road changed from Zeff Road to River Road.

Those bridges are a replica of the distinct differences in my life, the beauty of the past before the hellholes, to the dull of the present, he thought.

Stalker saw the lights of the truck coming at him so he stopped and knelt down, acting like he needed to tie his shoe. The left blinker came on and the truck slowed to a stop.

About the time he thought there would be no problems the truck didn't turn, it slowly started to come at him. Stalker bolted heading into the brush for cover before taking another look.

He believed the employees at the warehouse didn't care for homeless people hanging around their cars in the parking lot so the trucker probably wanted to scare Stalker away. He waited for the driver to park and go into work before leaving and making a clean getaway without being seen.

AFTER LEAVING NICOLE PRICE, AJ HAD TO JUMP BACK into the case. Despite him knowing they would all be waiting for him in the briefing room, his priority was finishing the written portion of the search warrant for the motel room and Nathan's Jeep. The Detective secretary and AJ were close to being done and his reputation with judges regarding his timeliness and thoroughness was at stake. The briefing would have to take a back seat.

"Man, she's an awesome secretary," AJ said with a smile, waving the final draft of the search warrant when he walked into the briefing room.

"The judge will be happy," Seth said.

"You know she will," AJ said. "For you young bucks, the lesson of the day, at least thus far, is keep a judge you have to wake up in the middle of the night on your good side. Lord knows you'll end up in their chambers at some point." Willie's eyes were locked on his phone, and he hadn't paid attention to anything AJ said. Allison Thompson, a detective not assigned to AJ's team, walked into the room. She did a finger point to herself, then to a chair to get AJ's approval, which he did. AJ loved to see young officers and detectives who wanted to learn.

AJ knew a majority of the detectives did not like to have briefings along the way, but AJ generally didn't care what the others thought...he was the lead investigator and felt they were important.

Beyond everyone having the latest information, briefings helped AJ to pass out assignments based on what needed to be done and who the best person was for each particular task. The disgruntled looks of some other detectives would not be enough to deter him.

Seth was the exception. He and AJ hit it off immediately. Seth had the same beliefs as AJ on handling cases, and the amount of effort everyone assigned should put in. They worked together on the last seven homicides where AJ was the lead investigator, with their clearance rate being double the remainder of other detectives in the unit. The two never said anything about it and let their actions speak for them.

Reviewing the case, AJ started:

"The initial officer on the scene told me nobody answered the motel door so he got a passkey, and only after he told the clerk he'd kick the door when the clerk refused. He went in, saw the guy taped up on the bed, and pushed the bathroom door open with his left hand to clear the room. Said he checked for a pulse but the guy was clearly dead. Says he didn't touch anything else."

"Knoxy?"

"I'll compare his prints to the ones I got off the door to eliminate them," Knox said. "It was a pretty straight forward crime scene. The drinking glass with lipstick and prints had liquor in it, I believe it's going to be whiskey. I found the beer can on the floor between the beds. The interesting thing about it is it looks like it has a pinprick hole in the top. We'll get the contents analyzed by the Department of Justice lab. Of course the duct tape will be important, but we'll have to get it at the autopsy."

Knox looked down at his notes.

"This is kinda weird, I found a strange wet spot on the carpet right outside the bathroom door, almost up against the door frame. It smells like piss. I cut it out along with the padding. The last thing is I lifted a set of prints from the top of the toilet lid, not the seat. Someone left it in the down position, which seemed kind of strange to me."

"See if you can do up those prints from the toilet seat lid as soon as possible," AJ said. "What about the Jeep?"

"There wasn't a whole lot there," Knox said. "I got a print, probably a thumb, off the rearview mirror. I found a couple of strands of longer hair off the driver's headrest area. They didn't look like the dead guy's plus they sort of have a red tint."

"Compare the print from the Jeep to the dead guy's and to the toilet seat lid," AJ said. "There's a good chance there'll be a match. Send the hair to the DOJ lab, too."

AJ noticed Sergeant Boykin leaning against the doorframe with arms crossed. AJ acknowledged him with a slight head nod, hoping he would stay so AJ did not have to waste time later catching him up on everything.

When AJ looked at Willie he wondered if Willie would come clean. "Willie, you're up."

Besides the waitresses in the diner, Willie told them he identified a drunk, a trucker, and a couple of kids groping each other in a booth. Willie's stomach turned a little with his decision to pass over other information, or lack of it. He figured he would be hanging himself if anyone realized he didn't do what AJ told him to do. He also said he put in the request for the nine-one-one tape to be transcribed, along with a booking photo of the dead guy from the sheriff's office from when he got arrested on a drunk driving manslaughter case.

"Seth and I split up the room-to-room search," AJ said. "Nobody answered any doors on the north side, we did find one witness a couple doors down from the victim." AJ provided everyone with Adam Riley's information after he described the interview.

"Knox and Willie, I want you guys to make sure you get everything logged in, book the stuff staying here, then Knox can get the other evidence up to the DOJ Lab. When you're done, Willie you can go get a little sleep. I may need you later," AJ said as he stood to leave.

Everyone began picking up their notes preparing to leave.

"Hey Willie. Are you sure no one else was in the restaurant?" AJ asked, loud enough for everyone to stop.

Willie looked at Knox real quick, the look on his face begging for help. He looked down at his notes, unable to make eye contact with AJ, the feeling everyone's eyes in the room were beating down on him.

"Yeah, I didn't see anybody else in there. Why?" Willie asked, not really wanting to get into a discussion

"I could feel we were being watched. Arsonists are not

the only ones who like to see what is happening at their crime scene. It's pretty cold outside, so it's likely with all the windows around the restaurant a person would watch from in there. Maybe do things like count how many of us there are, watch our routine, see what every person did and how thorough we were...not to mention the nine-one-one call came from the pay phone outside the restaurant."

"It did?" Willie said, the tone and his pale face giving him away.

AJ stared at him long enough to let everyone know Willie had lied to him.

"I bet if I go ask the older night waitress, not the young one who's trying to find a husband, how many customers were in the restaurant at the same time the cop asking questions was there she could tell me. Now, unless you want me to get more information from her about who you didn't identify, then get you kicked out of the Detective Bureau, I suggest you get me information on what he looked like within twenty-four hours."

AJ grabbed his paperwork and headed for the door, Seth following close behind. AJ winked as he passed Sergeant Boykin who had a tight lip smile, until he glared over at Willie.

"I told you," Knox said emphatically. "I don't know how he knows things, he just knows. You should've listened to me. Stupid move." Knox walked away, heading to the evidence room.

Smiling, Allison said, "Man, kind of crazy how he knew you were hitting on the waitress instead of doing your job. Glad it's you and not me." She chuckled as she turned to leave, then repeated, "Glad it's you."

CHAPTER TWENTY-TWO

Dani had gone to work early. She liked the quiet time in the office before everyone started arriving and the pace quickened. This would be day three of Dani's first child-abuse trial. Sitting in her office going over the case, Dani sat back in her chair, her fingertips together as if she was praying. Something inside of her told her she had nothing to lose. The first two days of the trial she worried about every little thing going wrong and today, looking at her calendar she decided no more.

Today, Thursday, December 8, I am changing my way of thinking, she thought. *I'm tired of being timid.*

At a few minutes before ten Dani started the third day of trial by putting Azar's best friend, on the stand. She testified it had been five forty-five in the evening when she received a phone call from Azar. The woman said Azar sounded near hysterical, while at the same time she would only whisper. Azar told her she couldn't believe she did not help her son as her husband beat the boy black and blue with a belt buckle.

"I asked Azar when it happened, and she said a few minutes before she called me," she said.

"You testified earlier you suggested Azar take Cass to the Emergency Room. Why the suggestion?" Dani asked.

"I knew Azar would never call the police...they would," she said.

Later in the day Dani put a physician on the stand who was on staff at Children's Hospital in Oakland and considered to be an expert on causes relating to child injuries. She described her medical training in addition to her years of experience, and the Defense did not object. The judge declared her an expert.

Dani methodically worked the information in from the expert, leading the jury down a path of complete description of the injuries Cass had suffered, the mechanics of those injuries, and the doctor's expert medical opinion as to the causes of the injuries. Dani knew the defense would point to the wrought iron gate after Azar's earlier testimony, so she decided to attack the issue first. The expert testified only two bruises could have been from the gate, every other bruise or injury would have come from a belt buckle similar in shape and size to the one in evidence.

The judge called for a long break before lunch. Dani felt pleased with her expert's testimony, especially since she had not been able to warn her of the wrought iron gate defense until she had spoken with her after she arrived.

During the break Dani thanked the doctor and felt she had made a decent recovery from the original disaster. She decided she would rest her case.

Dani breathed a sigh of relief as she walked into the hallway and felt pleased with the turnaround of the trial. She began to regain some of her confidence she had lost in the beginning.

CHAPTER TWENTY-THREE

⟶ ◦ ⟵

Seth and AJ ended up at Perko's Restaurant. AJ wanted to hear what Seth found out while they caught up on food for the long day ahead.

The waitresses knew them as regulars from eating there at least twice a week. Seth had been going there from his early days in Patrol, gradually introducing AJ to all of them. Amber was by far their favorite, somehow always knowing when they needed privacy to discuss work. With two menus in her hand she motioned for them to follow, seating them in the farthest corner booth of the back dining room.

AJ knew what he wanted but Seth went straight for the one page menu with specials of the month. AJ felt his phone vibrate with a text from Bethany.

Sorry you had a call out. I wanted to say have a good day. I don't expect you to get in touch with me for a few days, I do hope you think about me. Know I'm thinking about you. Love you!!! B

Smiling, AJ put his phone on the table. Being relatively new to loving someone and being loved back, the text made him feel pretty good.

When Amber returned with their coffee AJ ordered his usual. Often more open to trying different meals Seth ordered "The Habanero Skillet."

"How's your father doing after the stroke?" AJ asked Amber.

"He's doing great," she said with a smile. "They gave him some wonderful drug and it reversed the stroke. They told us it was because we got him to the E.R. so fast."

"Fantastic," AJ said. "If you need anything all you need to do is ask. We'd be happy to help."

"Thank you so much for caring about us," her voice breaking a little. She left before AJ could respond.

AJ told Seth the old pay phone in front of The Diner only had smudges, no prints.

"When you listen to the call the guy comes across matter-of-fact like, no emotion, never giving dispatch a chance to ask any questions," AJ said. "Probably not much help."

"You think he's the killer?" Seth asked.

"I don't know. At first glance it looks like a woman might have killed Nathan and this guy's only letting us know there's a dead body. The problem is, something doesn't feel right."

"Yeah, especially with the call most likely being made right after the guy died," Seth said.

"Sandy said Nathan couldn't have been dead too long. He still felt warm and lividity had barely started setting in. Either the guy killed Nathan or he knew when the girl left and made the call after she finished him off."

"Hmmm, starting out with a little challenge," AJ said. "My kind of case. What'd you find out from the clerk?"

"She was kind of weird, didn't talk much," Seth said raising his eyebrows.

"Check this out. I ask her who rents the room and she slides the card under the teller's window they have on the side. The card has all of Nathan's information, including the Jeep. Then something told me to show her the Polaroid we took. She doesn't even hesitate, and says he's not the guy who rented the room. She only described him as a white guy not quite as tall as me. All the right info, not the right guy."

"Strange," AJ said. "We've got to figure out who the girl was with Nathan that was seen by the guy in 125."

Seth commented on Nathan being taped up like a Christmas present, not a wrinkle in the duct tape. They both agreed Nathan probably passed out and didn't put up a struggle, and also the woman could have easily taped him up if he were passed out.

"So then, where does the strange guy in black who rents the room come in?" Seth asked.

"Maybe I'm going to have to talk to Nathan's sister again. She said something about Nathan previously being charged with DUI manslaughter where he claimed a friend of his drove, not him. Maybe the same friend gets the room for him after Nathan tells him he thinks he's going to get lucky with this chick."

"What about his parents?"

"They're in Hawaii. Death notifications suck, although his sister made this one easier. I think she knew it as soon as she saw me."

AJ felt bad for Nicole and told Seth of her crying on his shoulder and him feeling like a dad consoling his daughter.

"She gets to bury her brother right before she heads back to school. Great holidays, huh."

Amber returned with their breakfast and coffee and told them she'd make sure nobody bothered them.

AJ cut his eggs so the yoke would run, unscrewed the lid from the pepper shaker, then poured generous amounts over the eggs. He put the lid back on and ate the fruit first, as always.

"Wipe the silly ass grin off your face," AJ said.

"You always want to come off as though you're tough, not wanting anyone to know you care and have compassion," Seth said. "For the record, going back to re-interview her is your way of making sure she's okay. We both know you could get the information on the mysterious friend a dozen other ways."

"You know, sometimes you're a pain in the ass," AJ said, smiling, before changing the conversation.

"Their Dad got the best lawyer in the area money could buy and poof, the kid walks, although Nicole did say she thinks Nathan was really the driver. She had no idea who Nathan's friend is that he had supposedly been with when it happened. She did say with certainty Nathan left alone last night around dinnertime."

Seth accurately described manslaughter as a viable motive to kill, either by one of the DUI victim's family members, or by someone they paid to do it. Still, they both agreed their problem would be Nathan mixing his drinking with his rich kid attitude, unfortunately providing a lot of people motive.

AJ sensed they were about to change directions again given the uncomfortable pause, along with Seth's stirring of his food with his fork. AJ quietly set everything down, grabbed his coffee and waited.

"Since we're sort of on the topic of women…I kind of need your help," Seth said.

"You got it. What is it, Seth?" He knew Seth and his wife had been having some difficulty about all of the overtime in the Detective Unit.

"It's nothing major really. It's…look, I don't need any more complications at home, so if it's possible I would kind of like to skip the autopsy. Sandy and I were doing a little bit too much flirting and I ended up feeling like crap. I need to stay away if you don't mind."

Seth was a good person wanting to do the right thing. AJ wanted him to know he supported him, so without hesitation AJ looked him square in the eyes.

"No problem," AJ said. "You need me to run interference, let me know. If you need to get home to your family, go. Look at me, twenty years as a detective without ever having a serious relationship. I've been married to this job up until six months ago when I met Bethany. Don't let this job, and all the crap it brings, become your family. Whatever you need you got it."

Seth's deep sigh confirmed he knew AJ meant every word. The validation of their deep friendship eased Seth's mind allowing them to finish breakfast talking about anything and everything, except homicides.

CHAPTER TWENTY-FOUR

D ani took a drink of water from the fountain spaced between the restroom entrances. Walking back toward the courtroom something felt different, although Dani could not figure out what. She contemplated the day until she got to the large wooden doors leading into the courtroom.

Forget about it; you have more important things to worry about. Focus.

Dani walked to the prosecution's desk where her OCD compelled her to arrange her notes and pads in specific locations. Thinking to herself which witness the defense would likely call first, Dani heard voices as the doors behind her opened. Turning to look the answer to her uneasiness came to her.

I haven't had the creepy sensation someone's watching me today, unlike all those other days, she thought.

Several minutes after the bailiff brought the jury back Dani told the judge the prosecution rested. Before the judge could respond, or Dani could take her seat, defense attorney Samuel Rothstein jumped up requesting a directed verdict.

"Your Honor, the prosecution has failed to meet their burden of proof in presenting a prima facie case against my client," Rothstein said.

The judge directed the bailiff to escort the jury to the deliberation room. Dani's mind started racing as she stood, while trying to portray confidence to the jury members as they filed past her.

"What do you base your request on Mr. Rothstein?" the judge asked.

"Well, Your Honor, the victim has never stated he is a victim of abuse from my client. Further, the child's mother testified Cass fell from a tree where he landed on a wrought iron gate. Although the doctor is a recognized expert, even she admitted at least some of Cass's bruises might have come from such a fall. The prosecution failed to put the child on the stand at the preliminary hearing so we have never heard directly from him as to exactly what happened. Even if you take the expert opinion regarding the cause of injuries to Cass, the prosecution has never proven my client is the person who inflicted such injuries. For all we know, Your Honor, it could have been the mother who beat her son, she's told different stories so who knows. It's quite possible her conscience got to her in court today knowing she could not send her husband to prison for something he did not do."

"Your Honor. If I may," Dani started.

"I'm sorry, Ms. Larson," the judge said, cutting Dani off. "I must admit I was already contemplating a directed verdict. I have thought about this throughout the entire recess expecting the prosecution might rest. I believe the prosecution has in fact failed to meet their burden, therefore I am inclined to order a directed verdict for the defense."

Dani hesitated. *Remember your vow to yourself earlier,* she thought.

"Your Honor, you would be making a huge mistake," Dani said, trying to look confidently into the Judge's eyes.

"Oh really," the judge almost snarled. "For what reason?"

"By allowing the mother's best friend to testify under the hearsay exception of excited utterance on its own is enough to send it to the jury. Further, despite what Mr. Rothstein claims about our expert, she testified the majority of injuries to Cass would have been caused by the belt, while only two could have been caused by the fence. Both of these are questions of fact for the jury to decide," Dani said.

She paused to take a breath, hoping to find more courage before she continued. Lowering her voice to a whisper so as not to embarrass the judge, Dani continued.

"We all know you hate being overturned on appeal, but there is a very good chance you would be if you order a directed verdict. Look, let's cut to the chase. We come into these child abuse cases knowing they are fifty-fifty at best. Prosecution knows it, defense knows it, and judges know it. Are we likely to lose or end up with a hung jury...sure. Still, this jury deserves to make the decision as to the questions of fact being enough to carry the burden of proof beyond a reasonable doubt, and not be excused because Mr. Rothstein wants to take the path of least resistance."

"Are you done," the judge said, her eyes squinted, a look of disdain on her face.

"Yes, Your Honor, I have nothing further," Dani said.

"Very well, Ms. Larson. If you want to roll the dice then we will," she said in a very low voice. She sat straight up, paused for a good thirty seconds as if contemplating, and then said, "The request by Mr. Rothstein for a directed verdict will be denied. Bailiff, bring the jury back so I can instruct them on what took place."

Walking back to their tables Rothstein whispered to Dani. "Took some serious guts girl. It might cost you your career, regardless, it definitely sent a message about your willingness to stand up for what you believe. Proud of you," he said as he winked.

Minutes later Rothstein rested his case without presenting a single witness.

Dani walked the jury through the facts presented by the witnesses with a relaxed, confident demeanor. Even though she knew her comment to the judge about her chances of winning the case was accurate, she had to do her best for the little boy.

Rothstein showed his years of experience as a defense attorney as he minimized everything Dani had said, even getting jurors to nod their heads in agreement as he turned Dani's expert into a defense witness.

STALKER ENTERED HIS HOUSE AND TOOK OFF HIS JACKET laying it across the back of the couch. He headed straight for the refrigerator, but glanced around to make sure nothing was out of place. He grabbed a water bottle from the fridge, then opened the left side of the dual appliance to take a Drumstick cone out of the freezer. Even though Stalker believed in being fit, he had long ago decided his love for the ice cream dessert would be his one vice.

Returning to the living room he thought about what he had accomplished. Although it had been a good day, he knew he needed to decide when the time would be right to follow Bethany again. Without thinking he walked to the rear of the couch, picked up the jacket, and hung it on the first rung of the coat tree by the entry.

Back at the couch he grabbed a ceramic coaster, placed the coaster on the coffee table and his drink on it. Setting down the Drumstick on the table he began to take off his boots. The boots were put next to the couch on his right side, with the back of the boots placed evenly up against the base of the couch.

Stalker carefully unscrewed the cap because he hated to spill liquid, even water. After taking his favorite gulp... the first swallow before it could be contaminated in any way...he picked up the Drumstick. He opened it as he had hundreds of times before, completely unrolling the paper cover so he could use it as a type of napkin while he held the cone in his other hand. Gently laying back on the couch Stalker half propped his back up on the arm as he slowly ate his ice cream, rehashing the details from his latest work.

His cat, Streak, lay on his perch of a carpet-covered maze. He knew better than to go directly to his master when he walked through the door, a lesson he had learned as a kitten. He waited patiently for the music to come on after the ice cream had been eaten. Streak stood to stretch, and quietly descended from his maze, softly walking to the couch without a sound. He jumped up on the end by the feet, making one last assessment before he gradually made his way up to lay on his masters' chest.

Stalker relaxed as Streak lay there, purring softly. He loved cats. He loved everything about them. He loved how they were so gentle, yet in an instant they could spring to kill for food. He loved their grace of movement and their confidence in how they carried themselves. He appreciated the fact they were generally a clean animal, having watched for hours how they bathed themselves as if cleanliness were a necessity.

Stalker had begun watching cats in the foster homes. There were constants in the numerous foster homes he had gone through in his early years; the filth from having too many kids under one roof, the abuse, though it took different forms, the lack of caring except for the money received per child, and the cats. Even if the foster home did not have a cat there were always some in the neighborhood.

After ending up at the boys home when he started ninth grade he met up with Boots, the charcoal gray male cat with white *boots* on all four feet who was one of the residents. Stalker had seen many animals, especially cats, become the prey of many a sick kid, so it surprised him to see a cat residing at the home. In less than three hours he saw why Boots survived…Boots clawed one of the boys as he tried to push him out of the way with his foot. When the boy ran off to get something to wipe up the blood running down his legs Boots sat, as if to say, "Don't mess with me."

The group home counselors were amazed at how Todd had befriended Boots in such a short period of time. Boots would not socialize with or let any of the boys pet him, except Todd. He spent hours watching Boots, all the while his appreciation increased. Not only had the cats been his private retreat, they often provided him a responsibility as he usually got assigned the task of caring for the animals. Although he cared for all of the animals with affection, he adored the cats and always provided them with complete compassion.

Years later he had seen Streak as a kitten when he walked past a pet store in a strip mall. Stalker stopped when something caught his attention in his peripheral vision. He looked down at the six kittens in the cage. While five of the kittens were moving around slowly, one kept streaking through the cage antagonizing the others, often bringing a smile to his face. He watched for nearly fifteen minutes. Twice the kitten stopped to look up at him, short breaks before he took off for another round of terrorizing his companions. Stalker became captivated by the kitten's beautiful mixture of black fur accented by four white paws. He knew the kitten's name before he ever entered the store.

CHAPTER TWENTY-FIVE

When AJ left the restaurant he drove north past the university and pulled into his driveway. Stepping from the Mustang he paused to look around, enjoying the peace of living in a cul-de-sac. AJ picked up the morning paper, tucked it under his arm and slid the key into the deadbolt.

He gave the door a light push as he stepped inside, listening for any sounds of life. He heard the distinctive sound of metal tags clanking against her collar and spotted her slowly making her way to him on her three legs, tail wagging as best as possible.

"Hop", short for Hop-a-long, was a shorthaired black and white mutt the size of a small Labrador he rescued shortly after buying the house. When he first spotted her lying on the side of the road she looked dead, her right front leg mangled. When he got closer he noticed her eyes were open. He had no intention of getting a dog until he saw her pleading eyes ... she became his family.

Kneeling, AJ petted her. Between her age, getting hit by a car, and arthritis in her back hips, Hop did not move fast anymore.

"You want to go out, old girl. Come on. I'll get you some fresh food while you're out there."

He patiently waited at the back door for her to work her way outside. AJ grabbed a can of dog food from the cupboard, a recent change after she started having trouble eating dry food. He didn't know how much longer she would live but he wanted to do his best to keep her comfortable until that day came.

AJ first noticed the fresh pine smell when he entered the house. His cleaning lady came every other week, except during the holiday season when AJ asked her to clean every week. He smiled when he saw Hop's clean oversized pillow bed. The cleaning lady left him a note to tell him she took the pillow to a laundromat to clean it in one of the large washing machines. Although her note read she hoped he wouldn't mind, she knew AJ well enough to realize he would appreciate anything she did, especially for Hop.

AJ pulled out his cell phone and sat on the couch while Hop ate. He touched the message icon, then Bethany's name so he could text her while he waited.

Thank you for thinking of me earlier. I'm so sorry about not being available for the next couple days. I have to run with this while it is fresh. I will get in touch with you when I can. I'm really looking forward to spending several days with you at Christmas time. Have a great day. AJ

Not knowing when he would be home again, AJ decided to freshen up. When he headed back out to the living room he found Hop fast asleep on her clean pillow bed.

DUE TO THE THICK FOG CHP OFFICER CASEY ANDREWS had been assigned to patrol Highway 99 in Stanislaus County until the fog cleared. Earlier in the morning she slowed traffic with her emergency lights on, weaving back and forth across all lanes trying to prevent multiple car pileups. Near eleven o'clock in the morning she drove northbound on Highway 99 when she noticed the maroon Camry on the shoulder. She had seen someone in the driver's seat on her southbound pass earlier. Seeing the car and driver still there surprised her.

Andrews flipped on her emergency lights as she pulled in behind it, hoping other drivers would see her lights as they came out from under the overpass of Crows Landing Road. Approaching the car on the passenger side she could see the driver's head against the headrest. She initially thought he could be napping, despite it being an odd place and time to stop.

She tapped on the doorframe with her flashlight to get the driver's attention. After waiting several seconds Andrews tapped again before she bent over to look in the front passenger window. She took a half step back, startled by what she saw. With as many dead bodies as she looked at over the years they usually did not shock her. Shining her flashlight in once more she saw large amounts of blood had come from the right side of the driver's neck, covering his clothing and much of the interior. She checked for a pulse she knew didn't exist and called for a Sheriff's Office homicide team and a coroner.

A young deputy from the Stanislaus Sheriff's office parked directly behind Officer Andrews's car. Based on what Andrews told him before he looked in the car he thought it would be good experience for him to see it. Although the deputy went solo one week earlier after being released by his training officer he knew not to disturb anything before detectives got there. When he looked in the passenger window he had to turn away, nearly throwing up. He backed away, happy to wait on the shoulder by the patrol cars chatting with Officer Andrews.

CHAPTER TWENTY-SIX

A J knew nobody from his team would be at the office so he decided to go to the DA's office to see what he could find about Nathan's acquittal. The morning fog lifted enough for him to see about a hundred yards in front of him, enough to open up his Mustang and let her fly.

On Highway 99 AJ neared the overpass of Crows Landing Road when he saw flashing lights from a patrol car rebounding off the fog. Rounding the bend he saw two patrol cars on the right shoulder before the bridge going over the Stanislaus River so he slowed to make sure the officers were safe. He saw a Sheriff's office patrol car, with a Highway Patrol car in front of it. He noticed two officers by the passenger door of the Sheriff's car with the driver of the maroon Toyota Camry sitting in his car. Seeing the officers were safe he sped up and noted the Camry driver looked pretty relaxed with his head flopped to the side.

AJ parked next to the downtown county jail in one of the reserved police spots. Despite all of the parking officers for Modesto Police Department knowing his Mustang, he still put a business card on the dash in the corner out of respect. AJ grabbed his folder and walked to the front of the building. Barely two steps into the lobby he heard his name and saw Deputy Lowell waiving him around the metal detector. The deputy started walking toward him with his hand extended.

"AJ, how the hell are you?"

"Doing well, Tom. How about you?"

"Still here, thanks to you and Bino," Lowell said. "I haven't seen you in so long, I don't think I told you about my newest tat."

"No, you haven't," AJ said.

Tom enjoyed talking about his numerous tattoos almost as much as he liked showing them off.

"For the last ten years or so every morning when I looked in the mirror I saw a damn scar where the dirt bag shot me and the docs had to reconstruct my shoulder," Tom said.

"My wife got tired of my complaining about it being ugly. The artists are so damn good nowadays she suggested a tattoo to cover the area. Now I see Bino with his badge every morning when I'm shaving. Took it right from the picture you gave me of him after he passed away. Seeing him every day reminds me to be thankful I'm alive. I can still see Bino nailing him. No offense, I didn't give you any ink despite the fact you killed the fuck for me." Lowell laughed.

Laughing with him, AJ said, "No offense taken. Glad my dog's name is memorialized, at least until your scrawny ass ends up six feet under." They laughed until one of the other deputies called for Lowell to help him. AJ patted Lowell on the back before he started up the stairs.

"Hey, Tom. I'm looking forward to seeing your tat," AJ said. Tom smiled proudly.

AJ headed down the main hallway to the lobby of the District Attorney's office and to the clerk behind the small open window. Before he identified himself, District Attorney Bridget Fletcher walked by, less than thirty feet away.

Seeing her focused on something AJ chose not to interrupt, despite the fact they worked numerous cases together back in her deputy district attorney days. Bridget briefly glanced as she passed by. After a few steps she stopped and looked back, smiling. She asked the clerk to buzz the door to let AJ in.

Extending his right hand he said, "Madame District Attorney."

Going past his hand Bridget gave him a big hug.

"AJ, it's been such a long time. How the heck are you?"

"I'm well, thank you for asking. How about you?"

Bridget got elected district attorney a few months after she successfully got a guilty verdict on the most notorious murder case Stanislaus County ever had.

"So-so," she said. "As I'm sure you've guessed, I'm not doing much as an attorney. I feel like the director of an orchestra when I'm not putting out fires or attending political functions." Bridget moved closer to AJ and whispered, "You know my husband and I are separated, right?"

"No, I hadn't heard. I'm really sorry, I always thought you two were perfect together. What happened?"

"It's all my fault really," she continued softly. "My ego wanted me to become the district attorney. Going from a trial with nationwide coverage, then straight into an election campaign for this position, and getting it, well…it only burdened our time together."

She paused, her eyes drifting down to the pile of folders in her hands.

"I don't blame him really. We're trying to work on it… it's been difficult. I've missed the last two counseling sessions after problems arose here. I think he might be on his last straw."

AJ could tell Bridget was worried when she kept shifting her weight from one leg to the other. He'd seen it many times before during their trials.

"I'm sorry to hear that. If there's ever anything I can do for either one of you please don't hesitate to ask. I respect both of you so much...I'd do anything for you guys."

Her eyes watering Bridget gave AJ a quick hug, holding on long enough to gather herself, then turned to the clerk and said, "Linda, please get this detective whatever he needs. Thank you." She partially turned back toward him.

"Great seeing you, as always. If you're ever up this way at the end of the day text me, maybe we can go have a cup of coffee and catch up."

Not waiting for a response she started to leave, took a couple steps, turned around, and said, "I really do miss working cases and going to trial with you, more than you know." Her eyes again watering Bridget walked away.

"How can I help you, Detective?" Linda asked.

As AJ watched Bridget walk away, a feeling of sadness overcame him.

"I'm sorry," he said when he realized Linda was waiting.

"I'd like to talk to the deputy DA who went to trial against a defendant, Nathan Price, not very long ago,"

Linda matter-of-factly began searching her computer. She found the information and was about to tell him when her phone rang. Half-listening she began writing down the attorney's name on a notepad. She tore off the top sheet, gave it to him, and pointing to a hallway mouthed the words, *Three doors down on the right.* Before AJ could say thank you Linda already moved on, typing into her computer again.

When AJ saw the open door to the third office on the right he walked in. The bland nameplate on the desk said

Dani Larson, same as the note. Despite Dani not being there, AJ decided to wait knowing most of the judges took their noon breaks within the next fifteen minutes. Having sat in numerous attorneys and judges offices while they were away, AJ did what he always did, he began snooping.

Dani's diplomas on the wall were from UOP in Stockton, with her juris doctorate from McGeorge Law School in Sacramento. Both were expensive, McGeorge costing quite a bit more than Humphreys Law School where AJ went. He figured she either had money, great scholarships, or she was school loan poor. Her desk appeared very organized with an obvious system for the huge stacks of cases she had been assigned. Considering the large number of cases deputy DA's always had going, her system alone impressed him.

Seeing several pictures on the oversized windowsill AJ walked around her desk. He first picked up an older picture with a family of four, then the one next to it with a young boy and a young girl.

Hmm, I wonder if they're twins, he thought.

"Ahem!" Dani Larson held her folders close to her chest, her head leaning to the side, staring with cold, hard eyes, her jaw tightening, the distinct look of someone pissed off about their territory being invaded.

"I'm sorry, these two beautiful pictures caught my eye," AJ said, replacing them on the windowsill.

Returning from the courtroom where the outcome of her child abuse trial now sat with twelve jurors, Dani found it difficult to be in the mood to deal with a stranger milling around her office.

"Excuse me, can I help you?" she asked in an annoyed tone.

"Do you mind getting back on this side of the desk," she added sarcastically. Walking inside, she neatly placed the folders on the center of her desk.

When AJ turned around after setting the picture down, Dani's folded arms went right along with the frustration he heard in her voice. She stared at him with visible disdain. Despite the stare, he could tell by her eyes she had to be the little girl in the pictures.

"My question still remains," she said.

"Oh, I'm sorry, I'm Detective AJ Conti, Turlock PD," he began as he worked his way toward the open chair by the door.

"Unfortunately, I need to ask you some questions about a trial you were involved in several weeks ago. Looking at your desk, it's probably the last thing you need, right?" AJ smiled, hoping it might relax her.

"I live in Turlock so I'm familiar with your name from the paper. What case?" she asked straight-faced.

"Have a seat," she directed.

So much for the smile softening her up, AJ thought.

"Thank you," he said.

Subtly letting him know who controlled the domain, Dani made sure he sat first before moving around the desk to take her seat.

"What can you tell me about Nathan Price?"

"He's a pompous, arrogant jerk who has no remorse for the young woman he killed," Dani said, the anger in her tone rising.

"I don't know everything about the case, I think I recall him being acquitted, wasn't he?"

"Yes, thanks to weak police work. I'm simply stating the facts. Not trying to be disparaging about your fellow officers."

"This took place in Turlock?"

"No. He got drunk in Turlock, the accident happened out in the county. CHP investigated it," she said.

AJ felt better knowing his agency didn't investigate it. "Can you give me a rundown of the case?"

Without needing to retrieve the file for review, Dani went into what sounded to him like her closing argument. He had been around enough deputy DA's to know, they are so overwhelmed with cases, only a handful become personal. *I wonder what it is about this one?* he thought.

"After the jury acquitted him the cocky jerk came up to me and said, 'Nice try, maybe next time.'" Dani said.

"Well, you don't have to worry anymore," he baited her.

"What? Why?"

"He was found dead in a motel room in Turlock this morning," AJ said, watching for her reaction.

"You're joking right?" Dani asked, her eyebrows raised.

AJ sat in silence staring at her.

"You're not joking. Oh my gosh, that's, that's quite a shock." She sat back in her chair, staring down at her desk.

"I don't feel anything for Nathan, but I do feel terrible for his parents. No matter what a jerk I think he was, he's still their son…I feel bad for them." Her tone softened when she commented on Nathan's parents.

Funny, the parents are who I always feel bad for, too, he thought.

After hearing Dani's choice of words when speaking of Nathan, AJ decided to try to find out what made this case so personal to her.

"I noticed all the pictures over by the window are old," he said. "It looks like you when you were little. Out of curiosity, how come you don't have any updated ones?"

AJ guessed she would not be prepared for the quick change of topics. Sure enough, before she realized it the words were coming out of her mouth.

"My parents and brother were killed by a drunk driver when I was ten. There are no new pictures."

The look on her face changed from slightly being shocked to disbelief he got her to open up so easily.

"I am so sorry," AJ said. "I shouldn't have asked such a personal question."

Standing to leave he said, "I know you're very busy so I won't take up any more of your time. Thank you for your help." AJ turned toward the door.

"Wait, Detective. How did Nathan die?" Dani asked.

"Right now it looks like a homicide, we don't have a lot of details yet. Thanks again," he said as he left the office.

CHAPTER TWENTY-SEVEN

⸺⸺⸺ ◦ ⸺⸺⸺

D etective Fuller from Stanislaus County Sheriff's Office arrived on the highway within fifteen minutes of the request. Fuller's first inclination was a passenger in the front seat or the back seat probably stabbed the driver. The wound on the right side of the driver's neck would have been difficult, if not impossible, for a person to accomplish from outside of the car.

After looking at the driver Fuller surveyed the area. He requested a K-9 unit, feeling the most likely way for a suspect to get away would be going down the grassy hillside off the passenger side. The trailer park at the base of the hillside seemed like a natural place to go to get away so Fuller had specifically requested the Sheriff's Office best tracking dog.

A little over an hour later the K-9 started his search from the passenger door of Adam Riley's car. Within seconds he picked up a strong scent and began tracking down the hillside toward the trailer park. Five feet before the asphalt canal running between the hillside and the trailer park the dog hesitated. He smelled the asphalt close to the grass for a couple of seconds, then the grass to his right. All of a sudden he made a hard right turn, staying in the grass next to the canal.

He tracked the scent for close to thirty seconds before slowing down and making a left turn which took him across the asphalt canal. Reaching the grass on the other side he took off again, pulling his handler with more strength, like he did whenever he located a suspect. Once the K-9 reached the cyclone fence he started barking aggressively.

"Dang it, it's one of the biggest junkyards in the county," Detective Fuller said.

"I hate to do this to you," he said looking at the handler, "even though we know he's probably not in the junkyard anymore, I still need you to take him around so he can do a search of the place."

***

STALKER KNEW HE NEEDED TO GET A COUPLE HOURS OF sleep before his midnight shift as a nursing assistant at the hospital. He decided to prepare another list so the thoughts weren't running through his head while he tried to sleep. He softly picked Streak up off of his chest and set him on the carpet, scratching behind his ears one last time. He walked into the spare bedroom he had turned into his den, and opened the drawer of his roll top desk.

A stack of latex gloves lay neatly in the drawer. As with many things in his life…he had a system. He always took the oldest pair from the top because every morning when he got home after working at the hospital he would place the newest ones he took from their stock on the bottom of the stack. After putting on the top pair of latex gloves he opened the drawer where he kept the special cards.

Each of the cards had the words "I'm sorry," on the face, usually with a picture. The inside of the cards were either blank or said, "I'm sorry. Please forgive me." Stalker grabbed one of the envelopes and the first card with a picture of a sad dog. He opened the card, and reached for one of the many brand new fine point blue pens lined up perfectly in a row on the top left side of the desk. He always took from the far left, using every pen before he would open a new package, lining them up as the ones before them had been. After reflecting for several minutes he printed on the inside cover.

Bethany Walker,

You could have done more. The dog on the front is sorrier than you were. You have never apologized to me or asked me to forgive you. Someday you will beg me for forgiveness.

From Your Past,
S

He printed Bethany's name and her address on the front of the envelope. Like always he left the return address area blank. After putting the card in the envelope he sealed it with a glue stick.

Unlike the first two notes he mailed to Bethany from other cities, Stalker already decided he would put this one in the mailbox in downtown Hughson as he drove by her house again on the way to work. He took out another sterile set of latex gloves, setting them with the card by his keys on the little table near the front door.

Peeling the latex gloves off inside out he used one of the gloves to pick up the pen he had used, sliding it into one of the finger holes of the other glove. He set the used items on the table near the card and keys so he could dispose of them later. Feeling satisfied, Stalker relaxed on the way to his bedroom knowing he would now sleep well.

CHAPTER TWENTY-EIGHT

After leaving the District Attorney's office AJ knew one of the parking enforcement officers had checked out his car when he saw his business card had disappeared from the dashboard. When he got to the driver's door he saw the card on the seat. AJ started the car to let the engine warm up as he read the back of it, recognizing the handwriting immediately.

A little cold to be driving with your top-down. If you need to warm up give me a call. Happy holidays.

AJ chuckled. He enjoyed their ten-year flirting game, happy it remained a game. If he did not need to get to an autopsy he would search the area for her three-wheeled vehicle. AJ had been known to do a little recon and follow her, leaving a return flirt note while she walked around giving tickets. His phone buzzing with a text from Knox telling him he had arrived at the coroner's office redirected AJ's thoughts.

Pulling up to the County Coroner's office he saw Knox at the corner of the building smoking a cigarette. When Knox saw him he ground the cigarette into the sidewalk and started walking toward AJ's car.

"Knoxy, looks like it's only the two of us. The department Christmas party is tonight so maybe we all need a mental break for a day or so."

"Yeah well, you might want to wait and reconsider," Knox said.

"Okay, you piqued my interest. What's up?"

"After we were done with briefing this morning, I took care of the evidence and decided to take a look at the drinking glass we retrieved at the motel room. When I got it under the good lighting in my lab it looked like there were a couple of nice prints on it. When I put the glass in the superglue chamber those prints were excellent."

"Good news, Knox. Great job. Next time you get back to it maybe you can get it ready for the AFIS system," AJ said as they began walking toward the building.

"Way ahead of you, AJ," Knox said proudly. "I've already got a hit in the system."

"How'd you get a hit so quick?"

"It's one of us," Knox said. "Well, it's kind of one of us. Sort of law enforcement for the county."

Stopping abruptly AJ turned to look at him.

"You're serious!"

Nodding his head, Knox said, "Yeah…it's a doozy."

"Come on, Knoxy, quit stringing me along and tell me who it is."

"Fine, fine," Knox said. He paused, enjoying his fifteen seconds of fame, almost as much as he did making AJ wait.

"I'm telling you, this case officially jumped to the top of the Political Case list. The prints belong to one of the deputy DA's here. Her name is Dani Larson."

"No way. I just came from her office. She definitely sent mixed messages." AJ hesitated, wondering if Knox might be pulling his leg.

"You're positive, right? You're not messing with me are you?"

"A hundred percent positive, and I'm not screwing with you on this one. You mentioned mixed messages, what did you mean?"

"Well, she seemed a little caught off guard when I first told her about Nathan Price being dead, then she kind of became cold and uncaring about it. I will say she seemed genuinely compassionate for Nathan's parents for what they were about to go through. Man, you're right, this is about to become a huge political case."

LINDA SAW DANI AT HER OFFICE DESK SO SHE KNOCKED on the doorframe as she walked in. She handed Dani a red envelope with only Dani's first name written on it.

"This good-looking guy in a suit gave this to me a few seconds ago, he asked me to give it to you. I offered to call you and have you come out to get it. I don't know," she shrugged her shoulders, "he wanted me to give it to you. So here you go." Linda started to walk away.

"Wait, wait. You don't have any idea who he was?" Dani asked.

"Nope. No idea. I will say he's better dressed than most of the guys here. Cuter, too." Linda smiled and left before Dani could say anything else.

Dani pulled a Christmas card out of the envelope. It had a beautiful picture of a street with houses on both sides decorated with lights and manger scenes. She forced herself to read the message on the right wishing for a happy holiday season first. On the left side of the card she saw a handwritten note.

Dani,

Would you like to have a cup of coffee or

hot cocoa with me? If so, I will be at Perko's across from the college in Turlock at five o'clock tonight.

Dani's emotions fluttered back and forth. Linda's description and the offer to meet for coffee were exciting, separate from the obvious concerns; she didn't know a thing about him or his name.

Dani walked to the front desk with the card. When Linda saw her she smiled.

"Okay, tell me, tell me. Was it romantic?"

Linda's excitement made Dani blush.

"He wants to know if I will meet him for coffee tonight."

"Hell, if you don't, I will," Linda said. "I'm telling you he's cute. Who is it? Do you know?"

"No, I don't have a clue." Dani started to give the card to Linda when she noticed something underneath the last line of writing. Looking closer she saw the two little stickers, one of Raggedy Ann and the other of Raggedy Andy. Shocked, Dani dropped the card.

"Oh my God," she said, her hands covering her lips.

"What? What's wrong?" Linda asked, as she picked the card up and looked inside, not seeing anything to cause such a reaction. She looked at Dani with questioning eyes.

Dani's hands were together directly in front of her lips as though she were praying. For twenty years nobody else ever gave her anything with Raggedy Ann and Andy.

It can't be him, she thought. *Not after all these years. Still, who else could it be?*

Linda's phone rang, so she handed the card back to Dani to answer her phone. Dani walked toward her office trying to rationalize who else could have brought her the card.

She knew it could not be anyone in the regular courthouse community otherwise Linda would have likely recognized them and Dani eliminated Linda covering for someone in the office.

There were very few people Dani ever told the entire story about what happened to her family, with even less hearing about the dolls. She knew she could not discount the slight possibility someone she told may have passed on her story to another person…although it seemed unlikely to her.

Looking at the clock Dani knew she had to head back to court. Putting the card in the envelope, she put it in her personal briefcase. She said a quick thank you prayer about only having to agree to some continuances defense attorneys would be requesting on three of her cases, knowing her mind would not be focused solely in the courtroom.

Dani felt relieved to see Linda still on the phone. She slowed long enough to mouth the words *We'll talk later,* to Linda when she looked up.

CHAPTER TWENTY-NINE

AJ had trouble paying attention to Nathan's autopsy, his mind on what Knox told him before they went in. Knox took photos and collected the duct tape as evidence, diligently paying attention to the coroner's every word.

AJ decided he'd have to go back to the DA's office to speak with Bridget Fletcher. He wanted more time to look into the case, and also knew if he were in her position he'd want to know as soon as possible. Inasmuch as the detective inside of him didn't like it, some information probably needed to be shared sooner than later.

"Hey, AJ, where's Seth?" Sandy asked as she walked into the room pushing a gurney with a covered dead body. She set her clipboard from on top of the body on the counter.

"Great to see you, too," AJ said.

"My bad, AJ. How are you?" she asked, smiling as she continued past Nathan on table number two. Past table number four she opened the freezer to put her gurney inside. After moving a couple of gurneys around so the order for autopsies would be accurate she pushed the button on the outer wall as she came back out, the freezer door automatically closing behind her.

Smiling from the knowledge he got to her, AJ said, "I'm fine. Thanks for asking. The answer to your question is I let him go home. He wanted to go spend some time with his wife while his kids were at school. We have the department Christmas party tonight so I only kept essential personnel. You're stuck with me and Knoxy."

"Sounds like fun," she said, trying to hide her disappointment.

AJ got across his point about Seth, so he could not see any value in capitalizing on Sandy's disenchantment any more. With her being an exceptional deputy coroner he did not want to fracture their working relationship, and changed the subject.

"I was surprised you weren't here when we arrived. Where've you been?"

"Picking up a guy from the highway who got killed in his car, parked on the shoulder," she said. "It's Detective Fuller's case from the SO."

"On ninety-nine north of Crows Landing Road?" AJ asked.

"Yeah. How'd you know?"

"I drove by there earlier on my way to the DA's office, saw a couple of patrol cars. I figured it must have been a car stop—I guess not."

"Nope, it wasn't a car stop. Oh yeah, I found your business card in the man's right front shirt pocket," she said.

"Really. What's the vic's name?"

Walking toward the counter with her clipboard of paperwork, she said, "I've got it over here. I remember he's from San Diego, or so his driver's license says." She opened her file folder and said, "His name is Adam Riley."

"Shit," Knox gasped. "Isn't he the one you told us about in briefing this morning?"

"Yep, same name," AJ stated. "Mind if I look at him, see if it's the same guy I spoke to?"

Sandy stole a look at the coroner who nodded and Sandy jerked her head for AJ to follow.

In the freezer she pulled the cover off the man's face on the last gurney on the right.

Damn, that's him, AJ thought before he nodded.

"How was he killed?" AJ asked as they walked out of the freezer, not thinking about the precarious position he put her in.

The coroner doing the autopsy on Nathan stopped, looking over the top of his glasses directly at Sandy. AJ could almost feel his eyes burning right through her waiting to jump on her if she crossed into his territory of cause of death.

"I have no idea AJ...you know that," she snapped, the squint of her eyes staring right at him making sure he knew he screwed up.

"All I do is pick them up and bring them here." With the outside of her palm she smacked the button to close the freezer door.

"Stupid question," AJ confessed. "Sorry, Sandy, I must be getting tired. I haven't slept for two days."

Satisfied with the answers the coroner went back to what he was doing. The instant he focused on dictating the contents in Nathan's stomach Sandy looked at AJ. Using her pen she jabbed it toward her neck like a knife. AJ nodded and she headed for the doors.

"Great seeing you guys. Have fun at your Christmas party," she said, exiting before they could respond.

AJ and Knox walked out of the coroner's facility and headed toward Knox's van. Knox lit a cigarette as soon as they got outside to quench his desire before he had to get back in the van. Slowing the pace to give Knox more time

AJ said, "If you have not sent anything to DOJ yet, hold off."

"Not a problem. Makes my life easier," Knox said. He was curious as to why, although not enough to ask.

"I know you can get me prints off of the duct tape if there are any," AJ said. "I'll try to keep people busy so they stay out of your hair. Are you guys going to the Christmas party tonight?"

"Nope. Unless you need me to do the duct tape right away I planned on heading out as soon as I got back. You probably don't remember, I wanted to surprise the Frau and take her to Napa for the weekend," Knox said.

"Oh crap! I forgot. I'm so sorry."

"Don't worry about it," Knox said, not a hint of disappointment in his voice. "So long as I can get home by six we're good. I asked her to pack for us for a couple of days without ever giving her any major clues where we were going." Knox smiled, proud of himself for never giving in.

"We should easily be to the hotel by ten if we can leave shortly after six," Knox continued. "Are you sure you're okay with me doing the duct tape on Monday? You know I don't want anybody else in my lab, so if you think you have to give them to someone before Monday I'll go do them right now."

"Man, don't worry about it," AJ said. "I want you out of here as soon as you can. You two deserve this weekend. Don't worry, I'll keep people out of your lab, you can do it all next week." AJ patted Knox on the shoulder and said, "Have a great time, and, thank you for all your help." AJ hoped Knox knew how much he appreciated his work.

Knox smiled, noticeably gratified by the comment.

DANI RETURNED TO HER OFFICE SHORTLY BEFORE THREE thirty. She tried to work on cases, only to find herself having to re-read police reports several times, unable to focus on anything besides her dolls. The image of her Raggedy Ann and Andy dolls sitting on the top shelf of the hutch in her living room, underneath the soft accent lighting, protected by the glass doors, kept coming to her mind.

Friday afternoons were the least busy time of the week for everyone at the office, so Dani could hear all of the other deputy DAs talking with each other in the common areas about their cases. Dani usually stepped out of her office to join in—not today. There was no way she would be able to pay attention to anything the others said, so she decided to stay in her office and wait for the mad rush to begin. Happy hour for her colleagues, usually forty of them, began sometime around four fifteen on Friday afternoons. She counted down the minutes.

CHAPTER THIRTY

A J sat in his car after Knox left trying to decide a course of action. He knew he should head back over to the DA's office to talk with Bridget Fletcher about the fingerprints. Something about the information Sandy provided them made him hesitate. AJ decided to speak with Sergeant Boykin first considering it could become a political nightmare in a flash.

"Sergeant Boykin," he answered.

"Hey, Sarge, it's AJ. I wanted to give you a heads up on my homicide."

"What happened?" Boykin asked, dragging out his words like he was waiting for the bad news. "This late on a Friday afternoon, it can't be good."

"Well, I think it's a little early in the investigation to say too much about the direction it's gonna take," AJ started. "You already know Knox lifted a fingerprint off of a glass inside of the hotel room near my dead guy. Well, the print comes back to the deputy DA who took him to trial and lost on a drunk driving manslaughter case." AJ hesitated, wanting the concept of a local deputy DA's fingerprint in a lower quality motel room to sink in.

"This could easily turn into a political hot potato so I wanted to let you know in case you wanted to run it up the flagpole," AJ said. "Clearly, I need to let DA Fletcher know about this, probably sooner than later. I wanted to give you guys' time to think about it and discuss it first. I planned on calling to set an appointment to see her at the beginning of next week."

"You're right, it's got all the makings of becoming a political nightmare," Boykin said. "Thanks for the heads up. I appreciate it. I know the chief will, too. I realize it's probably a little early…what's your gut telling you about her possibly being your suspect? You know the boss is going to ask me."

"I actually spoke with her today before Knox told me about the fingerprint," AJ said. "She seemed a little cold about the guy being dead, at the same time she showed a lot of compassion toward his parents. Then, one of the deputy coroners told us at the autopsy about a guy murdered in his car on Highway 99 near Crows Landing Road who happened to be our one witness. He saw our victim with a woman going into the hotel room."

"What are the chances that's a coincidence?" Boykin asked rhetorically.

"Exactly. I'm guessing our witness got killed after our deputy DA was already at work this morning. You can see why I said it's a little early to say what direction this thing is going to go. To answer your question, though, my gut says she's not my suspect."

"I agree, it's too early to say anything definitive," Boykin said. "You know as well as I the DA may think otherwise. Let me know when you plan to go see Fletcher in case there is any backlash. In fact, do you want me or the Chief to run interference for you by contacting her?"

"Trust me, I thought about it for a second. I decided she

141

and I have a pretty good working relationship so I'd like to do it. After I tell her I'm going to see if I can get her to hold off doing anything overly aggressive, at least for a while."

"Sounds good. I've got another call coming in. See you tonight at the party," Boykin said.

Bethany left Emanuel Medical Center shortly before five. Earlier in the morning she decided to go directly to AJ's house after work instead of going home. Despite Hughson being relatively close to Turlock, she did not want to make AJ late for his department Christmas party, provided he stopped working long enough to go.

Pulling up to AJ's she saw his work car parked in the driveway. Bethany parked along the curb in front of the house, not sure if he had made it home.

Even though a number of years may have gone by one never forgets the special feeling of first times. Whether a first date, a first prom, or in this case, Bethany being the first date AJ would be taking to the department Christmas party, a nervous excitement ran through her.

The front door was locked, so Bethany used the key he had given her. Hop greeted Bethany when she stepped inside, her tail wagging, happy to see her friend. Bethany's fondness for Hop grew every time she saw her and she loved AJ's compassion and caring for Hop.

I feel so at home here, she thought.

CHAPTER THIRTY-ONE

Dani walked out of her office carrying her briefcase with files she needed to work on over the weekend. The high noise level leaving the impression theirs was a busy place full of important people had fled the area, replaced with a ghostly silence. Most of the attorneys in the office were across the street nursing their second drink. As Dani approached the door near the secretarial desks DA Bridget Fletcher came out of her office.

"Hi, Dani. How are you?" Fletcher asked.

"I've been better, thank you for asking though," Dani said.

"I heard about your child-abuse case. Try not to let it eat you up. Those are hard cases to get a conviction. Regardless of the verdict you need to know we would not have given it to you if we did not think you were a good attorney. Keep your head up."

"Thank you so much," Dani said.

I needed that, she thought.

DA Fletcher took one step and stopped. Looking at Dani she said, "A piece of friendly advice, you might want to think about relaxing this weekend. Sometimes the pressure makes us try harder, which isn't always a good thing. Try to have a good weekend."

The drive from Modesto to Turlock seemed to take forever. Dani's mind had been racing between her conversation with DA Fletcher, and thinking about the unknown man waiting for her at Perkos. Sitting in her car in the restaurant parking lot she contemplated not going inside. She took the card out of her briefcase, read it several more times, and decided she needed to know who sent it.

Walking into Perkos the hostess could see Dani straining to look for someone.

"Are you meeting someone, Ma'am?"

"Yes, I'm supposed to meet a man here," Dani said.

"Oh yes, he's already here. Follow me," the hostess said.

Following the hostess Dani could see they were getting ready for the evening rush since there were more waitresses than customers. She appreciated having a little privacy. Halfway down the long row of tables she could see a lone man in a booth next to the windows on the east side of the restaurant. His suit looked exactly like Linda described it, he had to be the one who left the card for her.

"I see him, thank you," Dani said, dismissing the hostess from walking her to the table.

While the hostess walked away Dani paused to take a deep breath, trying to summon the courage to keep going. Before she could find it, he turned and looked at her...his face vaguely familiar. The softness of his smile made her take the first step toward the table.

He slid out of the booth and Dani stopped five feet from him. An uncomfortable pause existed as they stared into each other's eyes, neither knowing what to say. Finally, he extended his right arm with his palm up pointing to the opposite side of the table asking her to have a seat. Without removing her coat, Dani slowly sat in the booth while he took his seat across from her.

"Dani, I know this is very awkward, and I can see you're not even sure if you're going to stay since you still have your coat on," he began. "So I'm going to get straight to it and hope you stay to talk with me." He took his eyes off of her and lowered his head while he took a deep breath.

He's as nervous as I am. Good, it's not just me.

Looking at her he said, "My name is Chad Miller. Before you go running out of here I would ask you please hear me out. I know this may be hard to believe…I'm the one who pulled you from the burning car twenty years ago." Chad paused, praying quietly for her to stay. Dani didn't move, continuing to look into his eyes.

"I was seventeen when I took the Raggedy Ann and Andy dolls to you in the hospital. Something about the whole experience made me realize I wanted to change the direction of my life. Kind of like I helped you, someone helped me, too. Shortly after I left the hospital from visiting you I made my way to the soup kitchen in Turlock. One of the volunteers happened to be a middle-aged man who saw something in me…he helped me to change my life forever. Along with being a successful real estate agent he had his own broker office. Over time he taught me how to be a broker and I've been doing it ever since."

"How did … how did you find me?" Dani asked slowly.

"Believe it or not, a couple of months ago I sat right here having breakfast and reading the newspaper. On the bottom of the first page of the local news section a picture of you caught my attention. You were being interviewed on the courthouse steps after the jury in your manslaughter case acquitted the defendant. The picture had a good view of your face and I instantly recognized you. I have seen your eyes in my mind for twenty years and I just knew."

"You were able to tell…so many years later? I was ten the last time you saw me," Dani said.

"I couldn't be positive but something told me it had to be you," he said. "One day shortly after I saw the picture I took the morning off of work to go to the courthouse. I could easily tell who the attorneys were around there. After I asked a couple of them where you were at, I found you in one of the courtrooms. I sat watching you until the lunch break when I slipped out. Once I saw you in person I had no doubt it was you."

"Now it makes sense. I've felt somebody watching me in court several times the last few months," she said.

"I only watched you the one time. It has taken me all this time to build up the courage to take the card to your office."

Dani started to say something about his only watching her one time, deciding to come back to it another time.

"Look, I don't want to come across as being ungrateful. A wonderful family adopted me, they put me through college, then law school, and I have a terrific job I really enjoy. Still, there…there are so many times over the last twenty years that I wished you never saved me."

"I cannot say I know how you feel…I don't," Chad said. "Let me put it this way…my mother and father were not very good parents, they should have never had kids. Their lives centered on drugs…they still do." Chad took a deep breath to calm himself. Speaking about his parents stressed him.

"I left the house right after I started high school, went from one friend's house to another, always leaving before I overstayed my welcome," he continued. "Fortunately for me I got my GED before I started traveling with the hobos. I've never had a loving family. I prayed so many times, hoping the family you ended up with were good people, you had been through enough."

Dani looked at him. "I'm sorry to hear your family situation was not very good. My parents and brother were special people…I've felt terrible guilt because I lived…and they didn't." Dani hesitated, fidgeting in her seat.

"I'm thankful you risked your life for me, I am. It's nothing against you at all. It's just, I struggle with why."

The waitress approached the table with her pen at the ready. "What can I get you guys," she said.

Without looking at her Dani said, "Nothing for me, thank you."

"I think we will wait for now," Chad said, smiling at the waitress who shrugged her shoulders and walked away.

"You look really good," Dani said. "The last time I saw you, you looked pretty…disheveled. I'm really happy you were able to turn your life around. Are you married, any kids?"

"Thank you," Chad said. "I work for the man who helped me turn it around. I owe him everything." Chad paused, his eyes drifting down to the table. "No, I have never married. I have not really ever found the right person. As for kids, I'm worried I would not be a good parent. Mine never provided any good examples."

"I understand not finding the right person," Dani said. "I'm so busy with work, it doesn't help. But, I think you're wrong, you would make a wonderful parent. You got away from your parents due to their life-style and their lack of parenting. As kind as you were to me, I know you would be such a good parent to your children."

Chad cocked his head to the side as he looked into Dani's eyes.

"Thank you, you're very kind."

His eyes stayed locked onto hers, and when she felt herself getting a little flushed, Dani looked down.

"I need to go. I have quite a bit of work to do on some cases coming up for trial."

Chad did not try to stop her, knowing he had shaken up her world. He reached into his suit jacket pocket pulling out one of his business cards. Handing it to her, "Here is my business card. I'm really glad I finally found you and had the guts to get in touch with you. I have thought about you a lot over the last twenty years. I enjoyed talking with you. If you would ever like to talk, or get together, I would be happy to."

Dani looked into his soft caring eyes as she took his card. *I have thought about you more than you know*, she thought.

After she slid out of the booth she said, "Chad…thank you." She turned and walked away when her eyes began to tear up.

CHAPTER THIRTY-TWO

A J made it home in time to take a quick shower and change suits for the Christmas party. Bethany had taken care of Hop who had already found her way back to her bed. Although he physically prepared for the party, mentally AJ kept running scenarios of Dani Larson killing Nathan Price in his mind.

"Are you sure you want to go to the party?" Bethany asked.

"Yes, why?"

"You seem like your mind is anywhere but here," she said.

"I'm sorry, it's the early stages of my investigation. I've told you before I get very focused, and this one got an added twist a couple of hours ago."

"I know...it's just...I would have thought you could block it out long enough for us to go have a good time at the party."

AJ spun to face Bethany.

"I'll do my best. It's not easy to shut out the fact there are two families dealing with the loss of their loved ones who won't be celebrating Christmas."

Normally AJ did not let anything slip out he did not intend to say. Fatigue had started catching up to him and he knew the instant the words were out of his mouth he should not have said them. Not surprisingly, Bethany did not say much to him the remainder of the time at the house or on the drive to the party.

Walking from the parking lot AJ could see many of the officers and their spouses looking at them. AJ expected people would be surprised he actually brought a date since he had never done so before, although he did not expect the staring. Seth and his wife Teri were waiting for them close to the door.

"Good to see you finally made it," Seth said to AJ. "I wasn't gonna wait much longer...they started serving food." Looking at Bethany, Seth extended his hand, introducing himself and his wife to her.

"Very nice to meet you, Bethany. I'm glad there's somebody else besides me trying to get this guy to think about something other than homicide cases."

After giving Teri a hug AJ looked at Bethany and said, "This woman is a saint. Anyone who can put up with Seth for two decades walks on water in my book."

"Why, thank you, AJ. It's always a pleasure to see you," Teri said.

"Yeah, yeah, let's get inside and grab a seat while we still can," Seth said.

After they finished eating they watched Tom, the officer who dressed up like Santa Claus, hand out presents to all of the little kids. Seth and Teri reminisced about how their two kids enjoyed coming to the Christmas party when they were young. Teri almost got emotional talking about their teenagers choosing to stay home for the second year in a row.

"Seth, tell Bethany about our favorite Christmastime case," AJ said, trying to change the mood.

After they stopped laughing, Seth said, "Several years

ago when I was first hired and AJ was a young detective, we had a guy try to rob a convenience store. Pretty typical stuff, patrol officers surround the area to start searching for the suspect. AJ's called out after we discover one of the so-called witnesses inside the store is actually an accomplice and we take him into custody. Pretty soon the sergeant calls for an ambulance. He found the first suspect sitting in his car moaning, bleeding like a stuck pig. The guy tried to slouch down in his car to hide from cops while he waited for his buddy. As the sergeant got close to his car the fool tried to put the revolver down the front of his pants. Sure enough he shot off his own testicle."

Bethany began laughing and crying at the same time, right along with the rest of them.

"Tell her the best part," AJ said.

"No, AJ. She doesn't need to hear it," Terri said. "The entire administration is already looking over here wondering about us laughing so much."

"Who cares? It's a Christmas party and we're having fun," AJ said. He nodded his head at Seth who smiled.

"The instant I heard Sarge say the guy shot his own nut off, I immediately came up with a tune to a song everyone's familiar with, Bon Jovi's, *You Give Love a Bad Name*," Seth said.

"Really? How did it go?" Bethany asked.

Without hesitation Seth and AJ started singing together:
"Shot through the nuts, and you're to blame,
You give crime a bad name."

All of the veteran officers near their table started singing with them, soon followed by the entire area of officers laughing.

Thirty minutes later they were all laughed out.

"So, Bethany, tell us how you met," Teri said. "AJ never tells us anything."

Seth grinned, knowing AJ wouldn't get upset with Teri for asking.

"Well, about eight months ago I moved up here from Madera," Bethany began. "Right out of college I became a pediatric social worker at Children's Hospital. I got burnt out so I left. Now I focus on post hospital care at Emanuel Medical Center. Basically, I do total patient follow-through now and get them to the next facility."

When she looked over at him the corners of her lips raised a little.

"An eighteen-year-old had been beaten and left for dead, but he surprised everybody and lived. We spoke several times while the kid was in a coma and over the month before we transferred him to a rehab facility. It took AJ a month to build up the courage to ask me out. That was six months ago, we've been dating ever since."

"Okay, I'm going for more coffee," AJ said while standing.

Teri and Bethany laughed seeing him uncomfortable.

"I'll go with you," Seth said in a show of support.

Teri had been looking forward to talking without the guys around.

"I can see you really like him," Teri said. "He's a wonderful guy and for him to bring you here means he really cares for you, too."

"Thank you. It means a lot…"

"But?" Teri asked concerned.

"It's been hard adjusting to how invested he is on his cases," Bethany said, fidgeting with her napkin. "I thought married to his job meant he didn't date much. I admire him believing he's the victim's last voice, but it doesn't leave much room for a relationship?"

Teri laid her hand on Bethany's and said, "AJ and Seth are rare, they get totally committed...but they have to right the most terrible wrongs. I see their commitment as something they do for us as well. Sharing them isn't easy, trust me...then again, I wouldn't want to change them."

Teri knew it would take Bethany time to fully appreciate and accept AJ...if she could at all.

"I HOPE YOU HAD A GOOD TIME TONIGHT. I'M REALLY glad you came," AJ said, reaching out to take her hand in his.

Bethany remained quiet as they walked to his car. AJ got in and looked at her.

Bethany said, "I did have a good time tonight. Hence the problem."

"I don't know what you mean. What's the problem?"

"I enjoy spending time with you, AJ, and I would like for us to spend more time together. The problem is I feel like I have to share you with major case after major case. I told Teri I admire how hard you work to help your victims, I really do. Still, it doesn't leave much room for our relationship."

Where's she going with this? he thought.

"Look, I have to say this...I know it sounds selfish for me to want more of your time. Both of us have given up so much to help others over the last however many years. We have put our hopes and dreams on hold, so I guess I really want something more than satisfaction from my work. Tonight felt very nice, and I like nice. Selfishly...I need more of it."

They drove to his house in silence, AJ trying to take in everything Bethany said. Getting out of the Mustang he looked across the top of it and said, "I have given you more of me than I have given anybody else. I want more than anything to have a relationship with you. Patrol is no better though. Those guys are always mandated to work overtime. At my age it would be difficult to transfer to another special assignment. Retirement would be the only answer, and I can't say I'm ready to. So...I'm not sure I can give you what you're asking for, at least not right now."

"I'm not sure either, AJ," Bethany said. She turned, slowly walking to her car, the chirp as she unlocked it sounding louder than ever before.

CHAPTER THIRTY-THREE

S talker had gotten his normal six hours of sleep. He did not have to be to work at the hospital until eleven o'clock so he knew he had a few hours to work with. He put on his black jacket over his dark clothes to blend with the night, then placed his scrubs he wore at work in a paper bag. Putting on the latex gloves from the table by the door he grabbed the old latex gloves with the pen in them, his keys, Bethany's card and headed out.

He drove to the north end of Turlock. Passing by Pitman High School he turned into Dani's neighborhood, admitting to himself he actually liked the house Dani had purchased. He appreciated the fact Dani had a single-story house in an area where most of her neighbors were trying to outdo each other with their two-story houses and brand-new SUVs. He slowly drove through the neighborhood to get a feel for activity and he could see Dani sitting on her couch in her living room watching TV. He also saw several other people coming and going from houses near hers so he decided it would not be a good time to get what he needed. When he left he headed north to Hughson.

Slowing down on Santa Fe Drive, Stalker turned and the post office sat on his left. He decided to check out the area and drove around the block before deciding there were too many people. Changing his plans, he drove north about a mile before parking on Fox Road, less than two blocks from his destination.

He stood by his car to look around for activity while he put Bethany's card in his pocket. Not seeing anybody he began walking north for one block until it dead-ended into Little Avenue. Pulling the card out of his jacket pocket he walked to her front door. No lights were on so he opened the screen door enough to slide in the card and closed the door to hold the card in place. As he walked away he felt certain nobody saw him.

Crossing the street he intended to leave the area when Bethany's car came around the corner pulling into her driveway. He continued walking away as her garage door went up and she pulled inside. He smiled when he saw her use the garage, knowing it would be several days before she found the card in her front door.

After Stalker left Hughson he drove to downtown Modesto where he parked in a premium corner lot left empty for night owls like him. Walking toward J Street he took the latex gloves he had been wearing along with the ones containing the pen and placed them in separate trashcans along the walk. He continued to a small Mexican restaurant where he liked to go for dinner.

He watched a young family with enthusiasm, admiring how the parents interacted with their three children. He appreciated how they treated dinner as quality time, and no cell phones were visible. He couldn't help thinking of his family, how his parents used dinnertime as quality time, too. Without any fanfare he quietly paid for their meal before heading for work, long gone before they found out why.

DANI CHANGED INTO HER FAVORITE SWEAT PANTS AND long sleeve shirt when she got home and lounged on the couch. The television provided white noise with an occasional short distraction. She never watched a single show long enough to know the plot.

She could not stop thinking about Chad, the beautiful card he gave her with the dolls, and him sitting across from her as nervous as she had been. Dani knew her confusion about him really had more to do with her than it did about him. For years she had struggled between wishing he had not saved her, yet thankful he did.

Throughout the evening she found herself thinking about how good he looked in his suit, his hair short, and his face clean-shaven. He looked completely different than the last time she saw him years before. Although at times she tried to focus on the casework she took home, her mind drifted back to Chad.

CHAPTER THIRTY-FOUR

Despite his exhaustion, AJ had so many thoughts racing through his head he needed to go for a run. AJ knew once he got out to the canal bank parallel to Taylor Road he could relax, allowing him to think more clearly.

Even though AJ wanted a relationship with Bethany, he didn't know how to change his feeling he should be at the office pouring over information on Nathan's murder. AJ knew at some point he would need to tell Bethany about the likelihood the case would become more intense once he went to speak with the DA about one of her deputies being a possible suspect. After finding out how Bethany really felt, AJ could only imagine her response would not be good when he shared this news.

Putting his five shot Smith and Wesson .38 in his small fanny pack he headed out, hoping to find some answers.

STALKER CHANGED INTO THE OLDEST SET OF PURPLE scrubs he owned, putting his regular clothes in his locker. Within an hour his opportunity arose as he retrieved the bedpan from one of the elderly patients on the floor. He made sure none of the nurses were in the area when he went into the bathroom in the patient's room. Using toilet paper he dabbed feces from the bedpan on his scrubs. When he felt he had a sufficient amount on him he poured the remainder of the contents into the toilet along with the toilet paper and flushed.

Stalker opened the door to check for nurses, and seeing none walked to the dirty utility room. He rinsed the bedpan out in the hopper like the nursing assistants always did, cleaning it thoroughly before returning it to the patient's bathroom. Stalker then walked to the nurses' station to provide the charge nurse with his made up story of the patient jerking his leg and hitting the bedpan.

The charge nurse minimally paid attention to the story since those things happened all the time. Before Stalker finished his story she had the nursing supervisor on the phone requesting a set of scrubs from the Operating Room. In less than ten minutes Stalker was showering in the locker room. He put on the drab green OR scrubs with the words "Property of" in very small letters, with the name "Angelica" in big letters, both on the left chest of the scrub top. He threw his old purple scrubs in the red biohazard bag knowing they would be destroyed and went back to work.

At seven in the morning Stalker left the locker room wearing his regular clothes, carrying the OR scrubs in the paper bag he had used to bring his personal scrubs to work. The early Saturday morning traffic seemed light, so he made it to Walnut Road in less than thirty minutes. After a couple of turns he pulled into Dani's neighborhood.

There was no pedestrian activity, so he parked, put on a pair of latex gloves, and got out of his car. He walked the half a block to the south, then turned onto Dani's street, Greenfield Drive. One middle-aged man on a ladder putting up Christmas lights at least ten houses away appeared to be the only activity in the neighborhood. He liked the fact two of the houses across the street had no cars in the driveways, looking like the owners were gone for the holidays.

He walked to the gate on the side of her house by the garage and entered her backyard. He felt fairly certain she did not have an alarm system, never having seen any indication or connections in the doors or windows. He pulled his large knife out of the sheath and within seconds had the cheap doorknob lock popped allowing him into Dani's garage.

Although he did not expect to find many tools he figured she would at least have a hammer. Walking past her car he saw a small generic workbench with a pegboard back. Even though she did not have many tools what she did have were neatly in designated places. Not surprised, he admired her orderly quality. He took the claw hammer with a black and yellow handle before he left, making sure to lock and close the door behind him.

Before leaving the backyard Stalker put his black leather gloves over the latex gloves. He put the handle of the hammer up the sleeve of his jacket, wrapping his left hand around the head. He placed his left hand inside his jacket pocket, and slid through the gate to the front yard. He couldn't see anyone outside beyond the man hanging lights, so he confidently retraced his steps back to his car.

Inside the car he placed the hammer on the floorboard behind his seat before taking off both pairs of gloves. He drove out of the neighborhood, heading south on Walnut Road. When he got to Turlock Junior High School he pulled into the parking lot and disposed of the latex gloves in one of the trash cans.

He drove to Canal Drive by the County Fairgrounds where he parked in the lot of the quadraplexes at 724 West Canal Drive. He had done the same thing three times before to make sure people living in the area were used to seeing him and his car. He knew the chances were good no one in the area would cooperate with the police on anything; regardless, he wanted to take precautions.

Two sets of quadraplexes faced each other with a semblance of a grassy area between them. Stalker walked south on a dirt road behind the quadraplex on the east side. As he got to the end of the building he turned right, crossing the dirt and grass area. In front of him were six quadraplexes, exactly like the two on Canal Drive, each having a North Soderquist Road address.

He walked to the last apartment in the farthest south building closest to him. He looked inside the bare front window and saw the little boy sitting on the floor watching cartoons. He had on a thick jacket, a wool hat on his head, and a blanket covering his legs. Stalker could relate to the boy, having experienced much the same thing in foster homes exactly like it.

Since screaming, yelling and fighting were common in places like those, Stalker knew it might come in handy. None of those living there had jobs and what money they did have went for drugs, leaving no money for heat in the apartments. Had the boy not been home he would have dealt with the issue then.

Instead he walked away, confident the odds were slim he had been seen since no adult in the area moved in the early morning hours unless absolutely necessary.

CHAPTER THIRTY-FIVE

A J had only been able to sleep for four hours, so despite it being a Saturday he went to his office at six in the morning to get some of the dictation for his reports out of the way. At eight o'clock he unlocked his cell phone and found the contact for Detective Fuller. They had been to numerous detective training courses put on by the DOJ and had maintained a working friendship. When AJ called Fuller answered on the second ring.

"Jay, what's up, my friend?"

"I'm up to my you-know-what in a whodunit homicide. How about you AJ?"

"I'm up to my you-know-what in a homicide about to turn political. Not sure which of us is worse off. I will say mine at least has a potential suspect."

"Yeah, well, I'm not sure I'll find one in mine," Fuller said. "It happened on the side of the freeway and we tracked the guy down the hillside to the junkyard across the little canal down there before we lost him. It's a good thing you called, AJ, we found one of your business cards in our dead guy's pocket."

"Yeah, Sandy told us when we saw her at the coroner's office yesterday," AJ said. "She's the reason I'm calling. Your victim just happened to be the only witness we know of in my homicide the night before. I suspect it's the reason your guy got killed."

"Makes sense," Fuller said. "We pretty much ruled out robbery after we found a wad of cash in our victim's wallet. We also found a receipt in the guy's car dated yesterday from Tommy's Auto Repair in your city. We're going to have to get together soon so we can lay everything out to see if we have the same suspect."

"Interesting, Tommy's is literally on the other side of the highway from our motel where our victim got killed," AJ stated. "Did the coroner do your autopsy yet?"

"Yeah, early evening yesterday. He said the cause of death was a large sharp object, probably a knife, which entered the right side of his neck, apparently taking out his medulla oblongata. We don't think our killer got lucky, we think he had some training, or at least some previous experience."

"Man, definitely different than mine," AJ said. "My guy is the rich kid who had been tried on a DUI manslaughter case a couple months ago, acquitted by a jury. We found him in a motel room with his wrists and legs duct-taped and an NG tube down his throat. We think it might've been alcohol poisoning, not sure yet. Your victim told me he saw a woman get out of our dead guy's vehicle with him, then they went into a room."

"Hey, AJ, I gotta cut this short," Fuller said anxiously. "I've got to talk to my victim's mother, apparently she's on the other line. Poor woman, she's a basket case. Her daughter died early yesterday morning and then her son got murdered a couple hours later. And I gotta try to talk to her."

"She won't be able to give you any help at this point, at least for several days," AJ said. "I'd suggest you tell her how sorry you are for her losses and you'll call her in a week."

"You're right, I wouldn't get much," Fuller said. "Thanks, AJ. Stay in touch."

AJ sat back, pondering the two homicides. He had some difficulty reconciling Dani Larson physically committing the murders of Nathan Price or Adam Riley. He felt her playing a role in them seemed more likely, possibly paying someone to kill them…if she even did anything.

Looking at it from a defense attorney point of view, which AJ always liked to do, Dani would have most likely been at work when Adam Riley got knifed, along with having been in trial all week, so it seemed very unlikely she would have been tracking Nathan, much less would be alone with him in a motel room. Their one witness had been killed violently, so on its face it would appear the actual killer of Nathan Price then took care of the sole witness as well.

AJ began to write a list of the things he needed to do to help him determine Dani's culpability, or weed her out of the suspect pool.

DANI HAD FALLEN ASLEEP ON THE COUCH, EXHAUSTED from the long week of the child-abuse trial. She woke up at two, shut off the TV, and made her way to her bed where she slept soundly until almost seven thirty. Dani propped herself up on her elbows when she thought she heard noises in her house. After a minute of quiet she dismissed it. Still groggy, she went back to sleep for another forty-five minutes.

Lying in bed Dani's thoughts centered on Chad's comment about seeing her *eyes* for twenty years. The thought alone gave her a feeling she had not had in a long time.

Even though Dani still felt confused about why she lived, she realized she had fallen asleep thinking about Chad and woke up thinking about him.

Jumping out of bed she reached for her phone smiling as she knew what she wanted to do. She dialed his number before she lost the nerve to follow through.

On the third ring Dani started getting nervous.

If it gets to five I'm hanging up, she thought.

When Chad finally answered she knew she had to blurt it out or she would freeze up.

"You up for breakfast? I'm starving."

"Uh, sure. When…where?" Chad asked.

"Same place as last night. Thirty minutes. See you there," she said. After she pushed the button it hit her, she had not even given him the chance to agree.

Staring in the mirror while she brushed her teeth Dani could not recall the last time she felt this giddy. She jumped in the shower, wanting to make sure she looked good and smelled nice.

Am I doing the right thing?

CHAPTER THIRTY-SIX

AJ left the office and went through the drive-through at Coffee Plus. Along with his plain black coffee he got a medium caramel Macchiato for Bethany. Driving to Hughson he tried to think about what he might say to her.

Beats me, he thought as he ran his fingers through his hair.

Even so, AJ knew he needed to sit and talk with her. Bethany seldom slept in, so he figured she'd be awake. AJ parked in her driveway, careful not to spill coffee in his Mustang as he got out.

Walking up to the front door AJ saw a card sticking out from between the screen door and the doorframe. As he pulled the card out he saw Bethany's name on it. Though he saw a stamp on it, it did not have any postage markings, so AJ figured one of her neighbors left it for her. He rang the doorbell once. When he could hear her coming the tightness in his chest increased wondering what mood she might be in.

"Hi, Babe," Bethany said with a smile on her face. "This is quite a surprise."

The tone of her voice and her large smile relaxed him instantly.

"I thought a caramel Macchiato might be enough to get me in the door," AJ said.

Bethany laughed. "Bribery with a flavor often works well. Get in here, it's cold out there."

Walking in the door AJ reached out to give her the card. "One of your neighbors must have left this in your screen door."

"Thank you. I wonder who it's from," Bethany said.

Walking toward the kitchen she took the card out of the envelope and opened it. She stopped abruptly, the card falling on the counter.

"What's wrong?" AJ asked.

She never answered.

"Are you okay?" he insisted.

Bethany crossed her arms almost hugging herself. She walked into the living room, sat on the rocker recliner, and drew her legs up.

AJ set the coffees on the table, walked over, picked up the card and read it. Instinctively he looked at where his fingers were touching the card so he could point it out later. AJ set the card on the counter in an upright position with the flaps separated so he could see inside without having to touch the card again. He read it once more.

Bethany Walker,

You could have done more. The dog on the front is sorrier than you were. You have never apologized to me or asked me to forgive you. Someday you will beg me for forgiveness.

From your past,
S

AJ could see Bethany crying so he softly put his hand

on her shoulder and waited. After she wiped her tears with her sweatshirt sleeve Bethany composed herself and reached up and held AJ's hand. When she looked at him her eyebrows were pulled up, a thin crease between them, her lip quivering.

"Can you tell me what this is about?" AJ asked softly.

"I wish I could," Bethany said, her voice trembling. "I don't have any idea who these are from. Each one has gotten nastier…and this one left in my door …" Bethany began crying again so she got up, walking over to get tissues.

"This is not the first one?" AJ asked, more of a statement of his growing concern than a question he already knew the answer to.

Bethany walked into the kitchen and opened a drawer. She returned to the living room with two other cards and envelopes that she gave him, sat back down in the recliner, drew her legs up underneath her and crossed her arms. She started rocking the recliner while AJ read.

He could tell the writing most likely originated from the same person, with the blue ink on them similar to the one on the counter. The first card was the smallest.

The kid on the front has a better house to live in than I did. You could have done more.

The second card looked similar in size to the one on the counter with a picture of three brand new baby kittens whose eyes were closed.

You abandoned me when I was fragile like these kittens. You failed me and you will pay.

All three cards started with "Bethany Walker," all were signed the same, "From your past, S."

AJ looked at the envelopes, noticing the first one had been mailed from Madera in early September, the second one mailed from Stockton at the end of October, and the last one had Bethany's full name along with all of her residential information on it and a stamp, yet it had been hand delivered to her doorstep without using the mail system.

They were clearly getting more aggressive and threatening, although AJ did not want to make it worse for Bethany by telling her he agreed with her. Someone wanting her to pay and beg for forgiveness spoke of a deep-seated anger, not one based on something recent.

Bethany lived outside of AJ's jurisdiction so he decided to call Sergeant Boykin to see if he could get authorization for their agency to investigate. If he were successful, AJ would officially take himself out of the investigation into who may be sending Bethany the cards, although he had no intent to leave it up to someone else.

It took Sergeant Boykin the better part of four hours to connect with all the various administrators on a weekend to get the authorization for one of their detectives to work on Bethany's case. AJ appreciated Boykin assigning Allison Thompson as the lead investigator.

Allison had been with the department for twelve years, a detective for five. AJ had tried to convince Boykin to put her on his team when he had an opening a few months back…instead he got Willie. AJ had serious doubts about his junior detective ever being able to be the lead detective in any case. He had no such feeling about Allison.

Being very thorough, compassionate and a good listener, AJ could see Bethany had become comfortable with Allison. Despite Allison's conscientiousness, there wasn't much to go on beyond the basic presumption this had to be from when Bethany worked at Madera Children's Hospital. With three cards and envelopes, Allison made Bethany feel there may be a good chance they could get a fingerprint, or possibly DNA evidence from the envelopes being licked closed. When Allison looked at AJ while Bethany went to the kitchen the look on her face told him she did not believe it any more than he did.

After Allison left, AJ sat next to Bethany, his arm around her as her head rested in the crevice of his neck.

"AJ, I'm so sorry. I've been upset and stressed by the first two notes for quite a while now. I haven't been sleeping well, half expecting another one. I knew you were busy so I didn't want you to worry, and in the meantime I became bitchier towards you. You didn't deserve that. I should have told you sooner, I'm sorry."

"It's okay, don't worry about it," AJ said, kissing her softly on the forehead, and stroking her hair.

AJ spent the remainder of the weekend with Bethany, trying to comfort her. She told him there was something disconcerting about the anger in the words, and the person wanting to hurt her made her believe she could be in danger. As much as he tried to convince her threats are seldom carried through, AJ could not help thinking she might be right.

CHAPTER THIRTY-SEVEN

D ani sat in the lobby of Perko's waiting for Chad to arrive. Her left leg could not stop bouncing, and she kept fidgeting with her fingernails. Seeing him walk through the outer glass door leading to the foyer she liked the contrast of light blue jeans with a dark Cal sweatshirt instead of the suit he had on the night before. When he walked through the inner glass door leading to the lobby Dani stood and smiled.

"I'm not sure which I like best, seeing you in a suit, or in a pair of jeans," Dani joked.

Chuckling, Chad said, "I could say the same thing. I'm just glad you tacitly admit you like seeing me. How about that for some lawyerly language."

Dani felt her face begin to turn red and turned towards the hostess desk.

The hostess had seen Dani greet Chad so she already had their menus. Seeing Dani blush she changed her mind on seating them, directing them to a booth in the larger meeting room area for some privacy.

After they had ordered breakfast and coffee Dani looked into Chad's eyes. "Thank you for coming. I wasn't sure if I should call you, if you thought I was weird for asking you here, or even if you would come," Dani jabbered.

"Thank you for asking," Chad said. "Last night when you left I hoped you would call…I have to admit you surprised me by calling this quickly. I'm really glad you did."

Feeling her leg bouncing uncontrollably, Dani decided to get Chad to talk so she did not have to.

"So, I know you told me you are a real estate broker, now tell me, who is Chad? What do you like to do? What are your hobbies?"

"Well, I really like my job because the people I deal with are always excited about the new home they are buying. It makes it easy to go to work. In my spare time though I'm a Big Brother, it's been very rewarding for me. I've done it for fifteen years now. I often think if I had had someone there for me when I was a teenager I might not have run away from everything."

"I'm glad you did," Dani confided. "It's because you ran away you were there to save me."

Chad slightly nodded, his lips pursed with a small smile. He looked into Dani's eyes, eyes unchanged from the first time he saw them. For a long time he thought he would never see her again. Now, he felt blessed to be looking into her beautiful blue eyes once more.

"Tell me a little about Dani," Chad said.

"Not much to tell. I knew I wanted to be a lawyer when I was young," she said, her fingers playing with the green wrapper once used to hold her napkin.

"I wanted to put people away who caused pain to others. I started working at the DA's office right after I graduated law school, and it's everything you're warned about, no life if you want to be a successful attorney."

Dani looked at the table, feeling awkward talking about herself.

"I sometimes think there are things I would like to do, or to get involved in. Then I look at the stack of cases I have on my desk or on my table at home on a weekend...a normal life seems impossible." Looking back at Chad she said, "Pretty boring, isn't it?"

"Are you happy? Does being an attorney make you happy?" Chad inquired, concerned about possible reasons.

Dani had to reflect on the questions, her eyes staring past him as if she were looking outside.

An answer in itself, he thought.

"I love the law and I loved law school...I think I needed to do this for my own sanity, to try to right the wrong done to my family. Recently, I've realized I'm not in control of outcomes. So, I'm not sure of the answers to your questions. I think I might be happy being an attorney if I could ever get past why I did this in the first place, maybe if I could get back to loving the law being enough to satisfy me."

Dani paused, looking at Chad, not quite sure if she should share her feelings.

"I think I am ready to have a life. I think I would really like to find the right person and get married, maybe have some kids. If I ever did have kids I would want to be the kind of parent both sets of my parents were like, involved in their kid's lives and not wrapped up in their own. I'm not sure it's doable as an attorney."

Dani paused again, a warm feeling inside from opening up to him, and more importantly from his actually listening to her.

"I'm pretty messed up, aren't I?" she asked.

"I don't think so," Chad said, slowly shaking his head. "I think you are fortunate to be able to be coming to these realizations so you can do something about them. I think a lot of people get on some course for their life they don't know how to change."

"Well, I'm really glad you added some change to my life," Dani said. She smiled warmly as she looked into his eyes.

"Me, too," Chad said. "I got close to chickening out a couple of times…I'm glad I didn't."

"Are you sure you didn't come watch me in court more than once?" Dani inquired. "Yesterday you said you only watched me one time."

"I thought about it several times, for sure. I'm positive I only came to the courthouse once to watch you in trial. The only other time I went up there was when I brought the card and dropped it off with the girl in the office. Why do you ask?"

"I've had the feeling for a couple months now someone is watching me," Dani said.

"Maybe you…I don't know, really felt my presence there so it's made you more aware of who's in the courtroom," Chad said.

"Could be. Most of the time I get so caught up in my case there's no way I could tell you who is sitting in the courtroom watching the trial. You're right though, I know I have been more aware lately," Dani said.

CHAPTER THIRTY-EIGHT

———————

AJ called the team together for a Monday morning briefing. He wanted to see what Willie found out about there possibly being someone in the restaurant watching them the night of the initial investigation. More importantly, he wanted Willie to experience being on the hot seat.

AJ generally considered himself easy to work with, with one exception. He could not put up with someone being lazy when it came to working on a homicide. Lazy on a property crime never really bothered him, whereas the death of a person changed his expectations of everyone around him.

While AJ gathered his materials for the briefing his mentor walked into his office. One of the other two non-rotating detectives, his mentor had been a detective from AJ's first day with the department, training AJ when he first came into the Bureau. AJ had only seen him in uniform for ceremonies, department pictures, or officer funerals.

Thanks to his mentor AJ got to do what he was meant to do for the rest of his career, investigate crimes against people. His mentor convinced the administration a dozen years earlier to make a third non-rotating position for AJ based on seeing AJ's passion for working those kinds of cases.

Beyond being AJ's mentor, nobody in the department had the number of informants he had. He had spent his entire life in the Turlock area, garnering a respect like no other officer from the various nationalities throughout the city, well beyond his native Hispanic community.

Several years before AJ gave him the nickname of E.F. Hutton. AJ recalled the old E.F. Hutton commercial on television about "when E.F. Hutton talks, people listen," and he knew the name was perfect.

"E.F., to what do I owe the honor of your presence," AJ said, putting his stuff on the desk to give him a hug.

"AJ, it's good to see you. I heard you brought Bethany to the Christmas party the other night. I wish I'd been there. My daughter got called into work, so I had to babysit my granddaughter at the last second."

"I understand," AJ said. "I missed you, though. I really wanted you to meet her. Maybe the three of us can get together for dinner sometime?"

"I look forward to it mi amigo. I know you're getting ready to hook up with your team. I wanted to make sure I caught you before I head to the coroner's office."

"I'm all ears. What's up?"

"I got a call from one of my informants last night," E.F. began. "They said there's a prostitute who goes by the name of Cherie, apparently she freaked out a few days ago. They asked her if one of her john's hurt her. Cherie told my informant she took a guy to a motel, got paid to leave him there, and then the guy ends up murdered in the room she took him to. I thought it sounded a lot like your case from what Sarge told me."

"Damn, sounds a lot like mine. I probably know the answers to my next questions, otherwise you would have given them to me if you had them," AJ said.

"Yep. No idea what motel, or even if it's our city, only they did say they hadn't seen Cherie for over two days. They promised to call if they see her. I trust this informant... they'll call. I'll let you know right away if I hear any more."

"Thanks, E.F."

"Gotta go, man. I'm in serious need of coffee before I watch an autopsy. Catch you later," E.F. said as he walked out.

AJ picked up what he needed for the briefing and headed to the conference room. He had asked Knox to put up a couple of easels with flip chart paper, an old school method he chose to keep. He used them to track assignments given, as well as those accomplished, along with motives and theories as they progressed.

All members were encouraged to share their thoughts to cover all possibilities. AJ especially encouraged them to think like a defense attorney, so hopefully they would properly eliminate anyone in the suspect pool who did not belong, while solidifying why those who remained legitimately belonged there. The flip chart paper allowed him to tape them on the walls of his office when the meetings were over as his way of keeping track. AJ often had all four walls covered while he worked on older cases along with new ones. Only on rare occasions were the current homicides low enough to allow him or E.F. to be able to spend reasonable amounts of time on older or cold case homicides. AJ did his best not to forget.

Approaching the conference room he heard Knox telling the team about his weekend trip with his wife. AJ smiled. He enjoyed hearing when others were excited about their families. He stopped outside of the conference room to wait for Knox to finish. When the volume in the room lowered

AJ walked in, taking survey of the personnel. He saw Willie open his folder to review his notes and he looked pretty nervous to AJ as he fidgeted in his chair.

"I know it probably seemed strange with me not calling anyone in over the weekend," AJ said. "I just felt like we all needed the rest. So we all know what's been accomplished, let's do a quick review."

"The autopsy didn't produce much," AJ said. "We'll know more about Nathan's BA level when the blood work comes back. Knox has the duct tape and he'll be trying to locate some prints today. Willie, what did you find out about the guy in the restaurant?"

"Ahem," Willie said, clearing his throat. "I finally located the older waitress you wanted me to talk to. She had a hard time remembering some of the information."

"You went in this morning on your way to work, didn't you?" AJ asked. When Willie's eyes shifted down to his binder AJ knew he did.

"Don't answer...tell me what she said."

Embarrassed to look up, Willie focused on his notes.

"She remembered a guy sitting by himself in the corner. She thought it was strange he specifically wanted the large round table in the southwest corner...he sat facing the motel. She didn't remember much about him other than he seemed very polite, plus he left her a five dollar tip, even though he only had coffee."

"No description?" AJ asked.

"She said a white guy, dressed in dark clothes, she couldn't remember any specific type. She had no idea how tall, or how much he weighed, although she did say he looked like he was somewhere between twenty-eight and thirty-two. She also said the strangest thing about the guy besides only ordering coffee was he kept letting it get cold. She had to give him a new cup with fresh coffee twice."

"Great job, thank you," AJ said, wanting to make sure to end on a positive note with him. He could see the surprise on Willie's face from the praise.

"Willie, get your supplemental report dictated as soon as you can. I know you have your cases to work but I still would like the report by the end of the day. Knox, the duct tape is the focus for you. Seth, I know you know the guys in the Street Crimes Unit better than I do so hook up with them and see if they know a prostitute who goes by the name of Cherie." AJ paused as he wrote assignments on the paper.

"Seth, you have the description of the girl who got out of the Jeep. We need to find out if it's one in the same…if so we need to talk with her. All right, that'll do it for now. Thanks everybody. I've got to head to the DA's office for a meeting."

Everyone stood, sliding their chairs under the table. As Knox headed to collect the flip chart paper to return it to AJ's office, AJ said, "Oh, by the way, our only witness from the motel I interviewed, Adam Riley, somebody murdered him in his car on Highway 99 near Crows Landing Road."

AJ could see the shock on everyone's face except for Knox.

"Gotta go, see you guys later," he said, not having time to explain. Grabbing his binders he saw Knox looking at him, so he winked. Knox nodded his head, which for AJ meant Knox would not say anything about the print from the glass, or share any information about the dead witness until AJ let him know he could.

CHAPTER THIRTY-NINE

AJ made it to the DA's office about five minutes before the start of the meeting. Bridget Fletcher surprised him when she came out of her private office on time on a Monday morning considering the overall office could go from a well-oiled machine to a train wreck in a matter of minutes.

"AJ, I knew for you to want an appointment meant something had to be up. Come on in," Bridget said as she walked into her office, expecting him to follow.

AJ knew Bridget well enough to know she probably arrived for work around five o'clock and this would not be a good time for small talk.

Pointing at one of the large chairs in front of her desk she said, "Have a seat."

He knew she was all business when she sat at her desk instead of moving over to the more relaxing area she had set up in the corner of her office.

"Thank you for meeting me, Bridget. I'll get straight to the point since I know you are very busy. Unfortunately, I think this is going to make you even busier."

"Somehow I already knew," Bridget declared, a solemn look on her face.

"Look, you know me, I don't like to hide things from

my bosses, or the important people in a case. I know you might be called away at any time so I'm going to start with the punch line. We can always get back together later if we don't have time now to cover everything."

AJ could see he had Bridget's full attention. As a seasoned trial attorney she had become accustomed to waiting her turn, all while sitting forward with her pen on a legal pad at the ready.

"We have a fingerprint on a glass sitting on the table next to my latest murder victim," AJ said. "The fingerprint comes back to one of your deputy district attorney's, Dani Larson. Furthermore, our victim is Nathan Price. You may or may not recall she was the prosecutor in Nathan's DUI manslaughter trial a couple months ago. He got acquitted on all charges."

AJ paused, mostly to let the information sink in while Bridget finished with her notes.

Bridget looked at AJ, put up her index finger toward him, then leaned forward to pick up the desk phone. Seconds after pushing a button she said, "I do not want to be disturbed for the next twenty minutes. Move my next meeting back by thirty minutes. Thank you." Hanging up the phone Bridget candidly looked at AJ.

"The twenty minutes I gave you will more than likely only be about ten before people are lining up at my door. So, to the point right back at you…what's your gut say AJ, do you think she had anything to do with it?"

He expected Bridget to ask the question early in the conversation. AJ thought about how he would answer it the entire drive to Modesto.

"Something tells me she isn't directly involved, although I have not eliminated her from the suspect pool yet."

Bridget cocked her head, raised her eyebrows and said, "Not directly involved. What is it you're trying to say?"

"In a nutshell, a witness saw a women at the motel driving Nathan's car. The two got out, went into the room, then Nathan's found lying on the bed, duct tape around his wrists and feet, with an NG tube in his nose. We think he died from alcohol poisoning, we're still waiting for the lab results.

"Dani is still in the suspect pool due to the possibility she might have been the woman seen going into the room with Nathan. The homicide took place in the late evening or early morning hours, so we need to look into whether or not she has an alibi." AJ paused again, partially to let her catch up, but primarily for effect.

"The reason something tells me she isn't directly involved is someone murdered our only witness the next morning in his car on northbound Highway 99 north of Crows Landing Road. It's an S.O. case, and I've spoken with Jay Fuller, the lead investigator, he told me the guy got stabbed in the neck. His murder took place somewhere between eight and eleven in the morning so I'm pretty sure when I look into it Dani will have been here or in a courtroom."

Bridget stopped writing, slowly sitting back into her chair. AJ could tell her wheels were spinning.

"Another reason I'm unsure about her culpability is one of our guys has an informant who told him there is a prostitute who is very scared and seems to know something about our homicide. Given we no longer have a witness to positively identify the woman getting out of Nathan's car it will be a little more difficult to say if it was Dani or some other woman, like maybe the prostitute.

"And lastly, when I saw you on Friday I came here to meet with Dani. I didn't know about her fingerprint then.

Initially she seemed very surprised when I told her Nathan had been murdered, then her demeanor changed a little, acting like he got what he deserved."

AJ took a deep breath pleased he got all of the major cards on the table before Bridget had to leave. Another long pause as Bridget looked at her notes, taking in everything AJ said. She placed her notepad on the desk at the same time she looked him in the eye.

"I really like Dani. I've always had a soft spot in my heart for her. Her family got killed by a drunk driver, including her twin brother. If I had to guess, we might say the same thing if a drunk driver killed our family and we worked Nathan's case. We all have our own baggage and sometimes our baggage can be used to make us a better person. I can't believe she would kill somebody…on the other hand, we've both seen really good people do some really bad things."

"We are way early into this investigation," AJ said as he stood. "I wanted to give you a heads up, the same as the Chief, so neither of you would be caught off guard by anything. I hope you don't react to this too quickly from a political position."

Bridget stood and began to walk around her desk. Approaching him she said, "Your compassion for those involved in your investigations is what makes you special. You were direct with me, so I'll be direct with you. Don't be surprised if I put Dani on administrative leave with pay. I can try to keep it hushed, for whatever it's worth. Somebody will likely leak it to the press. I think the best thing is for her not to actively work on cases while you sort this out. I hope you can sympathize with my position."

"I do. I think administrative leave with pay is fair. Thank you for meeting with me on such short notice."

Bridget smiled and they hugged. Stepping back she said, "Thank you for keeping me in the loop on this. Can you do me a favor, please let my secretary know when you go out I need five minutes before she lets the next person in my office. Thanks again, AJ." Bridget turned and walked to her chair.

AJ headed for Dani's office knowing once Bridget put her on administrative leave his chances of her talking to him would be minimal. Approaching the office he could hear Dani talking as though she were on the telephone. He stopped in the hallway to let her finish the conversation and when he heard her hang up he walked up to her desk, taking a seat before she had a chance to offer it.

"Detective Conti, back so soon," Dani said.

"Yes, I needed to ask you some questions, so I thought I would pop in to take care of it while I happened to be here. So I can make sure I covered all the bases, can you tell me what you were doing last Thursday, the eighth, between ten in the evening until one in the morning?"

"Sure. I worked on this case right here," she said as she picked up one of the three files spread out on her desk.

"I worked on some pretrial motions in preparation for us to start picking the jury on Wednesday of this week. The truth is, I didn't get very far, my mind got stuck on a child-abuse trial in the hands of the jury last Thursday…I didn't have a very good feeling of how it would likely end. At about eleven thirty, maybe even midnight, I turned on the TV to try to relax and take my mind off of the case. Why do you ask?" Dani asked.

"You've done enough trials, you've seen enough defense attorneys to know if we don't look into every possibility they will make us both look like fools. Obviously, when the jury acquitted Nathan a couple of months ago it looked like a loss for you. Any defense attorney in their right mind would want to know if we questioned you, I mean, it's not unreasonable to think someone with your background might get angry enough to take matters into their own hands."

"Are you referring to the fact a drunk driver killed my family?" Dani asked, the muscles in her face starting to tighten.

"Yes. If you'd stop thinking like a deputy district attorney for a second and think back to law school when professors made you argue both sides you would see the logic in me needing to shut the door on this possibility," AJ said in a soft calming tone.

Dani took a few seconds to reflect on what he said. Thankfully she realized his comment might have merit.

"I'm sorry, you're absolutely right. As I told you before, even though I did not care for Nathan Price, I did not kill him."

"Two questions off of what you said earlier. First, what is the name of the case in the folder you were working on at home? Second, do you recall the TV show you were watching?"

"The case is People vs. Munoz. It's a stolen auto case out of Ceres where the guy tried to force one of the cop cars off the road before he lost control and slammed into a tree. He's a gang-banger looking at twenty-five to life. I can give you the docket number if you need it."

"No, what you gave me is fine," AJ said.

"I had the TV on the History Channel. As I recall it had to do with the Queen of England, well mostly about who will take over when she steps down," Dani said. "I didn't pay a great deal of attention, although it seems like

185

Charles doesn't want it despite his current wife wanting him to be the king. William seems like the popular choice though. I watched until almost one in the morning, then I went to bed."

Looking for the element of surprise AJ changed topics.

"Can you give me any reason why we would find a drinking glass with your fingerprints on it on the table in the motel room next to Nathan Price?"

"What? What are you saying? Are you serious? Of course not, there's no way. You can't be serious."

The level of the tone in Dani's voice climbed with each outburst. The look of anger on Dani's face returned, which pleased AJ. Knowing innocent people often get angry when accused of something they did not do, Dani's demeanor had been what he hoped for considering his gut kept telling him she probably had nothing to do with it.

"Look, I'm not messing with you," AJ said. "I'm trying to help you out here. We did in fact find a glass at the crime scene with your print on it. Try to calm down so you can process it. Is there any way you can think of for the glass to have gotten there?"

Dani stood and started pacing behind her desk.

"I have no idea how it got there, you have to believe me. I'm telling you I did not put it there. I've never even been to that motel." Dani stopped pacing. She took a deep breath as she looked at AJ.

"It's true, I probably took the Nathan Price trial too personally. In fact, it bothered me for days when the jury acquitted him. I felt I let the victim down...I let her family down. Look, I'm telling you, I have had so many cases between then and now I haven't had time to think about Nathan Price."

"One last question. Can you think of anybody who would try to frame you by putting the glass there?" AJ asked.

The shock of his implication about someone possibly framing her almost took Dani's breath away. She sat in her chair, her elbows on the desk, her fingertips together in a pyramid, her forehead leaning against the side of her index fingers. After nearly a minute Dani looked at him with watery eyes.

"I cannot think of anybody."

AJ could see by the paleness of Dani's face he shocked her with everything he asked, so he stood.

"Thank you for talking with me. If you have any questions you know how to get in touch with me." He set one of his business cards on top of the file directly in front of her before he turned and walked out the door.

CHAPTER FORTY

Bridget Fletcher poked her head out of her office to speak to her secretary and saw AJ across the room heading for the exit. She knew he had been to speak with Dani, which meant Dani would not be mentally capable of dealing with her cases the rest of the day. Instead of telling her secretary what she wanted, Bridget asked her to let Dani Larson know she needed to see her right away.

In less than ten minutes Bridget's phone rang, Dani was outside waiting to meet her. After telling her secretary to have Dani come in Bridget stood and walked toward the door to meet her. When Bridget saw Dani's face she knew she made the right move…Dani seemed lost.

"Dani, it's good to see you. Come in, please," Bridget said. She softly placed her palm on Dani's shoulder while directing her toward the couch.

Dani sat, pushing her hip into the corner by the arm. Without thinking her feet crossed almost simultaneously with her fingers interlocking. Bridget sat in the chair at the end of the couch.

"I can see you have probably spoken with Detective Conti this morning."

"Yes. Obviously he has spoken with you as well," Dani said.

"Yes, he has."

"I had nothing to do with Nathan Price's murder. You need to believe me."

"I do believe you," Bridget stated. "I need to make sure we all do the right thing here though, this conversation has nothing to do with whether I believe you or not."

"Are you firing me?"

"No, of course not," Bridget exclaimed. "I am going to put you on administrative leave with pay. The truth is you would have a hard time staying focused on your caseload, at the same time we could easily be accused of looking the other way if we did nothing. I hope when your head stops spinning you can see this is best for everybody. I promise to do my best to keep it hushed. The only person I have told is the Assistant District Attorney of course, I need her to be aware of personnel matters like this. We will simply tell people you needed to take some personal time for family matters."

"I can't believe Detective Conti did this to me," Dani said. "Coming here, telling you...putting me in this position."

"You should be careful about what you're saying," Bridget said, a directness now in her tone Dani had never heard before.

"I've known Detective Conti for many years now and we've had several major trials together. You would not want anyone else trying to clear your name. I can tell you this, he does not believe you are the suspect in his investigation. What he's trying to do is save your career, so the defense attorney community will not be able to say anything you have done could impugn your reputation."

"Are you serious? You're saying I should trust him?"

"I'm dead serious." Bridget paused for effect.

"He even voiced his concern with what actions I might

take against you; he didn't want me to be heavy-handed. He knows as a friend and colleague I trust his gut feelings. Unfortunately, my position is political, so I have to take into account many other things besides his gut feelings. So for now, this step seems to be best for everybody. Go home, try to relax, and don't worry about this place. You know the wheels of justice never stop turning."

Bridget stood so Dani would know the conversation had ended. Walking toward the door Bridget said, "I want you to go back to your office, get your personal things, and then close the door behind you. By leaving everything on your desk it makes it look like you had to leave in a hurry so nobody will be the wiser." Bridget softly touched Dani's shoulder for reassurance as she opened the door to usher her out.

Dani struggled not to run to her office. She closed the door, a rare occurrence around there, and sitting in her chair her mind could not focus on what to do. Dani took her phone out of her suit pocket, went to recent calls and started to touch Chad's number. She paused, something inside telling her if she started talking with him she would break down.

She took a deep breath, counted to three and stood. Dani set the case file on her desk like Bridget told her, grabbed her things and walked out, closing the door behind her. Traversing through the common area she could already feel the eyes of office staff on her. For some reason Dani felt they already knew the truth and the personal emergency ruse would not fool anyone.

Not a single person wished me luck or acted in any way like they were there to support me, she thought.

STALKER SAT IN THE BACK OF THE COURTROOM AGAINST the wall reading a paper. He recognized the two men at the defense table immediately. He had never seen the woman in the pantsuit at the prosecution table. He listened intently while trying to give the impression he could care less as he read the paper.

When the judge opened the door to her chambers the bailiff brought the room to order. Prior to the jury being brought in she smiled when she saw the Assistant District Attorney.

"Counselor, strange seeing you here," the judge said.

"It's been awhile, Your Honor," she said. "Ms. Larson had a personal emergency, so I'm filling in."

"It should be short. I'm sure you can handle it," she said sarcastically, smiling at her former colleague.

"Thank you, Your Honor," she said, returning the smile.

"Bring in the jury," the judge said, the smile replaced by a more authoritative presence.

In less than ten minutes the Wardas were smiling, thanking Rothstein for convincing the jury they were innocent and had not beaten their son.

Stalker glared over the newspaper in front of his face, disgusted with the system and the jury. Everything about the way they were acting told him they knew Cyrus had done it. A little boy being too scared to testify supposedly provided them reasonable doubt. To Stalker, Rothstein seemed almost as dirty as the Wardas. Despite the fact Rothstein wasn't celebrating like them, his role of convincing the jury Cyrus did not beat the boy made him an accomplice.

Stalker wanted to get out of the courtroom before the Wardas or Rothstein walked his way. He did not want them to see him directly. Walking through the wooden doors he noticed two females in professional attire in the anteroom to his left. He overheard one say, "Dani's been put on Administrative Leave. I'm not sure why, I heard it all happened this morning after a detective met with the DA."

Stalker grinned and kept walking.

Ahh, the scales of Lady Justice are beginning to tip, he thought.

He milled around outside to the north of the courthouse, fitting in nicely with the diverse crowd. Forty minutes after Stalker walked outside he saw Rothstein come out of the doors used by employees only.

Two steps onto the sidewalk Rothstein had his cell phone out making calls while walking, unaware of anyone around him. Stalker followed him to the multi-story parking garage on Eleventh Street, less than a block north of the courthouse. When Rothstein took the stairs to the third floor Stalker felt he could make his move.

Rothstein had the phone to his ear when he reached his car. Setting down his briefcase to free up his hand he reached in his pocket to retrieve his keys. He started to look up when the reflection in the door window caught his attention. Before he could focus on it, Stalker's elbow caught him in the face.

Rothstein stumbled backward, dropping his phone. Stalker kicked him in the groin, doubling Rothstein over before falling to the cement. Hearing a woman's voice on the cell, Stalker stomped on it.

Stalker got on top of Rothstein, grinding his knee in the middle of Rothstein's back while pulling up his head with a hand full of hair, all the while looking through the windows for any movement in the garage.

"You think it was justice what happened today? Letting the fucker who beat a kid walk off scot free?"

Stalker bounced Rothstein's face off the cement once.

"Since you think it's okay for someone to beat another person like he did, I know you won't call the cops about this, will you?"

Through the blood Rothstein spat, "No," while trying to shake his head.

"Good. Because if I hear anything about you calling the cops, you're going to find yourself in the same predicament as the guy in the car on Highway 99 a couple days ago. You get me?"

Rothstein nodded his head as best as possible.

"You better. Now, count to thirty while you stay face down. Do not look up at me unless you want to wear my shoe on your face."

Rothstein shook his head.

Stalker stood, keeping his eye on Rothstein to make sure he listened.

"One more thing," Stalker said. "Ms. Larson said you're welcome." Before Rothstein could move Stalker's foot came down hard on Rothstein's heel, shattering bones and tearing tendons and ligaments. Rothstein passed out from the pain, his bladder emptying on the cement.

Stalker calmly walked away, leaving the garage the way he entered, turning north on Eleventh Street.

CHAPTER FORTY-ONE

———◇———

Though AJ thought Bethany should not go to work, at that moment his opinion did not hold much clout. She possessed a strong will not to let anyone know she might be vulnerable. Although he appreciated her inner-strength, her exhaustion from very little sleep over the last several days had him concerned.

AJ made sure to text Bethany before he got too involved. He asked how her day had been going and if she needed anything, not really knowing what he could do to help. His pleasure at her quick response changed with her sharp toned response, only telling him things at work were fine. She made no offer of further conversation.

Bethany had never been a needy girlfriend like those of some of his colleagues. Her comments after the Christmas party were the first hint she wasn't as strong as she portrayed. And with the threatening cards, he felt submerged in foreign waters, unsure of which way to go. Worse yet, AJ wanted to tell her he would see her in the evening, but he knew he could not guarantee it. He knew a broken promise would not go over well. A week ago he would have texted it without hesitation, but now he stared at the screen unsure. He settled for a wish for a great day and a smiley face. *Stupid emojis!*

AJ updated the sergeant on his meeting with DA Fletcher

before he tracked down Allison. When she saw him walk around the corner she did a quick shake of her head, along with pointing her index finger. They met up at the outside tables in the garden…the Chief's idea of trying to provide a place to destress. AJ had never seen its value nor taken advantage of it. This time, sitting there with Allison felt more relaxing than in the noisy chaos of the bureau office, giving him cause to think about using it again.

"Got anything?"

"Not much," Allison said.

"I didn't figure you would."

"We checked for prints, DNA, anything to possibly give us a clue. Nothing."

"Hmm, not good."

"Kind of scary actually."

"Allison, you know I trust you. Give me your best read on this."

"In a normal investigation I would try to sugar coat it a little…look, I'm concerned. This guy is very clean, he knows what not to do, and he's very methodical. Each card mailed from a different location. The last one is malicious, and he delivers it to her doorstep."

They sat in silence, AJ trying to take it all in.

Allison asked, "You know Dr. P., the department psychologist?"

AJ snickered. "Yeah, we've met once or twice."

"Sorry, stupid question. You've had more shootings in your career than most of the department put together."

"Doc says shit follows some people more than others." They both chuckled. "We have lunch once a week, I've grown to trust him. What's his take?"

"All BS aside, he says we better take this guy seriously."

CHAPTER FORTY-TWO

Dani drove to Turlock in a daze, unable to recall her trip. She parked on Main Street two blocks from Chad's office. Crying, she wanted to have him hold her, and tell her it would be all right like he had years before.

In a brief moment of clarity she realized the untenable position she would put him in and decided to leave. Wiping away tears, she noticed the clock on the dash read six minutes before noon. Overwhelmed with despair, she had no idea where the last two hours of her life had gone.

HAVING HEARD SOME OF THE DEPUTY DA'S TALKING about Dani before he followed Rothstein, Stalker elected to again go by her house. He sat in his car to survey the activity. He knew there would be little in a neighborhood filled with up-and-comers, two income, no stay at home types. He decided to try to get a glimpse of Dani in the house, hopefully suffering.

Stalker looked around enough to believe she did not make it home yet. Like before, he went through the gate by the garage and finished his recon. Convinced she wasn't there, he sat in one of her swivel patio chairs, rocking while he contemplated.

Not only had Dani not been in court, Stalker had no doubt about what he overheard. There should have been no way he would beat Dani to her house, unless she stayed in her office crying, being consoled by bottom-feeding attorneys who secretly hoped she got fired so they could move up. He smiled, happy with the unplanned drama.

Sitting quietly, rubbing his palms together, he sat straight up. A small grin formed as he ran his new idea through his head. He loved how new ideas popped into his head, especially ones fitting perfectly into his overall goal. First Rothstein, now this; he could not keep from smiling.

Pulling his knife from its sheath, he popped the side garage door open as quickly as the first time. Walking to the workbench he knew what he wanted.

Reaching for it, the garage door opener came alive and the door started to creak. Grabbing the item, Stalker sprinted to the side door…several seconds later when the car pulled into the driveway he knew he had not been seen. Putting the knife and his new instrument of death from the workbench away, he slipped out, closing the door behind him. Holding the knob to keep it from opening accidentally, he leaned against the door to listen. First he heard the large door descending, followed closely by the sound of the house door slamming.

Nodding to himself, Stalker opened the gate, surveyed the area, and headed for his car.

A better day than I expected, he thought. *I'm gonna sleep well.*

CHAD TOLD HIS BOSS HE HAD AN EMERGENCY AND LEFT

work when Dani called him crying. Pulling into her driveway he had no idea what happened, her sobbing made everything hard to decipher.

Opening the door Dani ran to him. She hugged him, laying her head between his shoulder and neck. The sobbing breaths remained enough to make him sense the crying could start again any second. Stroking her head and back he felt he could stay there forever, then feeling self-conscious Chad looked to see if anyone might be watching, suggesting they go inside.

Dani walked into the living room, sitting sideways in the recliner, drawing her knees up and hugging the pillow.

Looking around, the recliner had distance from all the other seating. Chad looked once more at Dani nestled into the cave of the chair protecting her and moved, finally settling on the couch across from her.

"I got put on…Administrative Leave today," Dani said, her voice shaking.

"You what?" He was on his knees taking her hand before he knew it. "For God sakes, what for?"

"Nathan Price, the defendant in the trial you came to, he was murdered in a motel room here."

Chad's back stiffened, his head leaned slightly as his shoulders rolled up, his eyebrows almost touched.

"They found a glass with my fingerprints."

"You can't be serious."

She turned to look at him, the tears welling up making him a blur. She could not stop the familiar wave from overtaking her once again.

Please, tell me you didn't, he thought.

Waiting, listening, he prayed he knew her well enough.

"I didn't…you have to believe me."

His eyes shined as the corners of his lips raised. When his hand touched her cheek she laid against it, her heart settling.

For Dani the day had been a complex array of negative feelings. Then, she lifted her head and looked deep in his eyes, seeing his belief in her. For the first time all day she had a positive sensation.

"Have you eaten anything," he asked heading for the kitchen. "I'll fix some soup and hot tea. Then you can tell me everything."

Control…we need to be in control, he thought.

Twenty minutes later she sat back into the recliner, her fingers wrapped around her cup of tea, the half empty bowl of soup on the tray. Watching Chad clean up, Dani realized his kindness and quiet strength. She no longer wanted to curl up in the recliner and she moved to the couch…her left leg on the cushion, the sofa arm against her lower back.

She looks stronger already, he thought while rolling his sleeves down.

He sat, facing her, smiling.

Over the next thirty minutes Dani spelled out what she could recall of her conversation with AJ and about the trial. Chad sensed the best thing for him to do was to listen.

As the evening progressed Dani felt more tranquil, thankful Chad was there for her…again.

Hours later Chad cleaned up the kitchen from the pizza he ordered and finally settled in on the couch next to her. Dani nestled into his arms and fell into a deep sleep, the best rest she had had for months.

CHAPTER FORTY-THREE

AJ got to Bethany's house shortly after seven and was shocked at her greeting him at the door with such happiness. Christmas lights were on, music playing, and the signs of wrapping presents were strewn about.

"I knew you wouldn't be here until late so the chicken won't be done for another few minutes. In the meantime, how about a glass of wine."

"Sure, thank you."

Bethany walked up and gave him a long hug. Stepping back she took his hands in hers.

"I'm sorry for this weekend. I have no idea why I reacted the way I did. I decided I'm not going to change my life based on some cards with their stupid threats. Saturday morning you made me so happy when you brought me a Macchiato…I ruined the moment."

"You have nothing to be sorry about. I'm thrilled you have such a positive attitude tonight." AJ smiled, trying to hide his concern.

"What? There's more, I can tell by your face."

"Look, Allison and I agree this guy seems serious. I think you need to be cautious."

The buzz from the kitchen interrupted them and Bethany walked away. AJ heard what sounded like the oven door, along with a few knobs turning. Walking back in, she stopped in front of him again, only this time with a sly smile.

Raising her right hand she said, "I promise to be cautious, I cross my heart," which she did. Then she raised her eyebrows as she took his hand. "Except for now. Dinner can wait."

STALKER WANTED TO SEE DANI SUFFERING BEFORE HE went to work and drove through her neighborhood several times. Comfortable, he turned his lights off and pulled forward gradually until he could see in her front window.

Who the hell's the guy on the couch, he thought.

What he expected had not materialized and his increased blood pressure gave rise to his red cheeks.

His agitation only increased when he realized time had gotten away from him and he hated being late, anywhere. Speeding became a must. Taking several deep breaths he made himself focus. He had the rest of the night to dwell upon her.

CHAPTER FORTY-FOUR

A J arrived later than usual with Knox waiting for him near the back door smoking a cigarette.

"Glad to see you could finally make it," Knox said.

"Go ahead, finish it." AJ's mind had been dragging a little anyway. Encouraging people to work harder came easier with some than others. Between not keeping him from his weekend with his wife in Napa and giving him regular smoke breaks, AJ knew how to keep Knox happy.

Crushing his butt on the side of the smoke canister Knox said, "Got some good news...got some bad news."

"Go ahead."

"No prints on the duct tape good enough to get a hit in AFIS." He knew AJ liked the bad news first. He threw the butt in the canister as they walked inside.

"I did get some partials of what looks like the tips of fingers, along with some good outside palm prints, although they're probably outside of the scope of what you would get from a normal set of prints in AFIS. I think those have enough points of comparison for a positive match if we ever get a suspect."

AJ followed Knox as they headed to his lab, taking it all in. When Knox explained the process he always used AJ stopped listening intently, purely out of his trust for Knox in his domain. Knox was good in his lab and well recognized in the county's trial world.

Looking at the palm prints AJ agreed. Now he needed to get Knox some suspects so he could nail down whether they stayed in the suspect pool or got eliminated.

"I'll start with the deputy DA. See if she will cooperate."

"Yeah, I could let you know a result pretty quick once I get them."

"Good. I'll get back to you." AJ turned to leave.

"Ahem."

"What?" AJ asked, turning back around.

"Well ..."

"What? Say it."

"Best I can figure, when I first arrived at the motel I ran over to The Diner for a quick relief, before you got there."

"Would you cut to the chase?"

"Got a couple good prints of Willie's on the duct tape. He must have snuck into the motel room when I went over there. He had to have picked up Price's hands. Thumb on one side of the duct tape, fingers on the other."

"The mother...is he here?"

"Yeah. Got here a few minutes before you."

AJ took a couple of deep breaths to prevent letting loose with a string of obscenities.

"I'll fix him," AJ said, pulling out his phone. AJ sent him a straight forward text.

Knox smiled, patiently waiting for his explanation.

"I'll let him explain to the entire judicial world why he did it. I told him I want a supplemental report by noon explaining his actions in the room, specifically lifting the victim's taped wrists. Plus, I cc'd it to Boykin."

"Told you," Knox said.

"Told me what?"

"He's worse than a teenager. Welcome to parenthood." Knox chuckled as he patted AJ on the shoulder.

Not the best way to start the day, AJ thought as he left Knox still chuckling.

Thinking about Willie touching things at a crime scene frustrated him and he decided to try to get his mind on something else. He headed down the hallway, hoping the Detective secretary had come through.

Walking past her desk her left hand reached up with a folded white paper, her eyes never leaving her computer screen. AJ snuck a quick peek before putting it inside his suit jacket pocket. Never question the detective secretary on how she got things, and always keeping a private stash of her favorite dark chocolate…two of AJ's policies.

AJ briefly thought about calling Dani. He needed to get away from the office before he ended up on Administrative Leave himself.

Pulling into the neighborhood AJ realized how much the city had grown. Mostly Bay Area workers willing to drive two hours one way to be able to afford nice houses, similar to Dani Larson's.

The all white Kia Sorento in the driveway fit and looked well maintained. Dispatch informed AJ the 2016 Sorento belonged to a Chad Miller, along with his local address, a different one than Dani's.

AJ opened the screen door, rapping twice in quick succession, ready to knock again when the door swung open. The guy filling the doorframe looked to be in his mid-thirties, average build, wearing a nice shirt and slacks. The young man's attempt at the tough guy face did not fit.

"You must be Chad Miller."

Chad's eyes squinted for a couple seconds before the nod. Shaking his head and looking down at the ground replaced his *wannabe* tough guy face.

"I'm Detective—"

"I know who you are. What do you want?"

"Is Dani Larson—"

"She doesn't want to talk to you."

"You cut me off again, and she won't be the only one not talking." AJ stared at him long enough for Chad's feet to start squirming as he crossed his arms.

"Tell Ms. Larson she needs to get an attorney. I recommend Tom Sullivan. Then have him call me so I can help her clear her name. You *got* that?"

AJ turned and walked away on Chad's first nod.

***

STALKER WATCHED THE DETECTIVE PULL UP IN FRONT of Dani's house. Sitting in his car three houses down on the opposite side of the street he was close enough to recognize the detective he had seen at the motel.

Stalker researched on line about AJ. He discovered Detective Conti had been with the department for close to two decades, and in the Detective Bureau for most of it. Stalker appreciated seeing him following up on the person's prints left on the glass in the motel room.

Early on Stalker had envisioned Dani not thinking straight, and when talking with the detective, maybe incriminating herself in some way. Further reflection about her being an attorney changed his expectation to her not saying a word to a detective without another lawyer present.

When the man from the night before answered the door and Dani never spoke with Detective Conti, Stalker struck the top of the steering wheel. He had hoped to see her panicked by the detective's appearance. Turning the key he put his car in drive and took off making sure not to look at the detective as he walked toward his car. Instead, Stalker looked right, reaching for the radio knob. Looking in his rearview he saw Detective Conti stopped, looking his way.

Yeah, I'm keeping an eye on you, Stalker thought.

CHAPTER FORTY-FIVE

AJ could feel it again…someone's eyes on him like the night of the call out to the motel. He slid the edge of his suit jacket back, barely putting his fingertips in his pants pocket. He wanted his gun close…just in case.

Walking down the driveway AJ saw the black, four door VW Rabbit passing in front of the house. The driver reached to his right toward the dash making it impossible for AJ to see his face. But, the familiar feeling in AJ's gut told him he needed to be careful.

He looked to follow the car, trying not to be obvious or write anything down. It turned out the plate was easy to memorize. Even though the car stopped at the stop sign up the street a bit longer than normal, AJ kept walking to his car as though it were nothing.

AJ gave dispatch the plate to run, while taking note of the Minnesota Twins license plate cover. *It might come in handy in the future*, he thought.

DANI APPRECIATED CHAD BEING THERE FOR HER AND wiped away the little grin before Chad turned around. She knew he'd be no match for Detective Conti.

"What's with him?" Chad asked.

"According to the DA, she worked a bunch of cases with Detective Conti and assured me he is looking out for my best interest. I don't know what to think. He's right though... Sullivan is the best. But he's crazy if he thinks Sullivan will work with him, no way."

Sitting at the kitchen table Dani proceeded to tell Chad everything leading up to her Administrative Leave. The night before she had only touched on main points, mostly wanting Chad there for support. The entire time they were talking the detective's suggestion kept surfacing in her thoughts.

Reaching for her phone she located Sullivan's number on the website, dialed and listened to the secretary's well-practiced spiel.

"My name is Dani Larson. I would like to set up an appointment with Mr. Sullivan to possibly represent me."

"Yes, Ms. Larson, he hoped you would call. He's in the office now, give me a second," the secretary said, putting Dani on hold before she had a chance to respond.

"Dani, how are you?" Tom Sullivan asked, the polite thing to do, not waiting for her response. "How soon can you get to my office? I have an opening at two, or you can meet me here at four-thirty."

"Four-thirty works best."

"Great. See you then." Tom hung up.

Dani looked at her phone, then at Chad, her eyebrows nearly touching from her confusion.

CHAPTER FORTY-SIX

A J received a text from Seth saying they needed to head to Sacramento ASAP. He told Seth to meet him at a restaurant parking lot on Taylor Road...AJ knew Seth would want to drive.

AJ had barely closed the door when it began.

"I'm king of the car, this is my domain," Seth said, his hand sweeping from the glove box, to the left edge of AJ's seat, and everything in his direction.

"You get to take care of your seat and your phone. I'll take care of everything else," he said straight faced, before busting up laughing.

"Glad I get to come along for the ride," AJ said.

"You're welcome."

Seth made it easy to see why people either liked him or loathed him.

Seth ran down a call he received from Dean, one of the Street Crimes guys they both trusted implicitly. Dean said Cherie had been staying in Sacramento with a relative due to being afraid she would be killed if she stayed in Turlock. She adamantly refused when he tried to get her to come to Turlock to talk with them. He told them to meet her in the Golden Corral Restaurant parking lot off of Highway 99.

209

Seth had already gotten clearance with Highway Patrol, so they cut off twenty minutes getting to the restaurant. It appeared the lunch crowd had left and very few cars were in the lot. Cherie made herself pretty easy to spot pacing on the side of the building, puffing on a cigarette as if in a hurry to be someplace else.

She put her cigarette out the instant she spotted them, walking towards them before they had a chance to get out.

They had already decided AJ would do the questioning while Seth took notes. They would both watch her body language, even though they didn't expect to see much given the less than ideal conditions of interviewing her in a car.

"I'll get in the back," AJ said. Her canted head and mystified expression made him let go of the door, backing up to give her space. Only when he opened the back door did she get in.

AJ knew she was a prostitute, but up close in her jeans, sweatshirt, and straight hair, she looked like a normal young twenty-something girl, except for being a little thin from the meth.

They identified themselves, showing her their ID's.

"I need immunity," she said.

"It doesn't work that way," AJ said.

Fucking T.V., he thought.

"Then I ain't saying shit."

"Look, I got a feeling you got roped into this without realizing what you were doing."

"You're damn right. That's exactly what happened."

"Great, now here's the thing. I'm not the DA, so I can't offer you immunity, I can only share with the DA my feelings on whether you deserve it or not. Now, I've been doing this for quite a while, so my opinion is usually listened to."

"So what's the problem then?" she snapped back.

"I can't vouch for you until I have heard what you have to say, I mean everything, and I have to believe it's true."

"So what happens if I say I don't want to talk?"

"Not much really. We probably arrest you, charge you with murder. In California we have the Felony Murder Rule. You help in the murder of someone, no matter how small your role, you get treated the same as the person who actually did it."

The tears started rolling down her cheeks as she buried her face in her hands.

"Look, Dean helped us find you," AJ said. "I'm not going to screw him by letting the word on the streets get out he can't be trusted. I want to help you, but two things are not negotiable. First, before I go to bat for you I need to hear what you have to say. Second, I can only promise I will speak with the DA about your cooperation. You need to decide if you trust us."

"The mother fucker is scary," she said between the long sniffles before she finally blew her nose.

"Tell me about him."

An hour later Cherie got out of the car holding their business cards. Her description of events tied in with what they knew about Nathan Price's evening, along with what their dead witness had told them. She cleared up the fingerprint on the toilet lid from when she set it down to sit on it while she waited. Plus, her admission about urinating somewhere by the bathroom door would convince anyone she literally got scared about the real possibility of dying. Her lack of sharing information about the sole beer can being tampered with initially frustrated AJ, until she came clean once he brought it up.

AJ handed her cash and they left.

"Why did you give her fifty bucks?" Seth asked on the drive back.

"I don't know, something told me she needed it. It'll probably go straight to buying meth, maybe I'm hoping it's one less person she has to steal from tonight."

"You going to ask for her immunity?"

"Oh yeah. This guy killed at least two people we know of. There's probably more. He's scheming and he's dangerous. She could possibly be the one to help us get a conviction."

"If she doesn't get dead first," Seth said, stealing a quick glance at AJ. "He took care of one witness, what's one more."

AJ received a text from the detective secretary. After reading it he looked at Seth.

"We aren't done yet. Head towards the courthouse in Modesto."

TOO AMPED UP TO TRY TO SLEEP, STALKER KNEW HE could call in sick like many of his coworkers. He'd add one day to his regular days off, Wednesday and Thursday.

Having been in Bethany's home, he knew she had presents under her tree and he wanted to surprise her. He decided to go to the mall in Modesto where his odds were better of finding something to fit his plan.

While browsing through the numerous shops he thought about the Wardas. He continued to struggle with what to do about the boy's mother, not wanting the boy to end up in foster care. Could or would she ever turn her life around? Those odds seemed drastically low to him. His knowledge and comprehension about why she would probably replace one asshole with another did nothing to quash his disgust for her testimony in court.

Stalker left the card shop pleased with his two choices, a small ceramic heart and a wooden Holy Spirit sign, although he had no use for the Holy part. He had made sure to wear his thin leather gloves when he picked up the items and put them on the counter. He loved winter…no one noticed gloves.

The gift-wrapping made everything easier. When he got to the car he put on latex gloves to carefully open the package. He snapped off the word Holy, and set it aside. He made sure the other two items were as he wanted them, wrote a small note and stuck it inside of the package before re-wrapping it, much nicer than the young clerk had done.

Merry Christmas, Bethany, he thought.

Stalker enjoyed his drive to Bethany's home in Hughson. His frustration when leaving Dani's turned into feeling positive about his overall progress. He pulled into her driveway and acted like he belonged. Despite not having seen any activity in the area, he played the role in case he missed someone. He completely understood why burglars were so successful given the way he went in and out of neighborhoods and houses seldom seeing a soul.

Bethany never locked the inner door from the garage. He popped open the outer side-door and went in as he had several times. He bent down by her tree and read some of the tags on the presents. Only one had been signed *Forever Yours*, made out to *My Love*. He wondered who her boyfriend was. It might be something to look into later, if he had time. He did not want to push his luck with how late in the day it had gotten, so he placed his present in the back under a couple of others and departed.

Backing out of her driveway he relaxed, pleased he could now focus strictly on the Wardas. Despite being late in the day he decided he could walk through their complex one more time, hoping something he saw might help him to decide what to do with the boy's mother.

CHAPTER FORTY-SEVEN

Tom Sullivan contacted Sergeant Boykin to let him know he'd be meeting with Dani Larson at four thirty, and he expected to be representing her. He also let Boykin know he may want to have a sit-down with AJ and Dani in the future.

When AJ received the detective secretary's text he knew Tom Sullivan made sure he went through all of the proper channels to prevent a look of impropriety, despite having AJ's cell number to contact him separately. The possibility seemed likely they would get a call for a sit-down shortly, so AJ had Seth head to Sullivan's office.

AJ SAW SULLIVAN'S PARALEGAL WALKING THROUGH THE parking lot. She walked to their car and AJ got out to give her a hug. He asked her about her husband and her children, all by their names. She appreciated him remembering them all.

"Is Tom still meeting with Ms. Larson?"

"Yes. I don't expect it to be much longer. You can go inside and wait in the lobby."

"No...thanks though. Can't make it look like we were already expecting it. Right?"

She smiled, gave him a hug and headed to her car.

Seth shook his head when AJ got back in.

"What? She's Tom Sullivan's primary paralegal."

Seth gave him his no shit look. He refrained from asking any of the several questions running through his head.

Fifteen minutes later they got the text from Tom Sullivan to meet him in his office. They waited in the car another fifteen minutes before they walked inside. They were met in the conference room by Tom, Dani Larson and Chad Miller.

"Still got your job, I see," Tom said with a huge grin.

"Thanks to you," AJ replied with a roll of his hand and a bow.

Confusion oozed from the other three, having no clue what they were referring to.

"The police department tried to fire me several years ago…they didn't like my integrity and lack of willingness to partake in their shenanigans after work. The great and wonderful Mr. Sullivan showed them how wrong their actions were."

"They made a fatal flaw," Tom said matter-of-factly.

Confusion once again.

"They held the final city hearing for termination on St. Patrick's Day, in the evening mind you," AJ said. "Tom proceeded to show them the error of their ways in a timely and expeditious manner."

"Never keep an Irishman from his favorite night of celebration," Tom said, sitting back in his chair proudly.

"Now, to the business at hand."

BRIDGET FLETCHER WAITED UNTIL AFTER FIVE TO HAVE her meeting with Claire, her Assistant District Attorney.

She knew Claire could be pushy, even bordering on inso-
lent at times, but she kept her around because of Claire's
willingness to give her candid opinion. Unlike most trial
attorneys who enjoy hearing themselves talk, she didn't. Her
reputation as a serious thinker put her closer to being in
the category of the research attorneys. Even though Bridget
knew she wanted her job, she had always been a person
Bridget could count on…up to now.

"You seem wound up. What's up?" Claire asked.

"Haven't you heard about Rothstein?"

"No."

"He got the crap beat out of him in the covered parking
garage down the street. He's in the hospital."

"After I saw him in court this morning on Dani's case?"

"Yes. And …"

"What?"

"I got a call, so I went to the hospital. Rothstein made sure
we were alone in his room. He told me he is not cooperating
with the cops, sincerely believing the guy would kill him if he
did. Said he could see it in the guy's eyes. The real reason he
asked me to come had to do with the guy saying, 'Dani Larson
says you're welcome.' This could be our political future."

The Assistant DA took it all in, processing every word.
Bridget hated waiting, although past experience taught her
not to press her.

"I think you politely demand everything TPD has on
their homicide up to now. We need to put this on the Grand
Jury calendar and start preparing. By not asking for an
immediate hearing it gives us some time."

"No matter what, we can't say anything about Rothstein,"
Bridget said.

Claire bobbed her head side to side before saying, "Okay, it definitely factors in though."

"Could Dani really be hiring this stuff to be done?"

"She fits the perfect young professional mold. You of all people should know they can be some of the most devious minds and nobody ever expects them. Besides, it doesn't matter," she said with a dismissive tone.

Wide-eyed, Bridget seemed caught off guard.

When she noticed Bridget's reaction she said, "Sorry, I didn't mean it the way you must have taken it," both palms open to her.

"I'm not sure there is anything we can do to help Dani, even if we believe her," Claire continued. "If we look the least bit hesitant to do the right thing, we go down in flames."

Bridget sat quietly shaking her head.

"What? Go ahead, say it."

"Truthfully, I really like Dani. She's kind of special. I hate the idea of saving our careers by ruining hers," Bridget said, downcast.

"Really?"

"What's that supposed to mean," Bridget said with an irked tone.

"I think you might have hired her for the wrong reasons, purely based on feeling bad for Dani losing her family in a drunk driving accident, and somehow becoming a Deputy DA would help her get justice in some unforeseen way. Now you might have to be the one who brings her more pain… all part of being at the top isn't it, you need to make tough decisions and not let other people's problems affect you."

Bridget stewed over Claire's comments and her snideness for a minute as she internally gathered her composure.

"Compassion is not maleficent."

"I understand," Claire said.

Bridget recognized her expressionless face, having seen it many times before...*the consummate politician* she thought. Still, Claire made her acutely aware of how she really felt. More importantly, Bridget started to rethink telling her, wondering if Claire might go behind her back. *I might have backed myself into a corner,* she thought.

CHAPTER FORTY-EIGHT

———◆———

D ani seemed to relax a bit when she heard Tom Sullivan represented AJ several years before. The realization he had been Tom's client made it easier for her to slightly lower her protective wall.

Maybe he does know what I'm going through, she thought.

Seth used to be uncomfortable sitting with defense attorneys. Like most cops he fell into the stereotype trap. Only after sitting in on several conversations and interviews with AJ did he see the value of the rapport AJ had with most of them.

AJ and Seth were unsure of talking to Dani with Chad present and Tom took notice.

"Mr. Miller is Dani's close friend. Long story, suffice it to say she trusts him and wants him here," Tom shared.

AJ looked at Seth and he shrugged.

"Okay, Ms. Larson—"

"Dani."

"Okay, Dani. Can you tell me why someone would want to frame you?"

Dani looked over at Tom.

"Look, Mr. Sullivan won't hesitate to stop you if he doesn't want you to answer. This is awkward for you...trust me...I know. Now, it will be a lot easier if you and I merely have a conversation until he says otherwise."

Tom smiled and nodded. Dani looked at Chad who pursed his lips, slightly raising one side before he nodded, too.

"No, I've asked myself the same thing," she said. "I can't think of anyone."

"Right now you are in the suspect pool." AJ watched her hand slide over and grab Chad's as she pushed her back into the chair.

"I want to eliminate you as a suspect, meaning you have to tell me everything. More importantly, you have to trust me. I'm not here to trick you."

"The DA said the same thing. She told me you were trying to save my career…and to trust you."

AJ held his eyes on her and his eyebrows raised.

"Okay, I'll do my best," Dani said.

It took some time before Dani provided an excellent time line of everything she did on the evening Nathan died, along with the next morning when the witness, Adam Riley, had been murdered. Clearly, eliminating her from direct involvement would be easiest with Adam Riley's death.

"I'm going to need your authorization for us to do a forensic analysis on your financials."

Dani's eyes widened and she shot Tom a glance. When he explained how it would go to show no large payouts of cash to a possible hitman her mouth opened slightly and AJ could read her face like a book. With everything that had happened to her in the last few days she never considered the reasoning.

AJ waited, knowing the shock would pass and she finally approved and agreed to get Seth everything he would need.

"So, what's your take on Rothstein?" Tom asked.

Seth and AJ knew him well. Gregarious, and at times even quirky, Rothstein always talked with cops.

They looked at each other, and back at Tom with the same *what the hell are you talking about* expression.

Tom went from being relaxed in the back of his chair to sitting erect, even leaning forward slightly as his palms slapped down on the table.

"You haven't heard about what happened to him, have you?" Tom asked in a higher octave.

STALKER HAD EXPERIENCED THE LIFESTYLE OF THE SAME people who lived in single story apartments like the Wardas. As dusk approached, suspiciousness amongst the residents gradually increased and activity picked up under the cover of darkness. Young kids, like he was in those early years before the boy's home, were forced to use it as a daily training ground. Until being put in foster care, he had never known anything about such a lifestyle.

His home before the accident had been in an upper middle class neighborhood. His parents did not smoke or drink, much less do drugs. Only after he got to the first foster home did he realize how loving his parents were, and how great the relationship between him and his sister had been. For his age back then he possessed strength, intelligence and quickness, both on his feet and in learning how to survive. Possessing those skills made him one of the fortunate ones—many others were not.

He parked a couple of blocks away and approached their place. Walking down the sidewalk between apartments he could hear things as if windows were opened. The apartments were of cheap construction, with no such thing as privacy within those walls.

Reaching the last of four apartments he heard yelling coming from the one on his right—the Warda's. Then he heard a slap. Stalker moved to the door, putting his hand around the knob in case.

"I told you, bitch, don't fucking ask about what we do," Cyrus yelled. "You have one job, to service me in any way I demand. I'll take care of everything else. Me and my crew is none of your fucking business."

Stalker heard a low guttural sound, like Cyrus had knocked the air out of someone. He peeked in the window and saw Azar doubled over on the ground, her son hiding behind her head. The boy saw Stalker and lowered his head—too late.

The door flew open and Stalker stood face-to-face with Cyrus.

"What the fuck you want?" Cyrus hissed.

Stalker's mind raced through the litany of issues, settling on now would not be a good time.

"Yo man, don't want no problem," Stalker said, his palms up and taking a step back. "I'm from Merced. Don't know my way around here. They told me I could pick up my shit here."

"What shit?"

Cyrus looked ready to pounce if Stalker gave the wrong answer.

"You know, man, my tar." Stalker's recon trips provided him knowledge about the next set of buildings being where someone sold heroin.

"You're in the wrong area. Get the fuck out of here."

"Like I said, dude, don't want no problem," Stalker said, backing up like Cyrus intimidated him.

"Can you point my ass in the right direction, man? So I

don't have to knock on every fucking door."

"Get the fuck out of here before I kick your fucking dragon-chasing ass," Cyrus snarled, clinching his fists and taking a step forward.

Stalker could see over Cyrus's shoulder Azar grabbed the boy's hand and left the living room. He figured he had diverted Cyrus long enough. He kept backing away waving his hands like he wanted nothing to do with an ass-kicking.

You best enjoy yourself tonight, it's your last one, he thought.

CHAPTER FORTY-NINE

———◆———

Seth and AJ were almost back to the restaurant where he parked his car when AJ received a text from Bethany. He let her know they were getting close to the exit and he'd be heading to his house after Seth dropped him off at his car.

"I'm waiting and I have a present for you!" she responded with a winky-heart Emoji.

AJ laughed.

Seth smiled, waiting patiently.

"It's Bethany," AJ said, not wanting to reveal the message.

"Seems like she isn't letting those threats dictate her life," he said.

"Not at all—at least on the surface," AJ stated.

Seth dropped him off and headed back to his house. AJ arrived at his place in less than ten minutes.

An hour later Bethany and AJ were sitting at his table eating the one food he had in the house, cereal. She only had on his oversized Pitman High School hoodie the principal had given him a few years before as a gag gift. She had her bare legs drawn up in front of her chest with the bottom of the hoodie pulled over them, the bowl perched on her knees.

"You ever get a strange feeling, like something's wrong, or like someone is watching you?" Bethany asked.

"Yeah," AJ said. "I've had a couple of those recently, one earlier today in fact. Why do you ask?"

"It's not so much like someone's watching me, it's more like I had the weirdest feeling someone had been in my house when I got home tonight," she confided without a hint of fear, other than not looking at him.

"I had to get out of there."

If she were scared AJ would never have known by her actions since he got home.

Bethany said she looked all around and found nothing out of place. When she could not shake the feeling she decided to go to AJ's house. She refused to let him go take a look at her house and made him promise not to say anything to Allison, feeling it was probably nothing and she did not want to be embarrassed.

Over the next hour they sat drinking decaf and talking. Dr. P had warned him Bethany might start rambling at some point, driven as much out of self-justification as out of fear. Bethany explained, in depth, how many child cases she had in Madera, year after year. She and her colleagues knew some of the foster homes were probably going to be taking in kids solely for the money. They had no way of knowing which homes those were or which home specifically a child would be going to. They would tell each other they were doing the best they could for the child, and blindly supported each other.

AJ tried to let her know they did the same thing in police work. He didn't know of a cop he worked with who believed Child Protective Services was worth even the cost of the electric bill to light their building. Every cop experienced taking a kid out of a home only to have them returned to be abused worse.

Taking her hand in his, AJ looked into her eyes.

"We all had to make the best decisions we could with the information we had. None of us had the final say, and neither did you. Somebody out there has misguided hatred; I've never known anyone who cares about their cases and their clients like you do."

Bethany leaned forward and hugged him, burying her head in the crevice of his neck, not letting go.

STALKER DIALED HIS CONTACT'S NUMBER. THE CALL went to voicemail.

"I know you're scared, which is why you didn't answer. I promise not to kill you for the false information about the social worker still working at the hospital in Madera. It all worked out. Forget about it. If, on the other hand, you don't answer when I call you back, I promise you will be dead in less than forty-eight hours."

Stalker liked him and did not want to kill him. The guy had a reputation of being scrappy and nobody around would dig as hard as him or go to the extremes to finish a job like he would. He needed the guy, at least for a little while longer.

Stalker smiled when his phone rang and he saw the name on the screen.

"Glad you called," Stalker said. "Look, I need you to get me all the information you have on the people who live at the address I'm about to give you. Especially if they bought any plane tickets anywhere in the last six months to a year. I need this fast, gotta cover my ass. I'll double your pay."

He could tell by the way the contact tried to convince him he wouldn't be disappointed he would have his information shortly. Stalker appreciated the fact he would have it in time to go over it before he needed it—he liked being prepared.

CHAPTER FIFTY

A J's mind turned on at five a.m. when he rolled over and he could not shut it off. He got ready for his run, pulling the covers over Bethany before he left. He stared at her for a couple minutes, a warm feeling inside of him, grateful she came into his life.

He took his normal route to the canal bank on the far north end of the city and ran along it for a half hour. He decided to return by heading east on Christoffersen Parkway, running on the side facing oncoming traffic. The morning commuters were out in force and part of the reason AJ enjoyed the serenity on the canal bank. He started paying more attention working his way home.

Nearing the intersection next to Turlock Junior High School, AJ saw a black VW Rabbit stopped facing south. Approaching the passenger side he could see the driver looked similar to the one the day before at Dani's house. AJ sped up, hoping to go in front of him for a better look.

The light changed before he got there and the car took off. The driver never looked AJ's way and he never got close enough to get in front of the car. AJ did get to see the last part of the license plate and the numbers were the same as yesterday.

Something about it bothered him, despite logic telling

him there was not a thing wrong. Nothing about the driver's actions were suspicious, and he knew the guy's car being in the same general area for a second day straight meant he probably belonged there. Still, neither thought changed his feeling on edge about the young man.

Thinking about the car and driver consumed him and he finished the run before he knew it.

STALKER HAD NOT SLEPT WELL, UNABLE TO IGNORE HIS thoughts for the day ahead. He went driving around and had already been to Bethany's house, only doing one drive by after he saw a Sheriff's car patrolling the area.

On his return to Turlock he went by Dani's house. He saw the same car in the driveway and started to get irked. Parking a few houses away he watched for activity. Feeling safe, he walked to the front of the house, relaxing some after peering in windows and seeing the man sleeping on the couch in the living room by himself.

He did not stay long because he needed to focus on the job planned for that morning. He stopped at the red light near the junior high school and looking around saw a runner on his right approaching. The man looked bundled up and Stalker could not understand why people put themselves through the misery, especially in December when it was cold outside. He preferred lifting weights, in the comfort of a temperature controlled room.

When the runner picked up his pace Stalker glanced at the light figuring the man wanted to beat the light before he took off.

Too late, he thought when the light changed.

He took off and looked in his rearview mirror where he saw the runner had to stop and wait for all of the cars behind him to go.

"Not your day, buddy," Stalker said. "I got someplace I need to be."

STALKER KILLED TIME AT PERKO'S RESTAURANT ON THE opposite side of the highway from where he took care of Nathan. He knew everything about the Wardas morning schedule, so he relaxed and enjoyed his breakfast and coffee.

He finished and the short drive to the apartments took less than three minutes, parking where he had in the past.

Stalker wore the hospitals operating room scrubs he kept and made his way behind the four apartments, taking a position behind a tree at the end of the Warda's complex. He heard the door open and the little boy came out first.

When the boy looked over and saw him, Stalker put his finger to his mouth and slid behind the tree as Azar came out and closed the door. The boy looked back one time, slightly raising his right hand, his fingers moving. Stalker smiled, raising his hand.

He knew the exact amount of time he had once Azar and the boy turned south on Soderquist Road if she stayed true to her habit. She always walked him to the cemetery gates and he walked the rest of the way to school with his friends. Azar's actions would determine her fate.

Stalker slid in the front door quietly, took off his jacket and threw it on the couch. The snoring told him which way to go and he had confidence he could hold his own if forced to fight, although he preferred not to. He crept into the room, tools in his latex-gloved hands.

Cyrus slept facing away from him and Stalker knew his first blow had to be accurate to prevent a confrontation and possibly drawing attention from neighbors. Stealth was paramount since he could hear movement through the wall of the next apartment over.

Stalker put the point of the Philips screwdriver less than an inch from Cyrus's temple. With one hard blow from the hammer the screwdriver plowed through skull and brain matter. The multiple blows with the hammer were Stalker's way of returning every ounce of pain Cyrus had inflicted on the little boy, and if he were being honest with himself some were probably for the foster fathers he had encountered.

Once he calmed down Stalker backed away and hearing the front door he slid over partially behind the bedroom door.

Azar took a few seconds to kick off her shoes and take off her jacket before heading to the bedroom. She took two steps in the room and froze. It took several seconds for the screwdriver in his head to register and when it did her eyes burst open wide, along with her mouth.

Before she could scream Stalker pounced on her taking her to the thin carpet. His weight on top of her took the scream on the cusp of letting loose out of her.

He put his left hand on her mouth as he raised the hammer in his right hand.

"You have one chance to live," Stalker said sharply, staring into her eyes. "Why did you lie for him," Stalker's head nodding toward the bed, "and not protect your son?"

He could see the hardness in her glare, brought about by the number of beatings she had received. She did not appear to be afraid, so he lifted his hand an inch off her lips thinking she had something to say.

"Fuck you," Azar said, evil replacing the glare. Before he could move his hand she bit into the outer palm of his left hand, tearing the latex glove as his skin started to give way.

Reflex drove the face of the hammer into her head before the pain in his hand arrived. Her actions chose her destiny. He did not have a desire to hit her again, so he put the hammer down and covered her nose and mouth until she no longer moved.

Stalker found a clean dishtowel in the kitchen, obviously seldom used based on the mound of dishes in the sink. He wrapped his hand, put on his jacket and opened the front door. He took a quick look to make sure nobody was around and left, closing the door behind him with his good hand. He placed his towel covered hand inside the jacket pocket until he got into the driver's seat and pulled away.

He drove several blocks and pulled over. He tore the towel into strips and only used part of it to bind his hand, tying it tight to stop the bleeding. He drove over the railroad tracks and turned into the strip mall, stopping behind one of the businesses with an alcove and a dumpster nearby.

Behind the dumpster he got out of the scrubs and into sweats, and threw the scrub pants in the dumpster. Being relatively new and clean he was sure they contained none of his DNA. He drove to the other end of the strip mall where he threw the scrub top in another dumpster. With the bleeding under control he put his regular gloves on covering the towel. He disposed of the towel in a residential refuse can in front of a house by an elementary school, knowing the garbage in the neighborhood would be picked up soon.

Parking on the east side of The Diner restaurant he threw his latex gloves in the dumpster before he took several deep breaths, replaying what he would say. He did not want the boy going home and finding two dead bodies.

"Nine-one-one," the police dispatcher said.

Stalker calmly told her of the two dead bodies along with the exact address and apartment number. When she tried to engage him in conversation he cut her off.

"She wanted me to use the hammer and screwdriver from her workbench in her garage. I'm not sure why. Do not let their son get home from school to find them."

Stalker hung up as the next question from her began. Back in his car he slowly drove away. His plans changed, the throbbing in his hand taking charge.

CHAPTER FIFTY-ONE

B ethany looked comfortable getting ready for work, and AJ had to admit he enjoyed her being there.

I might have to seriously evaluate what it is I want, he thought.

AJ never had the opportunity to get used to someone else being in his house on a regular basis.

He kissed Bethany goodbye and his phone started ringing before he made it to his car. Dispatch told him of a double homicide, gave him the address and told him an unidentified male caller reported it. They read him what the man said and had a printout waiting for him. He became alarmed when they told him the caller used the pay phone in front of The Diner restaurant and indicated the man was instructed by a woman to complete the murder.

AJ had an uneasy feeling, especially when he thought about the caller referring to a woman wanting the man to use a hammer and screwdriver supposedly belonging to "her." The comment seemed too convenient, a likely set up according to his gut feeling. Based on everything that happened within the last week the first person he would have to look into would be Dani.

With the exception of Knox, nobody else on AJ's team had yet arrived when we got there. He spoke with the Patrol

Sergeant present and she informed him the dead man in the house was Cyrus Warda, the man in charge of a group who were known throughout the county to steal cars, chop them, and get the parts off to various locations throughout the state.

The Sergeant told AJ about Cyrus lying on the bed with a screwdriver in his temple, and a woman on the ground with a hammer near her head. When AJ asked if she knew what brands the tools were she said they were both Stanley tools, black and yellow with the Stanley name on them.

While waiting for the rest of the team AJ called the Dispatch Center on the non-recorded line and found out Cyrus Warda had been arrested almost a year ago for abusing his son. Then he felt like she hit him with a ton of bricks when she told him Cyrus had recently been acquitted and his attorney got attacked in Modesto shortly after the trial.

So the call would come from someone other than AJ, he had dispatch call the DA's office and find out which deputy DA had been assigned to the Warda case. In less than five minutes he had his answer—Dani Larson. The importance of the Warda murders tripled, and AJ's team had not even begun their investigation.

As much as he hated the reality of it, none of the Administration would be interested in these homicides, mostly due to where they took place—provided AJ could keep a lid on the suspect the caller hinted at. AJ called Seth to make sure he would be okay with running the scene so AJ could go look into things.

"Absolutely. You going to explain why?" Seth asked, knowing AJ well enough to sense a problem.

"Look, right now the less you know the better," AJ said. "It's your case, be thorough."

AJ's head was spinning with thoughts about the possibilities of how people would respond. His issues were not going to be with determining a real suspect, they were going to be with high level politics. How the upper echelon people might be perceived by the public often superseded allowing qualified personnel to do their job.

AJ TOOK A DEEP BREATH BEFORE RAPPING ON THE DOOR with his knuckles.

"Detective Conti, this is a surprise," Dani said, only holding the door open enough for her head to fit.

"Ms. Larson," AJ said, tipping his head to the side and hesitating.

"What's wrong?" Dani asked, her tone rising an octave.

"Can you let me in, so I'm not standing out here for someone to see while I try to explain this to you?"

Thankfully her hesitation did not last long, although she stood in front of him in the foyer after the door closed.

"Let me start with…I *wasn't* here. I promise I will share what I can with you and Tom the first chance I get. Right now I need to look in your garage. Cyrus Warda, and probably his wife, have been murdered."

Dani went white, shuffling backward until she ran into the decorative table against the wall.

"Why would somebody do this?" she asked, as much to herself as to AJ.

He knew the reference had to do with her, not the murdered couple. Putting his hand on her shoulder helped her to refocus on him.

"I really need to look quickly. I need to get back before

anyone questions where I am."

Dani studied his eyes, standing dead still, deep in thought. Detective Conti's face, along with what she heard from the DA and her attorney told her to trust him. She nodded.

What AJ hoped for did not materialize. The workbench appeared organized, everything having a place, making it easy to see the Stanley tools, and more importantly, the ones missing.

CHAPTER FIFTY-TWO

Sitting in his car in front of Dani's, AJ pulled up a Modesto P.D. Detective's cell number.

"Hey, it's AJ. What can you tell me about your agency investigating an attack on Rothstein, the defense attorney?"

"Not much. He's been pretty uncooperative. Even said he didn't want a report, the Captain made patrol do one anyway."

"No information on who did it, or who called for it to be done?"

"Nah, like I said, no help."

Only after hearing one of Modesto's detectives tried to do some follow up at Rothstein's home and got sent packing did AJ find out Rothstein had been released, supposedly still recovering there.

"Look man, I need you to do me a big favor, no questions though," AJ said.

"You got it."

Driving away AJ wondered if what he asked for would happen before he made it back to Soderquist Road. He did not have to wait long before his phone rang. Pulling into the County Fairgrounds lot in front of the main gates AJ pulled it out of his jacket pocket. He nodded when he saw a number he did not recognize.

"Hello," AJ answered, not wanting to identify himself in case it might be someone other than who he needed to talk to.

"What's up? We're about to get called in to court."

"Whose phone?"

"My client's."

"Good. The defendants in her last trial, Rothstein's, they were murdered. Specific Stanley tools. Anonymous caller says something like 'she wanted me to use those tools from her workbench' before hanging up."

"Got it. I gotta go. They're looking for me."

AJ was only about three tenths of a mile from the scene, so he was back talking with Seth in no time. Seth barely finished giving him the rundown when Sergeant Boykin walked up.

"So, boys, how's it going?" Boykin asked.

Seth and AJ looked at each other suspiciously.

"I got this," AJ said, tapping Seth on the shoulder. He nodded to the side and Seth took off into the apartment.

"I hope you know what you're doing," Boykin said. "The only reason I'm here is someone in patrol apparently saw you leave the scene shortly after you got here and before anyone else arrived. I guess they had calls stacking up and needed to leave. The Chief called me, now I can say I did my due diligence."

"This is shaping up to be an elaborate setup," AJ said. "The last thing I want is someone's career blasted, solely based on the fact it looks bad. We can let street dealers go so we can get to the big dealers. Yet, we can't go after the serial killer without throwing the person he has a hard-on for under the bus due to politics."

"Speaking of politics, thought you might want to know

the DA's already heard about this and has requested you be removed from the investigation."

"There you go, exactly what I mean." AJ shook his head, frustrated with the person Bridget had become.

"Way ahead of you, Sarge. I put Seth in charge of this one. I haven't even been inside the apartment. I could see this coming."

"I haven't removed you yet, in fact, I told the Captain and the Chief I wouldn't do it. Who knows what they will do as pressure mounts."

Looking at the sidewalk AJ swept the gravel off with the side of his shoe.

"I appreciate your support, and going to bat for me. Tell you what...let's go with it. We know Seth will look to me for advice, and the two of us can work together without me officially being involved. It gives me time to go do some follow up. You can put a spin on it to the Captain and the Chief making both of us look good, and then the DA can't say anything."

"You sure?"

"Yeah, I'm good with it."

"Okay, I'll let Seth know," Boykin said, walking toward the apartment.

Walking to his car AJ mentally shifted gears, leaving the Wardas to Seth, at least for now. Going back to the office meant AJ might come across one of the political hierarchy. That was not about to happen, at least not now. Sitting in his car AJ formulated a plan to get things checked off his mental to-do-list.

Looking at his notes AJ looked for the address dispatch provided him for the black VW Rabbit. He headed to Rose Avenue, an older area of the city with several renovated homes, probably thanks to all those television shows.

Todd Wilson's yard appeared void of anything Christmas. The immaculate appearance of the yard stood out since no other yard in the area came close. From the outside the house looked unchanged, although it did possess a pristine paint job.

The black VW sat in the driveway, so AJ figured his odds were good at finding someone home. The outward appearance of everything gave him a comfortable feeling, but when he walked by the car the hair on the back of his neck stood up.

AJ knocked at the door and a clean-shaven white man in his late twenties answered, identifying himself as Todd Wilson. He opened the door wide and seemed relaxed with AJ's presence, even inviting him in.

"Have a seat on the couch," Todd said. "Coffee?"

"Sure"

"Got it," he said, heading for the kitchen. "What can I do for you, Detective?" echoed AJ's way.

"I saw you yesterday morning in a residential area over by the junior high."

"Oh, yeah, probably around mid-morning. I had been checking in on a good friend of mine," he lied, "Jason Barrett and his wife Cynthia, their house. They're travelers. Six months ago they were in the Bahamas, this time in Belize. I should've gone to college like they did."

He returned carrying two cups, the smell of fresh coffee filling the room.

"Black, right?"

"Excuse me?"

"Sorry. Your coffee, you want it black?"

AJ looked at Todd's face as he handed him the cup.

"I've noticed a lot of older cops, no offense, drink their

coffee black, at least the ones at night in Modesto who come to the hospital where I work. Only the young ones want Cappuccinos and Lattes, not the veterans."

AJ nodded and grinned, Todd's description being dead on.

Todd explained what hospital he worked at as a nursing assistant on the graveyard shift.

"So, this morning when I saw you at the intersection waiting for the light to change by the junior high—"

"Yeah, I went by and checked on their house again after I got off work this morning," he said with a quizzical look. "Wait, were you the guy running?"

"Yeah."

"Wow. Small world. All's I saw was a guy bundled up, and I thought the dude was crazy, no offense. Hmm, I almost waited for you, probably would have if there weren't three cars behind me. I didn't figure they'd be too happy. Sorry."

"No problem," AJ said, his neck hairs relaxing the more Todd talked.

"Have I done something wrong? I mean I'm a little confused why you're here."

"No nothing. In fact, it's starting to look like I'm having a bad day with my gut feelings, seeing you twice in less than twenty-four hours, in an area where your vehicle registration is on the opposite end of the city from where you lived."

"Oh, good." Todd sighed.

AJ stood to leave. "Sorry to bother you. Thanks for the coffee."

"You're welcome. Glad it turned out to be nothing."

"What'd you do to your hand?" AJ asked walking to the door.

"Ah, this," Todd said, holding up his left hand with a gauze bandage around it.

"Had a combative guy I had to help the nurses with this morning. Hand got caught between him and the bedframe, which is why you saw me so early this morning. They let me leave once the job injury paperwork got taken care of."

"Hope you recover quickly," said AJ.

"Thanks."

Walking toward his car AJ stopped and looked back.

"You like major league baseball?" pointing toward the back of Todd's car.

"Big Twins fan. I loved Kirby Puckett as a kid. I got hooked then," he said, a huge smile across his face.

"Me too. Nothing like baseball. I'm a Giants fan, gotta say though, Puckett was great. Thanks again. Sorry to bother you."

Todd waved and closed the door. AJ waited to see if Todd went to the window and looked out. After thirty seconds AJ got in his car.

Absolutely nothing about his body language looked out of place, AJ thought. *And everything he said made sense. Then why do I still have a funny feeling in my gut?*

STALKER STOOD INSIDE, HIS BACK AGAINST THE DOOR until he heard the detective's car leave. His research told him Detective Conti would be a tough foe. Despite having to pay his contact double to get the information, his preparation on the Barretts paid off. He relished the moment, pleased with his performance.

Totally shut him down, he thought. *Even had him saying his gut feelings were wrong. Quite convincing, if I do say so myself.*

Stalker sat in his favorite chair, reclining back and sipping on his coffee. With only eleven days to Christmas he decided he had done enough up to then and he could rest until the holidays were over. He knew he would have no time for anything else since he always volunteered to work as much as possible. He enjoyed letting others have time to spend with their families, so working double-shifts never bothered him.

On his days off, when not doing recon, he liked watching educational shows, especially The History Channel. The free information on T.V. and the Internet allowed Stalker to always be in the learning mode.

Turning on the television, he settled in to watch the show he used to help him hone his craft, Forensic Files.

CHAPTER FIFTY-THREE

"Place is pretty clean as far as evidence goes," Knox said. "Yeah, looks like the killer caught Cyrus sleeping, dead before he knew what hit him," Seth said.

"The woman, Azar, I think she saw it coming."

"I think so, too. Patrol said a neighbor saw Azar walking her son to school like always, and returning home alone. The neighbor heard raised voices, which apparently happens a lot at the Warda's place, then thought they heard Azar say, 'Fuck you.'"

"To the suspect or to Cyrus?" Knox asked.

"My guess is the suspect. No sign of struggle from Cyrus, it's shortly after Azar returns, and the neighbor says Azar would never say 'fuck you' to Cyrus, she cowered down to him. Other than Cyrus, she's kind of an ass to everyone else."

"I'm about to rain on your parade so remember, don't shoot the messenger," Knox said. "There's no way to sugar coat it, Willie picked up the hammer before I had it photographed, and by the neck where most of the prints would likely be found."

Knox knew his hands would be full trying anything he could to keep Seth from killing Willie sooner than later.

AJ DROVE TO MAIN STREET TO FIND THE MORTGAGE broker office where Chad worked. One of the most professionally dressed secretaries he could recall in a long time greeted him. AJ told her he didn't have an appointment and she started to say something when Chad interrupted her.

"I have an appointment in a few minutes, if you want to step into my office until they arrive," Chad said, his arm outstretched directing AJ.

AJ followed him to his office. Standard to the times, the all black ceiling in the entire building had exposed air and heating ducts. The offices were all glass and the high-end-looking furniture spoke of the quality a client could expect.

AJ sat across from Chad, who appeared unsure whether to lean forward or back, and even where to place his arms.

"Look, you're under no obligation to speak to me," AJ said.

"Then why are you here?"

"I guess I want to know where you fit in the picture, with Dani I mean."

"Right now we're nothing more than friends."

"Right now?"

"I'm…I'm hoping it turns into more. I'm not sure it will."

"Why not?"

"It's a long story. I was there when her family got in their awful accident on the highway. I barely pulled her out of the burning car in time. I was a teenager, bad home life, so I hung out with the hobos. I happened to see her in the newspaper recently so I went to the courthouse. That's the first time I saw her in person, besides the hospital. Right now I think she's just happy to have a friend."

"What can you tell me about the accident?"

"It happened on Highway 99 at Hobo Junction. A head on collision, it sounded like a bomb went off. I ran up there and—" the phone on his desk rang.

The way Chad looked at him, AJ could tell Chad's clients were in the lobby. AJ stood when he hung up and left him with the thought he would like to continue their conversation another time.

Passing the happy young couple headed to Chad's office turned AJ's thoughts to the excitement of sharing a life with someone else. Before leaving the building he texted Bethany and let her know how much he enjoyed her being at his house last night.

———

BETHANY SMILED WHEN SHE RECEIVED HIS TEXT. AJ seldom sent her one without her sending something first. Bethany's peers noticed the glow and she enjoyed the positive teasing she received the rest of the day on where her relationship may be heading.

CHAPTER FIFTY-FOUR

AJ no sooner made it to his car when he received a text. He smiled, thinking it would be Bethany responding. He sat, read it and stared, not believing it could have happened so quickly. Tom's message let AJ know Dani had already received notice from the Assistant District Attorney, she had been placed on Administrative Leave—without pay.

AJ kept his response short knowing Tom would be in court and asked Tom to do him a favor on his first break. AJ hoped Tom could help him get his foot in the door.

AJ received a text from Sandy, the assistant coroner, confirming Nathan Price died from alcohol poisoning. AJ thanked her for letting him know and not having to wait for the coroner's report, usually taking days or weeks.

This killer knows what he's doing, AJ thought.

AJ could understand his use of alcohol and a slow death to help point the finger at Dani. Coupled with Dani's prints and lipstick on a glass, the killer had the DA heading right where he wanted her to go. Bridget would see the clerk and Cherie's comments about a man being involved as nothing besides hired help.

Politically, Bridget had to follow the crumbs where they led her. For AJ to help keep Dani from ending up in County Jail, or worse yet, prison, he had to figure out the answer to the real question…why her?

AJ would have to work with Tom to find the answer. He figured Dani would be reeling from the news of the Wardas, and the call from the Assistant DA probably sent her into a deep depression.

AJ decided to head to Salida and hope Tom had been able to grease the wheels for him to see Rothstein. When he arrived seeing such a modest house for such a successful defense attorney surprised him.

A woman in her mid-forties, towel draped over her shoulders and sweat running down her cheeks greeted AJ at the door. She put her hand on her hip and stared at him, clearly not willing to speak.

"Is Mr. Rothstein available?"

Her stare intensified.

"I'm Detective Conti, Turlock P.D. I'm hoping Tom Sullivan—"

"Damn it. Let him in," a male voice yelled from deep inside.

Stepping back, she gave AJ the finger as he entered.

AJ grinned, making sure she knew he won this round.

"In the living room," the voice said.

The bruising around his eyes caught AJ's attention first, along with the still present swelling. Underneath he could see the Rothstein he had dealt with many times.

"Hope you don't mind if I don't get up."

"Not at all," AJ said, looking at his bandaged ankle.

"Forget about her. She used to be married to a cop. I helped her with her divorce, which led to mine, and us living here."

AJ shrugged his shoulders, not really interested in too much of their personal lives.

"You must be a little unnerved by this guy to not cooperate with Modesto P.D."

"Yeah. Something in the guy's eyes. I've dealt with enough of these kinds to know which ones are serious and which ones are full of themselves."

"So, why me?" AJ asked.

"Several reasons really. And your reputation. I know I can say no report and none will be done. Tom says you believe someone is trying to frame Dani Larson, and I admire you for not throwing her in jail and wiping your hands clean. And selfishly, I need someone to nail the bastard so I don't walk around looking over my shoulder the rest of my life."

"So then, you must not believe Dani had anything to do with it."

"No, I don't. Too convenient."

"What do you mean?" AJ thought so too, but he wanted to hear Rothstein's explanation.

"The outcome of the child-abuse case made him angry. I could hear it in his voice...he was pissed. Even said something about it wasn't justice how it ended. And it seemed like he had finished talking when he had the afterthought of throwing in 'Dani says you're welcome.' I didn't get the feeling he did the job for her, or the comment about her was important."

"Anything else?"

"He said if I told the cops I would end up like the guy on Highway 99. I had my PI do some checking and the guy ended up stabbed in his throat sitting in his car."

"Hmmm."

"What the fuck is that supposed to mean?"

"The guy responsible, I think he killed an acquitted defendant in one of Dani's trials hours before stabbing the guy. And, the victim on the highway just so happened to be our one and only witness," AJ lied, not willing to tell him about Cherie.

"Then he goes after me, throwing Dani's name out. He wants her all right. Hell, she's the one who ought to be looking over her shoulder."

AJ disagreed, although arguing with a defense attorney did not make much sense. If he wanted to kill her he would have already. He wanted her to suffer a great deal of pain and sadness, before losing her freedom.

"It got worse this morning. Your client, Cyrus Warda, he and his wife were murdered in their apartment."

"Holy shit…this may sound bad…I think I'm lucky to be alive. This guy is one dangerous son-of-a-bitch."

Not very often had AJ seen a seasoned defense attorney stammer. AJ could see Rothstein's eyes drift as his hands squeezed the arms of the recliner, the realization of it all beginning to set in. AJ decided he had bothered him enough.

Rothstein agreed to talk to AJ again if need be. Heading for the door AJ saw the woman leaning against the wall by the kitchen, looking at him through squinted eyes, like maybe trying to size him up. AJ nodded, pleased she kept her fingers to herself this time.

KNOWING HE WOULD BE PASSING BACK THROUGH Modesto AJ thought about stopping at the DA's office, but decided Bridget would be too busy to talk, if she would even talk at all. Instead he settled on heading back to Turlock to go to the Caboose Lounge for some follow up.

AJ texted Seth for an update and had not driven a block from Rothstein's house when his phone rang.

"How you doing?" AJ answered.

"Fine, I guess," Seth said. "You're not going to believe what Willie did?"

"Try me."

"He moved the hammer before Knox photographed it in place." Seth's tone changed, it had an edge to it.

AJ could almost feel his anger coming through the phone.

"So, where are you now?" AJ asked, trying to change topics.

"We finished serving a search warrant at Dani Larson's a few minutes ago."

"Really. What for?" AJ had to work at sounding excited.

"Based on the call from the anonymous caller, specific tools."

"Like what?"

"Yellow and black Stanley screwdrivers. He made it sound like the tools at the scene were part of a set."

"Sounds promising. What'd you find?"

"Well, she had tools, only miscellaneous stuff though. No one brand of anything. Looked like hand-me-downs. Every tool on the workbench had a label and I found every tool in the right spot, including a hammer. The ladies a bit of a neat freak."

"So, anything at all tool-wise?"

"No. Good photos if we need them."

AJ grinned, happy the call to Tom worked.

"What about Dani?"

"Crying mostly. Guess the DA's office put her on leave without pay. Seemed to devastate her...You?"

"Tried to do some follow up. Kind of got nowhere really. At least nothing I felt would be helpful. Headed to the Caboose Lounge now."

"Okay. I should be at the office in another hour or so. Autopsy on the guy is not until tomorrow."

"Speaking of autopsies, who picked up the bodies?"

"Sandy. Very professional. I took her aside, told her I'm devoted to my wife and kids, then apologized for misleading her."

"How'd she take it?"

"Better than I could've expected. Kissed me on the cheek, told me my wife is a lucky woman and thanked me for being honest."

"Good man. Proud of you."

Seth thanked AJ and hung up.

AJ felt terrible having kept things from his best friend.

I know I'm doing the right thing...but, lying to him?

CHAPTER FIFTY-FIVE

A J arrived at the Caboose Lounge shortly after the lunch crowd left. He met with the manager he knew from having done volunteer work providing the homeless blankets and jackets one Christmas.

The manager showed AJ his parking lot videos from the night of Nathan Price's murder. AJ already had a good idea of what happened inside the bar based on what Cherie told them. The outside views were what he needed to see.

AJ could see Cherie approach from the south before going inside. At one point a man dressed in dark clothing walked into view from the south, shortly after Cherie went in. He stared into the bar for less than fifteen seconds before walking across the lot to a small park and out of the screen.

AJ fast-forwarded to Nathan and Cherie going outside to get into his Jeep. She drove north in the lot before turning left on Main Street.

Seconds after the Jeep went west a small dark car backed up from the diagonal parking on Main Street before also going west. From their camera positions and the distance AJ could not get a very good look at the car or the license plate. He decided to take the disk as evidence, hoping to get it enhanced.

AJ went to the contacts on his phone and pulled up Kenny Love's cell, a fellow detective assigned to the county-wide computer forensic task force. They went to the academy together and AJ trusted him implicitly. Kenny outdid his reputation as a good cop by becoming a great tech guy, highly sought after by private industry.

"Let me guess, you need my help," Kenny answered.

"Nah, man. I'm being Mr. Friendly, just calling to see how you're doing."

"Bull crap," he said, laughing.

AJ laughed with him. They both knew AJ needed Kenny way more than the other way around. He never rubbed it in AJ's face though.

"I got a video of the outside area of the Caboose Lounge. Need you to see if you can enhance it, or know someone who can. After my victim leaves in his Jeep another car takes off. Not sure if it's related, although the timing is right."

"How soon you need it? We're getting close to going after a couple of teachers with a bunch of kiddie porn."

"I understand. Whenever, man, even after the holidays. I'm grasping at anything right now so it's not a priority."

"Great. Have Knox run it up. Would love to chat ..."

"Got it. Thanks."

AJ knew Kenny's time as a cop would be coming to an end soon. All the major players in the computer world were courting him. His wife already started looking forward to more family time. AJ envied guys like him and Seth with their family priorities.

AJ got a text from Seth with the name of a gas station where the owner was the father of one of their officers. He was an Assyrian man who brought his family to America for a better chance at helping his children get a good education.

He also happened to love cops.

He had made part of the station into a sandwich shop, with a special table reserved for officers. Gratuities were considered a department policy violation, so the father charged a dollar for anything a cop purchased. The Chief finally quit arguing so the price remained the same for years. Seth and AJ often met there so they could have privacy.

Seth walked in and went straight to the counter. He ordered his usual...a large pastrami with all the extras. He had not yet reached AJ's slow metabolism age, so AJ's salad seemed pretty plain.

"So, Cyrus took a screwdriver to the temple," Seth said. "Killer drove it in all the way to the flange. Knox and I figure he had no idea what hit him. Cyrus was a violent guy, lots of fights to his credit. Not this time, there are no signs of a struggle."

"How'd the killer get in?" asked AJ.

"No forced entry. Neighbor said the Wardas never locked their door. Everyone knew Cyrus would kill them."

"There's more to it than luck finding Cyrus crashed out."

"Agreed. Kind of think the killer knew his patterns."

"And the wife?"

"Normal habit. Around 7:30 a.m. she walks the son to the cemetery gates on Soderquist Road. He hooks up with friends, she walks home."

"Think she surprised the guy?"

"Not really, at least it doesn't feel like it for some reason."

Seth got his food and when he sat down he slightly turned his head, looking at AJ through narrow eyes.

"What?" AJ asked.

"You know something, I can tell."

"I can't say I know as much as I have a feeling."

"I can listen while I eat," he said, taking a huge first bite.

AJ shook his head, wishing he could still eat like Seth.

"I met with Rothstein today."

Seth's eyebrows shot up, the food stuffed in his mouth preventing a comment.

"He told me his attacker seemed pissed about the outcome of the Warda case, commenting about justice."

"Go on," Seth mumbled around the food.

"I suspect the attacker might have been there when the verdict came in, and if so, it seems likely he had been following the case. I don't believe he randomly showed up for the verdict. I think it's possible he reconned the Wardas long before the verdict."

Taking a big drink of soda Seth paused, trying to take it all in.

"Makes sense," Seth said. "If he knew how violent Cyrus could be, he would want to choose a time to his advantage, to avoid a fight. Less noise. One at a time."

"Exactly. Plus, he wanted the boy out of the apartment. He definitely cares about the kid, telling dispatch to send cops before the boy gets home so he doesn't walk in on it."

Seth wiped his face with his napkin and took a deep breath.

"The elephant in the room is, why the Warda trial?"

"I agree. My gut's telling me this all has to do with Dani Larson. I think our killer is sitting in on her trials, or at least knows about them."

By the way Seth put his thumb to his chin and contorted his lips AJ could tell he was contemplating the possibility.

"We know she did not kill our witness in the Price homicide," AJ said. "Cherie clearly made us believe a guy is involved somehow, which supports your lovely motel clerk. We know a guy attacks the Warda's attorney, Rothstein. Then the Wardas. I mean, come on."

"Yeah, it's all related. Do you think she could be orchestrating this? Like maybe she's gone off the deep end."

AJ shook his head.

"I don't think you do either. I think someone is after her. They want her to pay for something she's done. Whatever the hell that is."

Seth nodded, only long enough to take another bite.

"Look, I need to come clean with you on something. I hope you understand, if you don't, I won't put up a fight."

Seth put up a finger as he finished chewing. After several seconds AJ threw his palms open to tell Seth to hurry up.

Seth held up his finger again, took a drink, and then sat back. "You mean the Stanley tools?"

"Yeah. How'd you know?"

"The sarge at the scene, she said she told you about the tools. Then you left the scene before we got there. You couldn't have been gone long, I don't think long enough to put a full set of other tools in her house. Now, let's make no mistake about this, I don't want to know anything else."

"Man, I absolutely hated lying to you. I'm glad you know. I hope you can understand why."

"You always say 'right is right and wrong is wrong,'... you thought you were doing the right thing, simple as that. The way things are going Dani might be looking at life in prison even though you know she didn't do these murders. I know where your heart is, which is good enough for me."

AJ sat in silence.

CHAPTER FIFTY-SIX

The Christmas holiday season brought about statistical changes. The city tended to have less homicides and major assaults, while suicides were often higher. AJ had never been one to take time off during the holidays. He never had a real reason, other than to spend time with his sibling's families.

Bethany wanted to go to Reno to spend time with her two sisters and their spouses. Initially AJ resisted, until she hit him with the facts. She reminded him he had more vacation time on the books than he knew what to do with, not to mention more seniority than seventy-five percent of the department. Other than his own insecurity, AJ had no rebuttal.

They took off Thursday morning in AJ's other car, an SUV, planning to come back the following Tuesday, the day after Christmas. AJ did not know how to act. He had never left his cases for so long, and he surely had never met the family of someone he dated ... he felt like a fish out of water and the four hour drive ahead only serving to give him time to think about it.

Bethany's excitement filled the air. She smiled and talked the majority of the way, making it easier for him to have his mind anywhere besides the office. The way she described her two sisters gave AJ a good feeling about them being easy-going, fun people to be around. Despite the awkwardness, he had to admit he felt a little excitement, too.

CHAD KNOCKED ON THE DOOR ONE MINUTE BEFORE noon and Dani answered wearing a pair of black sweats and a sweatshirt with her law school logo. Chad expected a long face, maybe dirty hair, definitely no make-up. He found none of those.

"Wow, you look …"

"I know, I know. I looked bad last night. This morning, I decided I did not want to be a mess anymore."

"I don't know what to say, other than I'm impressed," he said, stepping inside.

"So, you want to hear my plans?"

"The woman went from disheveled to beautiful, and she has plans," he said.

Dani smiled, her cheeks turning a light rosy color.

"Do you want to hear about them?"

"Of course I want to. Lay 'em on me."

"Okay. I propose we talk about this," her hands turning circles, "whatever you want to call it. We talk in as much detail as either one of us needs to. Ask any questions, speculate, discuss anything and everything. One caveat, when we're done, we're done. Until after Christmas when I see Tom Sullivan again next week. What do you think?"

Chad paused. After a couple of seconds his left cheek rose as he half smiled.

"What?" Dani asked, grinning.

"Are you saying we're spending the holidays together?"

Dani slapped the air, shaking her head.

"Close the door the rest of the way. You're letting all the cold air in," she said, still grinning as she started to walk away.

CHAPTER FIFTY-SEVEN

"Are you doing okay?" Bethany asked.

AJ turned to look at her. He could see the social worker inside of her understood the discomfort of being in a new situation.

AJ nodded as he looked back at the slow moving traffic due to recent snows.

"Yeah, so far I'm okay."

"Thank you for being willing to do this."

AJ picked up on a sincerity to her voice he had not heard before.

"You're welcome," he said. "I've been entrenched in my way of life so long, all of this is scary." AJ looked at her soft eyes staring at him. "I want to change. I want to work on this...this thing in me so focused on my victims I forget about my own life. I want *us* to have a life."

Bethany's eyes watered, and she touched his cheek.

"That means more to me than you know." She opened the center console and grabbed a napkin to wipe her eyes.

"Look, I know you won't be able to not think about your cases, especially the newest one. I understand. All I ask is please try not to let it be the only thing you think about. Try to be...normal, at least part of the time. You might enjoy this."

THE SMELL OF FRESH CHOCOLATE CHIP COOKIES FILLED the air. Chad sat at the table taste-testing one while Dani made coffee.

"What's going through your head, I mean, being put on leave without pay?"

"Financially, it is not an issue. My parents made sure I was taken care of in their will. I guess, to be honest, it didn't have the shock effect being put on leave with pay initially did. I got totally caught off guard on the first one. This one I kind of expected."

Chad felt warm inside, at peace from her explanation. He knew she would be all right, no matter what happened.

"I forgot to tell you Detective Conti came to see me yesterday. At my office."

"Really."

"He wanted to know how I fit in the picture."

"What did you tell him?"

"Not much. I had some clients come in shortly after he got there so it got cut short."

"Ahh," she said nodding, looking at the ground. Her options played out in her head, then the feeling inside of her won out over logical reasons not to say anything.

"He came here early yesterday morning," she said.

She looked up, hoping not to see a negative, non-trusting face. She sighed when she saw his compassion, his wanting to listen and not judge. She saw he cared about her.

"I'm hoping you know how dangerous this could be, for me, and for Detective Conti, if I tell you everything, but my heart says to trust you …"

Looking in his eyes Dani saw kindness, the same kindness she saw years before. She could tell he would do whatever was best for her, no matter what.

"He came here and told me about the Wardas being murdered. Then he went out into the garage and looked at my workbench. When I followed him I noticed my hammer and one screwdriver were missing. He looked at me, told me he wasn't here, then left."

Chad felt like he should say something, he just didn't know what.

"Wow," he mumbled.

Dani looked at him, head canted, like she expected more.

Chad got embarrassed, feeling himself fidgeting in his chair.

"This is the weird part...about forty minutes later a guy shows up with a black bag. Says he's Sullivan's PI. He goes into the garage, totally replacing my tools, making sure things were in their place like I had them, then leaves. Other than telling me who he worked for, he did not say one word."

"Sounds like...like stuff you'd see on T.V. I don't know what to say. Why did he do it? Conti, I mean."

"Two hours later TPD shows up to serve a search warrant. For all intents and purposes, they kept their search to the garage. They did not take a single thing with them."

Dani paused, giving time for Chad to contemplate everything she said.

At the same time his eyes got big he sat back, slowly nodding.

She could tell the answer came to him.

CHAPTER FIFTY-EIGHT

"Good morning, Detective," the medical examiner said. "Good morning, Doc," Seth said. "I brought some Christmas cookies my wife made last night. They're on the table in the lounge. You probably ought to go get some before we get started and they're all gone."

"Thanks, I kind of have to watch what I eat," she said.

"Doc, it's the holidays. Nobody loses weight during the holidays. Besides, you look great, from a detective perspective."

Knox chuckled, which led to the doctor smiling. She walked out of the room, returning with three different cookies and a fresh cup of coffee.

"So, today's autopsy is the wife of the guy we did yesterday?" she asked, followed by a bite.

"Yeah," Seth said. "Hope hers is as straight forward. Christmas is Monday and I have hope still I can get some shopping done today. I hate the thought of doing it tomorrow or Sunday. The throngs of people…everywhere will be packed."

A couple of autopsy techs had previously moved Azar Warda onto the metal table, her head propped on the hard rubber neck support, her nakedness unnoticed by everyone.

The medical examiner was a visiting pathologist from Marin County, not yet certified as a forensic pathologist.

266

The holidays always brought about a relaxation of the specifications, even though nobody would admit it. The regular forensic pathologists both knew a county in the less-populated areas of California would not risk losing them by making one of them work around the holidays.

"When do you head back home?" Knox asked.

"Right now we only have three autopsies for today," she said. "I'm hoping by early afternoon. I need to get started if I'm going to make it." She put on a pair of gloves, grabbed her clear mask, and before long started recording her early findings.

Well into the autopsy the doctor called them over closer.

"I think there's something in her mouth." Before she took it out she let Knox photograph from different angles.

Taking a small pair of Kelly Clamps she pulled the stuck item from the back of Azar's top front teeth. Laying it down in a glass tray they could see some redness on it.

"Is that what I think it is?" Seth said hesitantly.

Bent over, looking through a magnifying glass, the medical examiner cocked her head to look at Seth. "If you're thinking latex, like latex gloves, then yes. The lab will confirm it for you, and we can hope the redness might be the killer's blood on it, too."

When she finished dictating she started to thank them, then hesitated.

"I know my opinion doesn't mean much, still, if you'd like to hear it I have a thought about your killer."

"Sure," Seth said.

"When we did her husband's autopsy yesterday, it appeared obvious the killer had no problem dispatching him, maybe even overkill given the screwdriver being all the way up to the flange. From what you told me today while I worked on her, the killer wanted the man to pay for hurting the child. The woman today, Azar, I think it is, she had not been struck hard enough on the head to kill her. In fact, it may not have even rendered her unconscious."

She paused to gauge their interest in her opinion before going on.

"The petechiae in her eyes confirms he finished the job by blocking her airways…not by strangling her or she would have had corresponding marks around her throat. I'm not sure he really wanted to kill her. I wonder if when she bit him she forced his hand, so to speak."

After a short conversation they grabbed their things and headed outside. Seth told Knox he was clear to take the rest of the day off if Sergeant Boykin agreed with it. While Knox drove away in the ID van, Seth sat in his car so he could send a text.

Autopsies are done. No surprise on Cyrus. Azar, on the other hand, not so clear. Even got a little bit of evidence.

CHAPTER FIFTY-NINE

Teri had a look of disbelief when Seth's phone rang shortly after ten. She couldn't believe he would be called out again.

Seth looked at the phone, then at Teri.

"It's AJ."

Her long face turned jovial as her head bounced sideways.

"I hope things are going well for them," she said, her fingers crossed.

"Hey, how's it going up in snow country?"

"Great. Sorry about calling so late. Left my phone in the room while we went up to Mt. Rose ski resort for the day."

Seth's eyebrows went up and his head drifted back.

Teri slapped his arm. "What, what?" she whispered.

Seth put the phone against his chest, mouthing the words, "He left his phone in his room all day."

Teri's facial expression almost mirrored Seth's.

"Skiing huh. Didn't know you skied."

"I didn't either. I stayed on the rabbit hills."

"You mean the bunny hills?" Seth laughed.

"Yeah, whatever. It's been a good day though. Her sisters are great. A lot like her. Very easy going. One of the brothers-in-law is cool. The other one's a dick; thinks the world has to revolve around him."

"Having a good time, are ya? Better be careful, you might start liking this family thing. Mess up your plans of being a hermit when you're older."

"Yeah, well, I'm pretty well convinced that ain't happening anymore."

"What're you saying?" Seth asked, unsure if he heard what he thought he heard.

"I had no idea what to expect, I felt pretty nervous about this quite frankly. We've been here a couple days now and all I can say is I'm not sure why I've been dragging my heels. I'm pretty sure I love her, man. I've really been doing a lot of soul-searching. Up here in God's country, self-analysis is much easier to do."

Seth laughed. "Man, AJ, I'm so happy for you. Wait 'til I tell Teri. She'll pass out."

"Don't shock her too bad. So, what's this about possibly some evidence from the autopsy on the woman?"

"Ahh, it's nothing. Thought we had something, when we looked at it closer it was nothing. Sorry to give you hope."

"It's all right. I know you were trying to keep me in the loop. I know you probably won't be doing much before I get back, if you do don't hesitate to call."

"When you coming back?"

"Christmas day. Her sisters have to fly out so we decided to drive home. Should be minimal traffic, so it'll be nice."

"Then we'll talk Tuesday. Enjoy yourself."

"Thanks. Tell Teri Merry Christmas."

Seth stared at the phone for several seconds after they hung up.

"I thought you said you had some latex from the autopsy," Teri said.

"I did. He sounded so relaxed, it seems like he's having a really good time. I knew if I said anything he might feel like he needed to rush back. I couldn't do that to Bethany."

Teri patted his shoulder and kissed his cheek. "Look at you. A romantic at heart."

CHAPTER SIXTY

"It's nice to almost be home," Bethany said. "I loved spending time with my sisters."

"Yeah, they were fun. I had a great time."

Bethany looked at him, smiling, and a sparkle in her eye. "Thank you."

"You're welcome…for what though?"

"Thank you for going. This has been special for me, in many ways." Reaching over, she laid her hand on his. "You know…this was the first time you said you love me."

"I know. I'm sorry."

"*Sorry*. For what?"

She squeezed his hand, like she had to brace herself for what might be coming. Her smile faded, her eyes open wide.

"No, no. I didn't mean that." AJ could almost see her sigh.

"I meant…I'm sorry I've taken so long. I was afraid to say it, even though I knew it. I think the unknown scared me is all. I do love you. I'm positive of it."

The corners of her mouth shot up and her dimples returned. She had one of those radiant smiles, the type to light up a room. Right then it seemed even brighter.

They pulled into her driveway so she could get a few clothes for work the next day before they headed to his house.

"It seems like Christmas has changed," she said as they walked in the house.

"What do you mean?"

"It used to be the kids were outside playing with all the new things they got. Now, there isn't a kid in sight. They're probably all inside playing with new video games."

AJ had nothing to add…right is right.

"Hey, what's the one present still under the tree?" AJ called out to her in the bedroom.

"It's the one from you silly."

AJ squatted. He picked it up by the corners. Call it gut-feeling, instinct, sixth sense—whatever—it did not matter. Bethany had said she felt like someone had been in her house before they went away, so somehow AJ knew it could not be good.

His silence must have bothered her because when AJ looked over she stood in the doorway to the room and stared at him with a long and foreboding face. She went back into the bedroom.

AJ had been in many houses where the owners freaked out when someone unknown had been in their home. Bethany was not one of those. The social worker in her tried never to panic, to understand people and help them get better. AJ knew she had been trying not to let this guy control her life, her vow to herself.

"We need to open this," AJ said walking toward the bedroom.

"No, *we* don't."

"You're right…it needs to be opened though, if for no other reason than to see if S left it"

"Who the heck else would it be from? I knew every other present under the tree. I thought you snuck it under there so

I left it. We know it's from him. I told you I knew someone had been in the house."

"I still believe it needs to be opened so we can try to have a better understanding of this S character."

She zipped closed the bag with her clothes, taking a deep breath before she looked at him. She became stoic, a resolve about her. AJ sensed she did not want to let S ruin what they had the last few days—a great time.

AJ walked out and found a plastic bag in her pantry to put the present in. Before she came out of the bedroom he walked outside and put the bag in his trunk. He wanted to support her, especially since they still had the rest of the day before getting back to the grind.

It can wait, he thought, *trying to convince himself.*

An internal struggle began between the detective who knew they needed to open the package to find out what S left in the box and the boyfriend in love for the first time and afraid to derail the wonderful time they had.

Other than the ride to his house being quiet, AJ would never have known she received the package, much less the fact S had been in her home to deliver it. At one point he told himself any other victim with her resolve not to let the guy get to her would never call the police and he would never know. The thought did not completely stop his desire to open the package but it did help him to loosen up and accept her position.

They spent a relaxing evening reminiscing about the trip, and talking about their future together, with Hop trying to catch up on the love and attention she missed.

CHAPTER SIXTY-ONE

———

The next morning AJ decided to forgo his run so he could get to the office early. Before he left, Bethany started fixing her hair, singing to one of Bob Seger's tunes playing on the radio. She never admitted to looking forward to work to share good news, but AJ could feel her excitement.

He took the bag inside and set it on his desk. Along with Allison needing to see it, AJ hoped she'd be okay for them to have Dr. P. there, too.

At 7:45 a.m. AJ sent a text to the two of them to schedule a time to Skype. They all agreed on 8:20 a.m.

"When my phone dinged with your name on the screen I knew it had to be BS or serious," Dr. P. said. "Should have known you weren't wanting to know how my holiday went."

"Hope you had a great Christmas, Doc. Satisfied?"

He laughed as he waived one finger at AJ. Allison chuckled, not knowing how to take them.

AJ pulled out the plastic bag holding the present. The wrinkles on Doc's forehead and his raised lip and cheek on one side told AJ he had Doc's attention.

"We came back to find this in Bethany's house, under her tree. She thought I put it there. I didn't."

Allison leaned away, raising her eyebrows at him.

275

"What? I bought her gifts, just not this one," AJ said, his fingers pointing at the bag.

Allison had a clownish smile with raised cheeks. AJ could see she enjoyed making him explain something he did not need to explain.

"Moving on," AJ said. "Let's not waste time, take me at face value. I know this is from the guy sending the notes. He signs everything S."

Their silence meant to him they *bought in*, at least so far.

Wearing latex gloves he carefully took off the wrapping and opened the box. AJ tilted it so Dr. P. could see.

"Can you see them?"

"Yes," Doc said. "One looks like a ceramic heart broken in half, as does the wooden spirit sign."

"This guy's a nutcase," Allison said.

"I don't think so," AJ said.

"Me, either," Doc agreed, shaking his head. "I want to run all of this by a couple colleagues, if you don't mind. My opinion: he is angry at Bethany for something she did. Or didn't do."

"This has to stem from when she worked with kids in Madera, right?" AJ asked.

"Most likely. She can easily figure out who she has worked with at Emanuel in the short time she's been there. This has the makings of someone feeling like she's to blame for them ending up in a bad environment."

"I know you have an in with an FBI profiler, I thought maybe you could run it by her. She's welcome to look at everything if Allison is okay with it."

Allison nodded, affirmatively.

"How's Bethany doing with all of this?" Allison asked.

"Better than me, for sure. She's said she is not going to

let this guy control her life, so she pretty much doesn't pay attention to it. Although, I do think I've convinced her she's better off at my house for now."

They both laughed.

"What?" AJ asked.

"You dumb ass. That's what she wanted anyway," Dr. P. said.

"Ditto, on both points," Allison said.

After they hung up AJ followed Allison to their next meeting, feeling a little foolish for not picking up on Bethany's desires.

He called Bridget Fletcher's office as they walked unsure if she would meet with him or not. Her secretary indicated Bridget would be out of the office until after the New Year. AJ thought it odd when she specifically asked for his cell number, telling him if the DA checked in, she could pass it along.

Allison had called in an evidence tech considered the resident expert on fingerprints. Now in her early forties she was a gregarious woman, one of those people who always wanted to help. The detail in comparing fingerprints fit into her perfectionist streak, not to mention she loved testifying in court.

After her initial look of the wrapping paper, the expert told Allison there were only a couple of decent petite prints, surrounded by a tremendous amount of smudges. She speculated a small woman wrapped them.

They ended up in Sergeant Boykin's office giving him an update.

While there, AJ received a text from a number he did not recognize. The text indicated he should return the call.

Along with everyone else, Boykin voiced his concern about the person involved in Bethany's case stepping up his game. Boykin seemed to relax when he heard Bethany would be staying with AJ until they had more information.

AJ left his office and went out back to the garden area to make the call.

Bridget answered, "I wondered when I would hear from you."

"I thought it best to give you some time. New phone?"

"It's a spare, for privacy. Very few people know I have it."

"I shall guard it with my life, madam District Attorney," AJ said in his best regal voice.

She chuckled. "You better." He heard a deep sigh. "Available for coffee, in say thirty minutes? At the Fruityard restaurant? It's kind of halfway between us. I'm pretty sure I can get us some privacy in the back."

"On my way."

Seth walked outside with a huge grin on his face as AJ hung up. He didn't come out for shop talk.

"So, did you propose?"

"No," AJ replied, dragging it out.

"You didn't sound very definitive. Am I sensing something's up, like you're going to?"

"I don't know, I've actually thought about it. I get all sweaty and jittery when I think about it."

"Dude, no guy avoids that crap when it comes to giving up your freedom and committing to one person. It's normal, happens to all guys."

AJ started laughing with him and the look in Seth's eye told AJ of his excitement for them. Seth could hardly contain his enthusiasm, so AJ figured Teri would know within seconds of him walking away.

CHAPTER SIXTY-TWO

AJ walked in the Fruityard Restaurant and was greeted by the hostess.

"Are you meeting someone, Sir?" she asked.

Bridget walked out of the restroom hallway and they saw each other at the same time. AJ pointed, thanked the hostess, and walked over to Bridget. She gave him a tight hug catching him off guard, almost like a family member would give when they had not seen you for a long time, while the weight of the world rested on their shoulders.

"How are you?" AJ asked, as they headed to the back area where she had a private table for them.

"Not so good," she divulged. She pointed to the chair against the wall, knowing AJ would prefer it. She sat to his left, not across as he expected.

AJ thought it was nice to see her wearing jeans and a sweater instead of a work suit. He could see the tension in her eyebrows, and the corners of her lips turned down. Her body language spoke of stress instead of being relaxed for the holidays and she looked exhausted.

AJ knew sometimes people need to talk, so he remained quiet.

"I don't know what to do about Dani. Worse still, I don't know what to do about my Assistant DA." Her eyes were looking at the table while her left hand twirled a fork.

"She's pushing for me to charge her and thinks we shouldn't wait to convene a grand jury. With the holidays it could easily be another two weeks before they are convened. Too many left the area for the holidays, and the presiding judge won't bring them back early."

Her head bowed, almost hanging, as she turned to him. He reached out putting his hand on hers and tears slowly rolled down her cheeks.

"What do I do, AJ?" she almost begged.

AJ handed her a napkin and waited for some semblance of peace.

"Bridget, we've been friends a long time."

"I know. And I miss our friendship so much." Her eyes met his.

He said, "Sometimes a desire to climb some special ladder equating to success really takes away from a person's true desire." Neither of them needed to acknowledge it now, although AJ knew she understood.

"As my friend, I think you're torn between right and wrong. Not on any legal level, on a human level. You know Dani didn't kill anyone, nor did she orchestrate anything. Maybe I can't prove it beyond a reasonable doubt, *yet*."

AJ paused hearing his tone becoming argumentative. He took a deep breath, softened his tone and said, "Bridget, charging someone with a crime for a political purpose is not you. It's not the person I went to trial-after-trial with who refused to cross the invisible line. You are one of the best people I know."

Through watery eyes Bridget's eyelids crinkled as her entire face moved up with a heartfelt smile. The squeeze of his hand spoke the words she could not say without again breaking down.

After a few minutes Bridget had collected herself enough to actually pour coffee from the carafe.

"I always wondered how you got so many evil people to roll in interviews without ever raising your voice. I feel like I've experienced being interrogated."

"It wasn't my goal, I hope you believe me. I'm touched I happened to be the person you felt a close enough friendship with to open up."

She grinned.

"What's the grin for?"

"I know you meant what you said a second ago. Still, I couldn't help thinking, now I know why so many defendants would speak to you in the courtroom, even when their attorney's didn't want them to. They used to say how you showed them respect, talked to them like they were a person who mattered. Now it all makes sense."

AJ closed his eyes for a brief second trying to hide his self-satisfaction. He could feel a broad smile as a flash of some of the defendants passed through his head.

"I saw a good friend of mine grow up with polio," AJ said. "He was older than me, and I learned so much from him about how to treat people with respect, no matter their plight or condition."

"Well, I know your heart's always in the right place. I think I need to take a page out of your book, maybe try to set something straight before it goes bad."

AJ recognized nothing else needed to be said about Dani Larson. They spent the next hour reminiscing about trials, good and bad.

By the time they left, Bridget stood tall, walked with confidence, her eyebrows returning to neutral, and the corners of her lips slightly raised. AJ felt certain she would be okay.

Getting in his car, AJ's concern for Dani started to ease somewhat.

WITH CHRISTMAS OVER STALKER TOOK TUESDAY NIGHT off work, giving him until late Friday evening to play.

When he got off work a few minutes before 7 a.m. he drove to Bethany's house and wondered if she would still be there. Parking far enough away to keep her from seeing him, yet close enough he could see when her garage door would go up, Stalker watched Bethany's house for twenty-five minutes.

He wondered about her expression when she opened the present he left her, and also knowing he had been inside her home. Picturing her fear and uneasiness brought a smile to his face.

With no movement he figured Bethany went to work early, and left. He would check Emanuel Hospital to look for her car and it would be late morning by the time he spotted her car in the employee parking lot.

Feeling the time had come to turn up the heat, Stalker found a pay phone in the downtown area. He wanted to dial nine-one-one but instead dialed an office number knowing his call would be tracked faster on the emergency line.

When the young woman answered he told her he wanted to talk with Detective Conti. She tried to give him some explanation, so he interrupted her. He told her he killed Nathan Price and he wanted to talk with Conti. He ended the call saying he would call back in ten minutes, and if he didn't speak with Detective Conti someone would die.

Exactly ten minutes later he called the police department from a different pay phone five miles away and he was patched through to Conti's cell.

LEAVING THE FRUITYARD PARKING LOT AJ'S PHONE RANG and it was Sergeant Boykin saying a man had called demanding to talk with AJ, saying he killed Nathan Price. When he threatened to kill someone else if he could not speak with AJ, they contacted Boykin and he told AJ to expect to be patched into the man's next call.

AJ did not have to wait long once he pulled over onto the dirt shoulder.

"Detective Conti," AJ said after the patch through.

"Good morning, Detective."

"Is it true...about Nathan Price?"

"What, no pleasantries first?"

"You're not after pleasantries; you're after showing me you're in control."

"Very true. And I am."

"Why did you have to shoot Adam Riley on the side of 99 near Modesto?"

"He got nosy, got in the way. Nothing complicated. I figured he could identify me. Now, let's cut through the crap, we both know I stuck my blade in his throat, left down the side of the hill and then through the junk yard."

"Fair enough, said AJ. "Had to make sure you were who you said you were."

"Whatever," he grumbled.

"What'd you do with the woman Riley told us about? Is she out in some farmer's field?" AJ had to try to protect

Cherie believing the caller in all likelihood killed Nathan.

"You'll find her soon. Someone will come across the body."

Now AJ knew the caller did not share everything either. AJ had no choice, he had to play along for her benefit.

"You got close to being interviewed inside of The Diner, if my detective would have been doing his job."

The three second pause told AJ he was right, despite the guy's denial of being in there. It also confirmed to AJ his gut feeling had been right—the man had been watching him.

AJ almost asked him why he attacked Rothstein but chose to leave Rothstein out of it, for now.

"We know Dani Larson had nothing to do with Nathan's murder."

"I've done my homework on you," said Stalker.

"So, I'm right then, she's nothing more than a pawn in your big scheme."

"You're good at what you do—so am I."

"Why Dani?"

"You'd never understand."

"Try me."

"Maybe another time. I've got someone to watch; I plan on killing again soon."

He hung up before AJ could say anything.

CHAPTER SIXTY-THREE

———◆———

AJ headed straight to the P.D. to give Boykin a rundown of the entire conversation and then he shifted gears.

"Another thing," AJ said, pausing for effect.

Boykin raised his eyebrows.

"I commented to the guy about how he almost got interviewed in The Diner if Willie would have done his job."

Boykin raised his head to look at AJ with wide eyes, his frustration starting to show.

"A long pause followed before he denied being in the restaurant. He was in there."

"What did Willie do exactly?"

"Instead of speaking with everyone inside like I told him, he flirted with a young waitress the entire time. I intended to deal with him, mentor him, you know, try to leave you out of it. First, he goes in my crime scene and touches the duct tape before I get there when Knox goes to take a leak, then he fails to interview everyone in the restaurant, and now, after what he did at Seth's homicides, I can't work with him anymore."

"Yeah, well, easier said than done. E.T. doesn't want him either, and he has seniority. You know as well as I do this could be a union thing."

"Whatever. I want you to know, I won't fight it. I'll take

my days on the beach without pay."

"For what? What are you talking about AJ?"

"The first time the weasel looks at me cross-eyed I'm going to kick the living shit out of him. Then you can assign my cases to him while I'm on days off without pay. Unless he ends up in the hospital."

"AJ, c'mon, you can't, it's not the way to handle things."

"Yes, I can. When someone's been here as long as I have, given as much time to this place as I have, and some young punk cannot do what I assign him, then he touches evidence on two homicide scenes ignoring all of the proper procedures, and the department won't do anything about it…I can handle it that way, and I will."

AJ left Boykin's office, not waiting for an administrative response.

Before he went home he wanted to clear his head. He drove to Pedretti Park believing he would have privacy since no baseball or softball games were scheduled in the winter.

The first trip walking around the ballfields helped to calm him down. The second trip allowed him to focus on his personal life, something he had not been used to doing. There certainly had never been anyone in his life as important to him as Bethany.

Now what? he thought.

FROM THE PARKING LOT ON COLORADO AVENUE, STALKER could see the hospital employee parking lot. He saw Bethany walk out with two other women, all of them laughing before going their separate ways.

He knew she would turn north when she left so he exited and drove over to Tuolumne Road, slowly driving west while waiting for her to cross in front of him at the intersection. When she did he sped up, turned right, and followed her behind four other cars.

Bethany drove as he expected, ultimately turning north on Geer Road heading toward Hughson. When she turned into a subdivision across from the university he perked up, never having seen her go there before. Within seconds she pulled into a driveway and got out.

Despite it being a cul-de-sac he decided to drive in and circle around it, hoping she would not pay close attention. Slowly making the loop he saw her insert the key into the door and let herself in. Coming out of the loop he looked at the face of the garage, spotting what he needed.

His investigator had redeemed himself when he got the information on the couple who lived near Dani and he knew he'd find out about this house too. Stalker made sure to pay him double so he'd be comfortable again when needed in the future…the future had arrived.

Stalker stopped across from the house while he reached in his pocket to retrieve his phone.

"I need you to get me information on the address I'm about to give you. I want the owner, who pays the utilities, you know, the basics," Stalker said to his contact. "I'll pay you double again if you get it to me before midnight."

When the contact asked for triple pay if he had the information in less than an hour Stalker agreed.

Sitting in a sports bar near the university watching a basketball game his phone rang. He wrote down the name on one of the napkins, never saying a word. Sipping on his draft, he could not believe his good fortune. This felt like a belated Christmas present.

So many possibilities, he thought. *This is going to be fun.*

Reaching for a new napkin Stalker began plotting his next steps, never leaving anything to chance. Knowing he would be awhile, he raised his mug to get the bartender's attention.

CHAPTER SIXTY-FOUR

Pretty much on autopilot, AJ turned onto the road leading to his house, when he saw lights from a car. When the car started moving he assumed it must be one of his neighbors. When the car turned left AJ saw Bethany's car in the driveway. It had never evoked a feeling when he came home, but seeing it this time made his skin tingle.

It delighted AJ to find Bethany in a good mood when he walked in. Her desire not to be affected by everything being real or not did not matter to him at the moment. She had been handling it all much better than him. He suspected her time as a social worker made her realize she could not be bogged down by every little issue out of her control. She seemed determined to make the most out of each day.

AJ did not want to be derailed by any of the hundred things on his mind, so he walked straight to her and took her hand. He led her over to the couch, silently asking her to sit with his shaking open palm. AJ sensed Bethany felt his other hand holding hers shaking too. Along with the shaking he could feel his throat drying and restricting.

Facing her he took her other hand in his. He'd been in several shootings and life threatening situations, none of which gave him the feeling of constant movement under his skin over which he had no control. He tried clearing his throat, then looked into her eyes.

"Bethany, I have no idea …" AJ realized he was in the wrong spot. "Sorry," he said while moving.

The corners of her lips turned up as her eyes became huge.

"Let me start over," he jabbered, now on one knee in front of her.

"I have no idea what took me so long, and right now I don't care. All I know is I love you…I want to spend the rest of my life with you. Will you marry me?"

She flew off the couch onto her knees, hugging him as the last word left his lips. He could hear her crying in his ear, and her body trembling.

"Did I…say something wrong?" AJ held his breath, almost afraid of an answer.

"No. Yes," she gushed, pulling back from his shoulder, her face wet, the smile and the sparkle in her eyes bright. She wiped her cheeks as she looked deep into his eyes.

"No, you didn't say anything wrong. And yes, I will."

She gave him another big hug, smiled, and grabbed her phone out of her back pocket.

"I need to call my sisters," she said with a huge grin.

AJ smiled and stood, leaving her to enjoy her rush of excitement. Walking away he realized his smile wasn't just for Bethany's excitement.

When she finished talking with her sisters they decided to go to their favorite Italian restaurant to celebrate. They toasted with glasses of wine while they indulged in the homemade lasagna, a recipe brought over by Nonna, the owner's grandmother.

A couple hours later when they got home Hop met them at the door. Hop ran as best as possible toward the back of the house, then up again towards them. As she turned and ran back once more AJ figured she must really need to go. When he let her out she barked several times as she ran around the side of the house. Her abnormal actions caught AJ's attention and he began to step outside.

Bethany asked if he wanted more wine so AJ stepped back inside to answer. Before he could go back outside Hop slowly made her way into the house and walked over and laid on her bed in the living room. AJ chalked Hop's unusual actions up to the excitement of the evening.

STALKER LEFT THE SPORTS BAR AND HEADED BACK TO where he last saw Bethany. He could not help himself, despite realizing the inherent danger of snooping around a police officer's house.

Bethany's car was no longer in the driveway and he knew the house had an alarm by the little sign in the window. He would worry later whether it was actually used.

The cold evening air one night after Christmas drove most people inside with little activity in the neighborhood. He easily made it into the back yard through the west gate and peering in the windows from the back patio he could see the dog. When it saw him it started barking without ever leaving its bed and he noted the dog to his mental checklist as he made his way around the rest of the house.

He saw the flash of headlights as the car pulled into the driveway. He walked to the gate on the opposite side of the house as quietly as he could where he heard them talking. He looked through the slats of fence, saw them kiss once, and then turn to walk up the front sidewalk. Looking through the side window he saw them enter and the dog greeting them. When the dog hopped as fast as it could to the back door, Stalker realized he had to leave.

He wanted to go out the gate he came in since he would have an easier time blending in like a home owner if someone were around. When he heard the dog barking he abandoned his plan and went through the gate closest to him.

Closing the gate quietly he heard what sounded like young men. The instant the gate latched he moved to his left and knelt down, putting his back into the corner of the two fences. Witnesses were his immediate worry and he would have to tolerate the dog for now.

The young men got into a car in an adjacent driveway. He heard the car start to back out, and saw headlights in the cul-de-sac facing Bethany's car. He laid down against the fence hoping to present as small of an outline as possible.

When the car sped away, the tires on the brink of spinning, he knew the young men were excited to be going somewhere. He felt pretty sure they never saw him. As he got back into a kneeling position he heard the dog on the opposite side of the fence. When Stalker growled, the dog took off back toward the house, unwilling to point him out.

Walking back to his car Stalker chastised himself for letting his desires get ahead of logical thinking and planning. He decided not to dwell on it, attributing it to fatigue.

He headed to his house for a little sleep before the fun began.

CHAPTER SIXTY-FIVE

While getting ready for work Bethany could almost see AJ's mind racing.

"What are you thinking about, you seem really focused on something."

"I got a call yesterday. I'm pretty well convinced it was Nathan Price's killer."

"Not the attorney?"

"No, in fact I think she's being framed by him for some reason. He said I wouldn't understand when I asked why her."

"Well, in my world the anger you're describing is often at a family member."

"The strange part is she doesn't have any living family."

"Really? That is strange," she said walking out of the room, leaving him to ponder by himself.

Before AJ left the house he called Tom Sullivan's office and left a message on his answering machine saying he needed to meet with Dani at 5:00 p.m. at Tom's office. AJ asked for a return call to confirm or cancel the meeting.

Bethany walked up and gave him a big hug and kiss, thanking him for last night. She could hardly contain her excitement.

AJ kissed her again before he left and let her know he

would be late if the interview came through.

Stalker parked a couple streets over on the side street he left the night before.

When he saw the detective's car drive down the road he began walking toward the house. He noted a couple of parked cars running to warm up.

He figured Bethany might still be in the house when he saw her car in the driveway. Making sure no one was outside he slipped into the backyard through the gate like the night before. He pulled out his knife to pry the side garage door open. Quietly closing the door behind him, he turned to see the convertible Mustang he saw the night of Nathan's murder. Stalker admired the car while killing time.

When he heard the front door close along with the slight shake of the walls he listened for her steps. He heard her walk up to her car and get in so he slid over to the door leading to the house. He waited a good minute after she drove away before going inside.

The instant he stepped inside he felt the bite on his ankle. There had been no warning by barking like the night before. Instead the dog went straight for him. In one jerk of his leg he broke free of the grip, circling his foot back around in an effort to strike the dog's head to prevent another bite. The dog moved slightly, hampered by the missing leg. Stalker's foot landed squarely on the one good front leg, totally disabling the dog from getting away. Stalker felt bad, bending down to assess the damage. Realizing the extent of her injury, and her age, the next shot crushed the dog's head against the tile.

Stalker made his way into the bathroom, grabbing the first hand towel he saw. He wet the towel to wipe the blood from his leg. After rinsing the blood out, and wringing out the towel he wrapped it around his leg and pulled his sock up to hold it in place.

He tried to move with purpose, figuring he did not have much time before the alarm would sound. Before he could clean up the bathroom completely, the wailing in his ears nearly deafened him. He scanned quickly, looking for any blood drops. Not finding any meant it would be harder to get his DNA. Time did not allow for him to clean to the extent he wanted.

Stalker left through the garage doors and relaxed as he realized a house alarm, like in most California neighborhoods, no longer got anyone's attention. He walked at a good morning-walker pace so he did not stand out, even checking his watch to make it look like he timed his steps.

Nearing his car it passed through his mind Detective Conti would be too smart. Knowing he could not prevent a DNA analysis of any blood he may have missed during his clean-up he decided to try and stall it. Perhaps the right move might keep the detective from rushing to get the analysis done.

CHAPTER SIXTY-SIX

A J had only been at the office for about ten minutes when his cell rang. He chuckled to himself when he saw the alarm company's name on the screen. AJ figured Bethany must have done something or forgot a step in the process. He told them he would go home and fix it.

AJ knew dispatch had not sent the call out to a patrol officer, they stopped sending officers to house alarms years before. A sign of the times the Chief told them, not as though any officers were clamoring to keep going to false alarms.

AJ pulled into the driveway, the deafening sound making him wish he had a set of earplugs from the firing range. He covered his ears with his hands until he got to the door and told himself to be smooth. Going too fast usually meant he had to put up with the wretched sound even longer correcting his own errors.

AJ wondered where Hop hid this time. The sound usually hurt her ears so she often tried to hide under one of the spare beds. He was surprised he could not find her right away after he shut it off, and even more surprised he did not hear her trying to find him.

When AJ walked around the corner toward the door leading into the garage he saw her.

"Ahhh," he screamed, his fists doubled up and ready to punch the wall. For a spit second Bethany entered his mind preventing him from destroying anything in the house.

He stepped over Hop and went into the garage. Enraged, his mind envisioned the silhouette of Stalker standing down range and AJ pumping round after round into his worthless body.

Instead, he grabbed an old aluminum bat and went into the side yard. The first thing in his line of sight was the four foot high blue recycle bin. His first swing nearly broke the lid in two and the subsequent swings destroyed the thick plastic altogether.

AJ dropped to one knee, catching his breath as sweat rolled off his face. The intake of oxygen helped to dissipate his anger and allowed a more clear thinking mind to emerge.

"You'll pay for this mother fucker," AJ screamed as he went back in the garage throwing the bat on the cement floor.

He closed his eyes and took a deep breath before he went back inside the house. Falling to his knees he started to slide his hands under her head to comfort her. He felt the warmth of the blood. Rubbing her head between her ears AJ saw her leg, pointing sideways.

AJ told her how much he loved her and how good of a friend she had become. Flashes of her running around the house when she used to be younger played through his mind. After several minutes he gently laid her head down. He stood, going to the bathroom to wash his hands and saw the blood smears in the sink, then noticed the missing hand towel.

He squatted back down to rub her head one more time, telling her he was proud of her for trying so hard to protect their home.

Seth arrived first, followed by Knox, Allison, and Sergeant Boykin. Every one of them had a somber expression, feeling bad for Hop. Everyone avoided the white elephant in the room of who and why, even though they all wondered if it could have been the same guy who went into Bethany's house.

AJ's phone rang and he saw it came from Sullivan's office so he threw his phone to Seth who stepped out of the area to answer it. When he walked back into the room with the look of being unsure about a meeting, AJ nodded. He heard Seth say they would be there at five.

When Knox finished processing the bathroom and the garage doors he slid outside to clean up the destroyed bin. He had some city workers who owed him a favor and arranged for a new blue bin to be at AJ 's before five p.m. Allison offered to take Hop to the vet's office for AJ , but he thanked her and told her it was something he wanted to do. Sergeant Boykin told him to take his time getting in, even offering him a bereavement day if he wanted.

AJ felt overwhelmed by the kindness. Hop had been special; she touched all their hearts almost as much as she had his. He wrapped her in a soft bath towel and gently laid her on the seat next to him so they could begin their last drive together.

AJ SPENT A LITTLE TIME WITH HOP ALONE IN ONE OF the vet's rooms before saying his final goodbye. He emerged emotionally drained. Somehow he needed to let Bethany know without ruining her day and further upsetting her that someone had not only been to her house, but now his and had killed his dog.

Leaving the vet's office, he drove in the general direction of his house, his mind not exactly on driving. He looked to his left and saw three athletic looking guys surrounding a young teenaged boy clutching his skateboard. One of the three yanked the skateboard out of his hands while another threw a punch and the kid doubled over.

Making a quick U-turn AJ pulled into the strip mall lot. He parked close to the alley and made his way to the corner. He stepped away enough to get an angle to determine which of the three was the leader…he had his answer in a matter of seconds. AJ knew taking out the leader first makes for an easier battle.

Walking into the alley, he yelled, "Why don't you leave him alone?"

The three looked at AJ in his bloody shirt and pants as the leader yelled, "Get the fuck out of here old man, this doesn't concern you."

"You three all over twenty-one?" AJ asked and waited a moment. "I'll take it from the bozo back there nodding his head you are. That's good."

"What's so good about that old man?" said the one closest to him.

"Because it doesn't set well with certain people in the public for an old guy to kick the shit out of three young punks, but since you're all over twenty-one nobody's going to care."

AJ took a few steps toward the skateboarder as the guy closest to him took two steps back. The leader didn't budge, almost chastising the other guy with his cold stare for moving back. AJ could see the leader doubling his fists and waited for his first move.

The instant the guy's foot moved toward him, AJ took

out his knee with a sidekick to the kneecap, dropping him instantly. The second guy hesitated for a second and then made his move. AJ side stepped him and grabbed enough of his shirt to sling him face first into the brick wall.

When AJ looked at the one who nodded earlier, the guy stepped back and threw his hands up like he wanted no part of it. The guy looked down and his eyes got wide ... AJ knew the leader was about to do something else. AJ spun and did a low roundhouse kick and caught the guy on the side of his head, causing him to drop his already drawn knife. AJ grabbed it and chucked it up on the roof of the strip mall.

The second guy made his way to his feet, put up his hands like his buddy and wobbled to the other side of the alley. AJ could see they wanted to run but abandoning their leader on the ground would bring trouble.

The leader spit out blood and looked at AJ like he still had something in him. AJ put the toe of his shoe in the guy's crotch, his heel on the ground and the rest of his shoe ready to crush his balls.

"No, no, no, we're done, I swear," the leader screamed in a high-pitched little boy tone.

"Somebody killed my dog today…then I see you messing with my friend…er, what is your name?"

"Ethan," the boy said, smiling back.

"You messed with my friend Ethan. Guess you won't do that again," AJ said, putting an ounce more pressure with his foot drawing screams of "no" until he let up.

"Ain't nobody calling the cops…right?" AJ said, his eyes shifting among the three. "Good, because if you do, it won't just be me who kicks the shit out of you next time."

AJ made sure Ethan left first and then headed to his car, pretty certain the guys or the few onlookers gathered around would not call the police. Especially about an old bloody guy who defended himself against three troublemakers.

AJ went back to the house to start cleaning things up so Bethany would not walk in on the mess, especially knowing he would be at Tom Sullivan's office.

His emotions seemed to be on a rollercoaster. He found himself smiling, thinking of some of the good times when he picked up Hop's bed and personal items. Not so when he cleaned the floor and the bathroom; his jaws were tight, red hot blood seething through his veins.

CHAPTER SIXTY-SEVEN

A t close to noon AJ's phone dinged. Sergeant Boykin
texted to let him know the guy called the department
again wanting to be patched through. AJ agreed to it, then
closed his eyes and took a couple of deep breaths trying to
calm himself.

When AJ answered the call the voice sounded familiar,
except for a distinctly different tone.

"Detective, I am so sorry about your dog. She surprised
me and bit me...I overreacted. I know you probably don't
believe me...I love animals, really. I can't believe what I did."

AJ stayed silent for several seconds, surprised by the
sincerity in his voice. He had done many interviews angry
at what the person he arrested had done, only to put on
a calm demeanor to protect the investigation. He needed
to do it here, although he found it harder than any other
interview...this one became personal.

"What were you doing in my house in the first place?"

"I don't know. That's the thing, I initially went there to
try to get to know you better, you know, as my adversary. I
promise you, I will never step foot on your property again."

"I'm not your adversary. Whatever's making you do these
things is what has control over you."

"Maybe so, I've never quite looked at it that way."

"How do you look at it then?"

"Let's just say I'm trying to balance the scales of justice, I've never felt like something has control over me."

"Can't you see your good and evil are fighting each other? You're killing people who get in the way, then you're almost distraught over killing my dog."

"When you put it that way, I guess I can."

"You're breaking into my house thinking you need to know things about your so called adversary, yet you have this unwritten code inside of you telling you to do so again would be dishonorable."

Silence. Long silence. AJ knew he struck a chord.

"I really am sorry about your dog. I have to go. You're probably tracing this." Beep, beep, beep.

"You mother fucker," AJ yelled, throwing his phone on the couch rather than against the wall like he wanted.

AJ needed to de-stress before he went to the office. More importantly, he needed to figure out what he would tell Bethany, and when.

He had no use for traffic or people at the moment so he ran on the treadmill in his spare bedroom. A college basketball game blaring in the background distracted his mind, even if only momentarily.

When he finished cleaning up after his run he texted Seth. AJ wanted to meet with him away from the office, hoping to relax while he tried to eat, along with talking about their cases. He needed to focus on something other than Hop.

They met at a sandwich shop close to AJ's house. Mid-afternoon a few days after Christmas confirmed his guess about very few customers. They sat in the last booth in the back.

Getting through the awkward moments of not knowing what to say or how to say it, AJ decided to change the mood and told Seth about proposing to Bethany.

Before he could share details, Seth speed-dialed Teri, who AJ heard screaming in Seth's ear when he told her. Considering how the day started, hearing their excitement gave AJ a good feeling inside.

Once the food came they settled into good-old-fashioned shoptalk.

"I know I made the right call," Seth said, looking down, his hands fidgeting.

"What are you referring to?"

"The other day, I kinda lied to you about the latex glove thing. Before you go getting upset, I did it...look, you sounded like you were having a really good time in Reno, and I did not want you rushing home."

"No problem," AJ said, biting into his sandwich.

Seth looked like he had a uni-brow the way his forehead squinched together while he rubbed his chin.

AJ kept chewing. His best friend looking out for his welfare seemed like nothing to be bothered by, in fact he appreciated it. His mental plate was already full of more important issues.

"We recovered latex from Azar's teeth, like she bit into the killer's hand maybe," Seth went on. "It looked like it had blood on it, too. I've requested DNA, but with the backlog at DOJ it'll probably be next Christmas before I hear anything back."

AJ said, "I got another call from the guy who killed Nathan. He apologized, first for killing Hop, then for being in my house. Almost sounded sincere. Not enough to keep me from shooting him if I get a chance, sincere nonetheless."

Seth chuckled for a brief second before turning serious. "Funny, the visiting pathologist commented about how my killer wanted Cyrus to pay, although she did not feel the same about Azar. When Azar bit him she forced him to hurt her."

AJ stopped the bite he was about to take. "Sounds oddly familiar."

"It's quite probable. Right?"

"Being one in the same? Yes. As strange as it sounds, I think the guy has a sense of good about him, he's not simply overrun by evil."

"He's still pretty cold," Seth said. "I mean, driving a screwdriver into a guy's temple."

"Yeah, think about it though. It's the perfect example of what I'm saying."

"How do you figure? It seems…vicious," Seth said, his face scrunched up.

"It is. No denial here. Still, he's going to kill the guy anyway since he wants Dani to pay for something, who knows what. The kicker is, the way Cyrus treated their son, he not only killed Cyrus, he probably felt he corrected a wrong in his mind. He did right by the little boy who could not defend himself."

"You've been hanging around Dr. P. too much."

"Probably so. You gotta admit though, it kind of sounds right, right?"

Even though he barely nodded, AJ took it as though Seth agreed.

After lunch, AJ headed to the hospital and decided as far as Bethany was concerned, Hop simply passed away. She did not need to think both of their houses had been broken into.

Strangely enough, AJ started to feel like his caller would not bother entering his house again. Or did he? He wasn't positive.

CHAPTER SIXTY-EIGHT

Stalker watched from a long distance, pulling into the front parking lot in time to see Bethany crying on AJ's shoulder. Stalker felt bad, he had not wanted to kill the dog and seeing its' disability only made it worse. It bothered him seeing them crying about the dog so he drove to the back lot of the hospital.

Stalker often wondered what would have happened if he had not ended up in foster care. He typically cut the wondering short by cognitively stopping it, believing it served no purpose. This time he didn't, letting his mind wander.

He had done a great deal of reading about killers. He did not consider himself a typical serial killer, like Ted Bundy, or even a lust killer seeking sexual gratification through killing. Stalker had originally become hardened based on Darwin's most basic theory: in a bad environment it is survival of the fittest. He never enjoyed hurting people in the early years, but he enjoyed the peace brought about by others being afraid of him after he hurt someone. Especially if the person happened to be bigger than him, or if they had a reputation of being a badass.

He began killing to gain experience with his end goal in

mind. To kill someone society would easily deem expendable made it easier for him, serving a dual purpose. He simply fixed a problem, or so he told himself. Even though the first kills were not smooth they allowed him to gain experience.

Stalker's love of reading helped. He would research police stories, killers who got away with crimes, and mistakes made during investigations. Stalker seldom killed in the same jurisdiction in the same year.

The Wardas were an exception—Cyrus needed to die. Every day Cyrus lived Stalker felt the odds were against the boy living a long life. Very few killings excited Stalker...he looked forward to Cyrus. When he saw the pictures in court of what Cyrus did to his son, Stalker instantly knew why those who hurt children are often targeted in prison.

He looked down at the large, square band aid on his hand and shook his head, a queasy feeling rising inside his stomach he did not like. He wanted Azar to live, telling himself she sided with Cyrus out of fear. He thought she would be thankful for freeing her from her misery with Cyrus. His nausea stemmed from sentencing the young boy to foster care, a hellhole, crapshoot system at best. Although he had lost his belief in God many years before, he regularly prayed for the boy to end up in a good home.

What can it hurt? he thought.

HIS MIND WANDERED FOR LONGER THAN HE EXPECTED. THE people flowing out of the back doors to the employee parking lot brought him back to reality. He found her car and waited patiently, focused on the doors. He needed to know her ultimate destination to successfully carry out his plan.

CHAPTER SIXTY-NINE

⸺⸺⸺⸺◈⸺⸺⸺⸺

As Seth and AJ pulled into Tom Sullivan's parking lot, AJ thought he recognized Chad's car, so he hoped they could get started right away. AJ wanted to get home to make sure Bethany was doing all right.

They were shown to a conference room and told Tom would be with them shortly. Dani and Chad were already there sitting facing the door.

AJ sat directly across from Dani as he would in an interview. He wanted to be able to read her body language if needed. She tried her best not to show her worry. Her face looked solemn except for her wide-pupils, and the hint of a couple wrinkles in her forehead.

AJ noticed the way Chad looked at Dani and gently put his hand on her shoulder when AJ first sat. He could see Chad's genuine concern for her. AJ broke the ice by apologizing to him for interrupting his day at work last week. Chad seemed unfazed by the visit, thanking AJ for the apology anyway.

Tom walked through the door and AJ started his questions.

"Dani, can you tell me about the car accident back when you were a child?"

Tom looked at AJ with alert eyes, one brow raised, choosing not to put a stop to it, yet.

"Well, there's not much to tell," Dani said.

All eyes were on her, causing her to shift in her chair as she crossed her feet. Her eyes focused on the table while her hands began rolling around each other.

"We were coming back from Madera after my twin brother played in a baseball game. We were approaching Hobo Junction when it happened. My mom screamed, my brother went flying in slow motion and I hit my head and was knocked unconscious."

Dani slowly looked at Chad as he rubbed her shoulder, faintly nodding to let her know she could do it.

"When I woke up Chad was there …" Tears slowly began as she lowered her head.

Chad handed her tissues and she wiped her tears and kept her head lowered.

"Both cars were on fire…everyone died, except for me."

At that moment Chad sat facing her, but his eyes shifted toward the others for a split second and his shoulders drew in.

AJ could tell Tom saw it, too.

"Chad, is there something you want to add here?" AJ questioned.

Dani wiped tears as she slowly turned her head, a questioning look underneath the pain. Chad's hand came off her shoulder when he slightly backed his chair away from the table. Many a suspect did the very same thing in interviews to gain a little distance, right before they had something important to say…or to shut down.

"It's all right, son," Tom said. "We need to know everything." Tom leaned forward, bringing his hands together like he might be praying as he looked directly at Chad.

Chad bolted upright, his chair sliding back for a brief

second before it flipped. "I need some air," he said, racing for the doorway.

"Chad," Dani cried out.

Tom laid his hand on Dani's. "It's okay. He'll be back. He probably has never shared everything with someone like you have. It'll be okay."

Before AJ could look his way Seth stood and headed for the door. Beyond all of his candor with those he worked with, Seth had a compassionate side to him when he wanted to share it, a side that often calmed people and helped them to open up.

It did not take long before Seth walked Chad back down the hallway, his hand on Chad's shoulder showing him moral support.

Dani and Chad's eyes met as he entered the room. He stopped for a brief second, making AJ wonder if he would be able to go through with it. Chad glanced at Seth, who gave him the very same nod of encouragement Chad had given Dani. Chad stepped in further, walked to the far end of the table and started to pace.

Tom reached for the phone, requesting cold water be brought in.

Dani had a "deer in the headlights" look on her face as she stared up at Chad, still pacing.

When the water arrived Seth poured a glass, walked to Chad, looked him squarely in the eye and patted him on the shoulder.

Chad chugged half of it, before he returned to his seat. The corners of Dani's lips went up as she tried to reassure him, although her wide eyes told all of them a different story about her uneasiness.

Dani reached out and Chad took her hand in his. Before he could respond, AJ's phone dinged.

AJ received a text from dispatch telling him his guy wanted to talk again. AJ did not want to tell him no, fearing rejection may cut off future lines of communication. He texted back to patch it through.

"I'm going to get a call in a second. I need all of you to be quiet, very quiet and very still."

Except for Seth, the others did not know what to say, almost freezing in their seats. AJ did not have time to tell them to relax or explain when his phone began ringing.

AJ answered the call, putting it on speaker. "Yeah."

"Am I on speaker?"

"Yeah. I'm with the detective who is the lead investigator of the Warda's case. I figured he might as well be able to hear what you have to say, too."

Silence from the other end, the caller contemplating whether to allow it or not.

"What am I supposed to call you?" AJ asked to divert the caller's contemplation.

"Stalker. Call me Stalker."

"Apropos. So, why did you kill them? The Wardas I mean."

"The guy deserved it, the way he severely beat the little boy with the belt buckle. The system sure as hell wasn't going to do anything to him."

"And the woman?"

"I didn't want to kill her. She chose her fate. She wanted to protect him instead of her son. I even gave her one last chance. I did not go there to kill her, though."

AJ looked at Dani and Chad sensing they were about to speak, pointed two fingers at them, then put his index finger to his mouth.

"So why the BS about the tools, trying to point the finger at the Deputy DA again?"

311

"I told you before, you wouldn't understand."

"Look Stalker, we can go round and round. At the end of the day all of this is for nothing if you can't share shit with me. This game is getting us nowhere. And, right now, you aren't high on my list of people I like after killing my dog."

AJ saw Dani's eyes shoot wide open with shock. He barely got his finger to his lips in time.

"I told you, I'm sorry. I did honor my commitment to you, though."

"Oh, yeah?"

"Yeah. I followed your girlfriend home, made sure she got in safely. I stayed away like I promised."

"I appreciate it." AJ actually did.

"I gotta go."

"Wait, wait. Before you go, take my number...call me directly. It's crazy to go through the dispatchers every time you want to talk. They're busy enough."

Before he could answer AJ read him off the numbers, twice. Without saying anything else the guy hung up.

The silence lasted about fifteen seconds.

"Is it true? Did he kill your dog?" Dani asked, her facial expression saying she knew the answer.

"Yes. I'm pretty sure my dog bit him when he broke into my home. When she did, he killed her."

"How can the DA still think Dani is responsible?" Tom Sullivan said, his voice raising with his anger.

"Relax. I met with her. Early on I think she listened to the weasel Assistant DA who wants her job. Claire thinks it'd be the right political move. I feel like I convinced Bridget to do the right thing and at least hold off passing judgment. I'm convinced she does not believe Dani could have had anything to do with this."

"Then why can't she go back to work?" Chad asked, his forehead wrinkling, followed by pursing his lips.

"Long story," Tom said to him. "I can explain another time. Now," looking at AJ, "what do you have on this guy? Anything?"

"Not really. We believe Azar Warda might have bit him, I chose not to say anything to him about it yet. At the autopsy she had latex in her teeth. There appeared to be some blood on the latex, the problem is it could be forever before we get DNA results back from the DOJ lab. They're backed up at least a year."

"Hell, find a way to get it to a private lab, my office will pay for it. Dani's life can't be on hold for a year."

"Welcome to our world, Tom."

CHAPTER SEVENTY

W ithout knowing exactly what, something about Detective Conti made Stalker like him. He could even see some of himself in Conti. He appreciated the fact the detective tried to understand the people he dealt with and wasn't solely focused on cashing a paycheck.

After making sure Bethany made it to AJ's house and the phone call to Detective Conti, Stalker processed his options while driving home. He knew he could always drop off the grid, maybe go somewhere else to start life over. It was doable. Then again, he hated something being left undone.

He could lay low for a while knowing other cases would take up the detectives' lives. Then he reasoned it would only be temporary before some lab somewhere would get a DNA profile. Getting identified could bring an all-out blitz to locate him.

His final choice, to keep going and play it out to the logical conclusion he had expected from the time it started.

Walking into his house he decided the time had come to treat himself to a Christmas present. It had been over a week since he killed the Wardas, a week doing something he truly enjoyed, letting others he worked with enjoy their families while he covered their shifts. He needed a total break for the evening, mental and physical.

Pulling out his phone, he scrolled to the M's in the contacts.

"Hello," the female voice answered.

"Ms. Cybil."

The madam smiled. Only one person called her Cybil. Although she never asked, she presumed it had to do with the many faces she had to put on depending on the caller.

"Michael, how are you?"

"Wonderful, Cybil. How about you?"

"Business is a little slow. You know, the holidays. All the gentlemen pretend they're good family men this time of year."

"Such dishonesty, I say," he said, with his best regal voice.

Cybil laughed. "What can we do for you tonight, Michael?"

"I covered for all of my colleagues at work so they could have family time over the holidays. Now, I think I need to treat myself to a gift."

"I agree, Sweetie. What is it you're looking for?"

"How about Asian, petite, and willing to do anything."

"You are treating yourself, aren't you? You realize, willing to do anything double's the normal amount you usually pay?"

"Cost is not the issue. Not tonight. Of course, it is for the entire evening?"

"Of course, Sweetie. Same hotel?"

"Same one. Hey Cybil ..."

"Yes, Sweetie?"

"It's been nice." Beep, beep, beep.

She looked at the dead phone, pondering the possibilities of what he meant.

CHAPTER SEVENTY-ONE

Dani stood and tried to walk to the door, giving way to a run. Chad took off after her.

"Aren't you worried this Stalker guy's not going to do something to you or your girlfriend?" Tom asked, looking at AJ like she could be vulnerable.

"Not really. It's kind of hard to explain. He promised he would never enter my domain again. The guy's got some warped sense of doing what's right against those who do wrong, and I don't think he perceives what I am doing as wrong. In fact, I kind of feel like he sees it as trying to do justice, like him."

"Oh, great. Meaning he thinks Dani has done wrong somehow, and he needs to make it all right."

"Yes, exactly," Seth interjected. "Similar to why he did not want to kill the mother of the boy, only the father. He is not beyond doing what he believes needs to be done. When she bit him, she forced him to kill her. So he did, although not to the same violent extent he did the boy's father."

"Is Dani in danger?"

AJ looked at Seth, neither one of them wanting to be on the hook for an answer.

"She is, I can tell by your lack of response," Tom declared.

"I wish I could say definitively," AJ acknowledged. "It's kind of like my situation. I feel like if this guy wanted me like he wanted Cyrus Warda, the deed would have already been done. Something tells me it's the same for Dani. At least so far. Still, she needs to be alert for any changes in the picture."

"I can't believe your girlfriend isn't freaking out," Tom said, shaking his head.

"Someone has been sending her threats lately, which she's chosen to ignore. She's not about to let the guy control her life. I doubt she would look at this guy calling me as any worse than her situation. I did make sure I didn't tell her he killed the dog though. She might want to go after him herself if she knew."

Tom almost chuckled as his shoulders raised up and his head bounced.

Dani and Chad walked back in the room. She looked a little pale.

"Are you okay?" AJ asked.

"Yes…Chad has something you should hear though. He just told me …" When she started to dry heave they all got the picture this could be important.

"I'm not sure what happened after what I'm about to tell you," Chad began, his eyes bouncing between all of them. "I know for sure Dani's brother did not die in the fire."

"What's that, Son?" Tom blurted as he sat forward, his arms resting on the table.

"I reached in the back seat of her car through the broken window, unlatched her seatbelt, and pulled her out of the car. Then I carried her away from the car far enough to try to get back in the front."

Chad paused, stealing a look at Dani. With tears in her eyes she nodded for him to continue.

"Dani's brother was lying on the hood of the drunk guy's truck. An ambulance arrived almost immediately and I'm pretty sure it came from the Merced direction. They loaded up her brother, then took off back towards Merced. Some CHP officer yelled at them to get him to Children's Hospital in Madera, and said he would follow up with them there."

AJ looked at Seth, who stood, pulling his cell phone out of his pants pocket as he headed for the door.

Chad continued, "A few minutes later an ambulance came from the direction of Turlock. They put Dani in and it headed back toward Turlock. I figured they went to Emanuel Hospital when I saw them take the Golden State exit instead of going north on ninety-nine."

"You mean her brother was alive?" Tom asked.

"I don't know. I thought so by the way all of the emergency personnel were acting. I had kind of focused on trying to get Dani's mom out ..."

IT TOOK SETH NEARLY FIFTEEN MINUTES TO GET TIED into the correct CHP office. Hobo Junction sat near the county line, so they had to figure out which office handled the accident investigation.

"Detective, I'm the shift supervisor," the woman said. "Lucky for you we're slow. Otherwise you would be told to call back during regular business hours, Lord only knows if you would find someone there willing to help you."

Seth chuckled after she did.

"If I give you the location of a head-on collision caused by a DUI where most everyone died, could you get me the officer's name so I can speak with him or her?"

She seemed happy to help, at least while the lack of action remained. She put Seth on hold leaving him with easy listening Christmas music, no singing.

He heard the supervisor click back in, then nothing for several seconds.

"I remember this," she said, the chipperness in her voice gone.

Really? Seth thought to himself.

Fearing he could screw things up if he said the wrong thing, he chose not to say anything.

"I did training back then. I had a new girl on a slower section of the desk. We dispatched Delhi Rural Fire to it while other dispatchers were handling the main call."

Seth knew by the pause something went wrong. When she sighed he could almost feel her trying to gather the courage to continue with the story.

"That accident became the catalyst to getting rid of the signal lights on Highway 99 at Delhi. Too many people lost their lives because of drunk drivers getting on the wrong side of the highway from those lights after leaving the bars."

"I had heard there were lights there at one time," Seth said.

"Our officer asked for quite a bit of assistance, before it happened...he got hit by a car trying to put out flares. The driver said he was looking at the cars burning and he never saw our officer."

"Oh, I'm so sorry."

"Thank you...exactly what are you looking for?"

"The young girl you mentioned, an ambulance took her to Turlock."

"Correct."

"We believe another ambulance arrived first and took one child south."

"Sounds familiar. Those kinds of things happened back then. An ambulance close by could jump in and take a patient…less control over those types of things if you know what I mean. Now they all have to be dispatched or approved if they roll up on something."

"Is there any indication of follow up done at another hospital?"

There was a long pause.

"I don't know how to say this except…the status of the investigation changed to closed the next day. The follow up report indicated there were no other drivers or cars involved, the drunk driver had been determined to be at fault, and we had a funeral to prepare for. I'm sorry."

"I understand."

Seth did not want to say anything about the accident being north of the Delhi traffic lights. The drunk driver had been heading southbound, meaning he would have had to enter from one of the cross streets to the highway and not the traffic light. Since CHP lost an officer they pushed to have the lights removed, so who was Seth to question it. Besides, she already seemed bothered by having to talk about it.

"You might want to contact Delhi Fire to see if any of their volunteers remember the accident."

"Thank you. You've been a big help. One last question. If another ambulance happened to pick up a young kid who flew through the windshield, where would they likely have taken the child south of the accident?"

"Madera Children's Hospital. Best of luck, Detective."

They all stopped talking when Seth walked back in the room.

"Not much to tell," Seth said, returning to his seat. "I

spoke with a dispatch supervisor who remembers the incident. The CHP officer working Dani's accident died when he got hit by another car, creating a huge mess. Whoever followed up with her case closed it the next day. Said both drivers died so no follow-up needed. They knew who caused it."

"Did the dispatcher have any other news at all?" Tom asked.

"Not really. Said we should probably get in touch with Delhi Rural Fire Department, maybe someone there remembers it."

"Chad, did you know about the CHP officer being killed?" AJ asked.

"No, I had no idea," Chad said, shaking his head. "When the ambulance left with Dani...I know this will probably sound strange to you guys, something told me to follow her to Turlock. When I got to Turlock I crashed with some guys I knew under the Golden State Bridge, then went to the hospital the next morning hoping to see her."

Dani looked at Chad and nodded, so AJ figured she tacitly agreed with him about the visit.

Before everyone left the meeting AJ made sure they knew there were possibilities of one or both of them being in some danger. AJ suggested they think about leaving the area, making sure Tom knew their whereabouts and how to get in touch with them. AJ got their cell numbers in case they called so he would not ignore the call.

Driving back to Turlock AJ began the process of trying to locate one of the old timers for Delhi Rural Fire who might remember something about Dani's accident. Shortly after he got back to the office AJ received a call from the Rural Fire Chief at the time of the accident.

The Chief told AJ the two cars were fully engulfed when they arrived. Turlock Ambulance paramedics were tending to a little girl off to the side of the road. He said the CHP officer never got the assistance he asked for, apparently there were several other accidents around the same time, leaving him to have to try to do everything by himself.

"You know, I do remember the officer looking for the guy who pulled the young girl out of the car. I guess the fire got too intense when he tried to get her family members out. The guy disappeared before the officer could talk with him, and then of course the officer got hit by a car."

When AJ explained to the Chief they identified the man he seemed relieved. He thought someone should recognize the man as a hero. From what AJ knew of Chad he would not want the attention.

"Some social worker called a day or two later," the Chief said. "I know she worked at a hospital, I figured it had to be Emanuel where they took the girl. Asked about survivors. I told her I only saw the one kid."

I've got nothing official, neither Ambulance Company exists anymore, and by all accounts, except for Chad's, Dani is the only survivor, AJ thought. *Then why do I feel like Chad's the one who is accurate?*

CHAPTER SEVENTY-TWO

———◊———

Concerned about Bethany, AJ went home. When he arrived he took out the trash cans to look around the neighborhood and see if anybody might be lurking. When he felt comfortable he went back inside.

Although Bethany didn't act like her happy self, AJ appreciated seeing she no longer seemed overly upset. He still felt as though he made the right call not to tell her how Hop died.

"I'm sorry if I ruined your day," AJ said. "I didn't want you to come home to an empty house and not know why."

"I spent the morning telling everyone our good news, so by the time you got there it didn't ruin anything. I feel terrible for Hop though."

AJ could only imagine how she would have felt if he had told her everything.

"How'd your day go?" Bethany asked. "I mean, you never told me how you knew Hop died."

"Something alarmed me, so I came home to check. That's when I found her."

"I bet you found it hard trying to focus on your meeting," Bethany said.

"Yeah, pretty difficult. I think we learned a few things. Dani, the DA I've told you about, the man who—"

Bethany's cell rang so AJ paused.

"It's my sister," she said with a large smile. Bethany walked into the living room and sat on the couch, curling both of her feet up beside her.

It wasn't meant to be, AJ thought. His cell rang and Doc's name appeared on the screen.

"Hey, I wanted to let you know I have not reached my profiler friend yet," Doc said. "She did text me to let me know she's on a major case."

"Not a problem. Let me know what she says when you get a chance to talk to her."

"I will. In the meantime, I spoke with my colleagues. They agree with me, the steps he has taken to threaten Bethany are planned, progressive, and they indicate he will go further."

"If I had to guess I'd say your profiler friend will probably say the same thing."

"I think so too. AJ, somehow, someway, you need to convince Bethany this guy's serious. I'd even recommend she get out of town."

"Thanks, Doc. I'll try again, I promise."

Bethany spoke with her sister close to an hour. By the time she finished, how his meeting went had become the furthest thing from her mind.

"Sounds like you guys had a great talk," AJ said. "I was thinking, maybe you should go spend a little time with her for a while. Give some time for this thing to blow over while you guys can do a lot of the wedding planning. I'm sure you would love it."

"It would be a blast," Bethany said, her dimples showing next to her smile and her eyes sparkling. She gently took hold of his hands. "I can't though, I don't have any vacation time. Plus, I want to build up time for our honeymoon."

AJ thought about telling her they could go to her boss with an explanation of the situation. He felt certain she would make allowances.

"What's on your mind?" Bethany asked. "Something's bothering you, I can tell."

"While you were talking with your sister, Doc called. He spoke with a couple of his colleagues and they all feel—"

Bethany put up her hand in front of his face, then turned and walked away. Before AJ could say anything she stopped, turning to look at him.

"This has been a roller-coaster of a day. It's simple, I had a great conversation with my sister and I don't want to ruin the rest of the evening talking about it."

Bethany headed for the kitchen, putting wine glasses on the countertop. AJ decided to give in; she nailed it with the kind of day it had been.

CHAPTER SEVENTY-THREE

Bethany and AJ had wine as they spoke fondly of Hop. It felt cathartic, helping to ease his anger, if only for a little while.

Due to the stress and fatigue and probably a little from the wine, AJ got one of the best night's sleep he had had in a long time. The morning air had been cool in his lungs during his run, leaving AJ feeling renewed. Bethany appeared chipper when he returned, once again singing along with the song on the radio.

At a quarter-after-seven AJ walked into the bathroom area to let her know he had to leave. Bethany gave him a long kiss, and hugged him, laying her head on his shoulder.

"Thank you for caring about me so much," she said.

AJ stroked her hair. "You know, it would be a lot easier if you weren't so hardheaded."

Bethany laughed. She softly kissed his cheek, and patted his butt.

"You better get going, Mister, otherwise we might be late for work." She winked and smiled.

Driving to work AJ had a funny feeling in the pit of his stomach. He could see her captivating smile in his head. He told himself it had to be Bethany's tantalizing personality and not wanting to leave her making him feel the way he did.

Bethany had just set the curling iron on the counter when she heard a noise from the front of the house. "Did you forget something?" she asked. She reached for the hairspray and took the top off, setting it on the counter. Hearing another noise she walked towards it. When she reached the kitchen she saw the dish towels swinging on the rack near the refrigerator.

He must have wanted one of his Muscle Milks, she thought. *I'm going to have to talk to him about getting his hearing checked.*

Walking back toward the master bedroom someone came out from behind a door, wrapping their arm around her neck. Instantly Bethany raised the can and sprayed behind her.

The man screamed as his arm loosened and Bethany started to move but felt an uncomfortable tingling across her right shoulder blade. She could feel the oozing warmth on her blouse as she separated herself. When she realized she was trapped in the master bedroom she ran for the walk-in closet.

She reached around with her hand, patting the shelf, her hand grasping AJ's Glock 19 and quickly turned toward the doorway.

The attacker caught up to her, his hand covering her wrist and pushing it toward the ceiling. The gun fired sending a round into the attic. Before she could fire again his fist hit her squarely on the nose sending her flying, a trail of blood spatter following.

Lying on the carpet in the closet Bethany realized she no longer had the gun as the man's silhouette loomed over her.

The pleading look on AJ's face after he asked her to go spend time with her sister flashed into her mind.

CHAPTER SEVENTY-FOUR

Seth and AJ were getting ready to head to Madera and needed to confirm a young boy showed up at the hospital the night of the accident. It would be a tough sell in person, definitely not the kind of information someone at a hospital would hand out over the phone.

Seth's phone rang and AJ could tell by the look on his face it wasn't good.

"It was Teri. She said our son fell off his skateboard going to school and it sounds like he put his hand down to break his fall, and ended up with a compound fracture of his wrist. They're going to take him in for surgery. I gotta go."

Seth leaving was the right thing to do. AJ acknowledged to himself there definitely had been a time in his career where he would have thought differently, probably even telling Seth he could not do anything for his son during the surgery so he might as well stay. But not anymore.

AJ drove to Madera in a little over an hour and despite being at the hospital for quite a while he had not gotten anywhere. He could not escape his lack of a warrant and the patient confidentiality laws that had everybody afraid of lawsuits.

AJ started to leave when he remembered Bethany talking about one of her co-workers in the Social Worker's office. He had nothing to lose.

AJ waited for nearly fifteen minutes in the lobby. He texted Seth to see how the surgery had gone, and when AJ looked up a petite woman close to his age, wearing half glasses on the tip of her nose walked towards him.

"AJ. It's great to finally meet you," she said after she introduced herself and they shook hands. "Congratulations on your engagement. Bethany's as special as it gets."

AJ smiled as they walked toward her office.

Bethany was not kidding when she said she had spent the morning calling people, he thought.

He sat in a chair across the desk. She had a simple office, similar to his with case files stacked everywhere.

"It made me feel good to hear Bethany's excitement when she called yesterday. The last time I saw her was a few months ago at Suzi's funeral."

She must have seen the confusion on his face.

"Bethany probably never told you about Suzi being murdered. She told us you were knee-deep in your own homicide investigation at the time."

Vintage Bethany not to derail him in the middle of an investigation. AJ loved her independence.

AJ explained how he had gotten the runaround everywhere else he had gone in the hospital. He told her he could use her help confirming if a young boy had been brought to their hospital several years before.

She said she would do what she could, making sure AJ understood she made no guarantees. He provided her the name of the child, the date and time of the accident, along with the ambulance company he believed delivered the boy to them.

While she worked her way through the system AJ sent Bethany a text to let her know whose office he was in. He did not expect a long response, but after ten minutes he was surprised not to have received anything from her.

This is the second time today I've had this funny feeling, he thought. *Something's wrong.*

STALKER ZIP TIED BETHANY'S HANDS BEHIND HER BACK. He then zip tied her to the bedpost of the master bedroom.

With Bethany secure, Stalker went to the garage, pushing the button to roll up the large garage door. He moved Bethany's car into the street, before walking to his car around the corner and drove into the cul-de-sac and backed into the garage.

Back inside he inspected the Glock counting fourteen rounds, thirteen in the magazine and one in the chamber. He slid the gun in the waistband of his pants at the base of his spine.

"Who knows, might come in handy someplace," he said looking at Bethany.

Taking his knife out of the sheath he walked over to Bethany and slit the zip tie holding her to the bed post.

"Why are you doing this?" Bethany asked after he pulled her to her feet.

"You don't remember me, do you?"

Bethany knew there was no good answer. To say no might anger him worse based on the cards he sent her. She sat quietly, staring into his eyes.

"You subjected me to a life of hell. You didn't even find out if everyone in my family lived or died."

"You realize, no different than now, my hands were tied in many ways," Bethany said. Despite not knowing him exactly, she could easily surmise the basis of his anger.

"There were only so many things we could do. Which foster home you ended up in was totally out of my control."

"Yeah, well, I'm going to show you exactly how you dropped the ball."

Stalker grabbed a handful of Bethany's hair and led her to the garage. He popped the trunk, forcing her to get inside.

He decided to leave the garage door open as he drove away, heading to his next destination. Dani had been home when he drove by her house before going to get Bethany. He figured she still would be, being on administrative leave.

Twelve minutes later he backed into another driveway. Getting out of the car he grabbed the Glock, half inserting it into his front right pocket. He rang the doorbell and did not have to wait long before she opened the door.

Stalker yanked open the screen door, pointing the handgun at her face. The wideness of her eyes coupled with the gaping hole of her mouth told him she would not resist. He stepped inside, closing the door behind him.

Dani kept shuffling backward until she ran into a small table, knocking off a vase. The shattering of the vase did nothing to take her eyes off of him and slowly both hands went to her mouth.

"You know who I am, don't you?"

No words would come. She slowly nodded her head.

CHAPTER SEVENTY-FIVE

Bethany's former co-worker returned to her office five minutes later, holding a paper in her hand. She looked back and forth between it and AJ.

"I don't want to put you in a bad position. All I need to know is if a boy arrived here the same evening."

She looked at the paper, more staring at it than reading it.

"Yes, a boy came in, and...Bethany got assigned to be his case worker."

AJ's back pushed against the chair as he took in what she said.

"His first name...was it David?"

"Yes, Larson. David Larson." The instant she said it she put the paper through her shredder.

AJ stood, trying to relax his face to appear calm, although he could tell by the way she looked at him he had failed.

"AJ, is something wrong?"

"No, thank you, though. The puzzle is starting to come together is all. Thank you for your help. I promise, nothing will be documented about this in any way."

The wrinkle between her eyebrows went away at the same time the corners of her mouth almost started to turn up.

"Oh, one more question. Do you know when Suzi died?"

When she told him the first week of September and someone stuck a knife in her brain while she sat at a park bench AJ's heart sank.

He thanked her again and left. His mind was racing to the point he could not recall how he found his car. AJ pulled out his cell phone before he sat.

AJ rubbed his forehead with both hands as he processed options. With Seth at the hospital and the Street Crime guys off after working through the night, AJ's options of people he could trust to go do some checking for him while he drove back were slim to none.

Once he got on Highway 99 he punched it. AJ called dispatch, asking them to send a car to Rose Avenue to look for the black VW Rabbit registered to Michael Wilson. He also asked them to call CHP to let them know he would be flying up the highway. Then he called Seth.

"How'd the surgery go?"

"He's in recovery now. Doc said it went well. You need me to do anything?"

"Nah. I'm heading back from Madera." AJ could be back before Seth could be to Turlock. Mostly AJ wanted Seth to be there for his son when he woke up.

"One quick question, though. Which side of Azar's head did your killer hit her with the hammer?"

There was a short pause before Seth said, "On her left. Why?"

"I'm trying to picture which hand she bit to get Latex on her teeth. Thanks. I'll come visit later."

"Hey...stay safe."

"Always brother. Always." AJ grinned after hanging up. They had a strong bond, so Seth could tell things were heating up regardless of what AJ said.

AJ sent a text to Bethany telling her to get in touch with him immediately. If he could only confirm she made it to work he would feel better. AJ waiting patiently would not happen, and he kept thinking of ways to get answers. He dialed the detective secretary's number at the office, asking her to call Emanuel Hospital for him.

Within a minute of each other AJ received confirmation there were no cars or any activity at the Rose Avenue address, along with his return call from the detective secretary.

"AJ...she..."

CHAPTER SEVENTY-SIX

Bethany knew he had not driven far, although she had no idea where they were. The throbbing in her shoulder and face had dulled to a constant ache and she felt pretty sure she had stopped bleeding from the wound by lying on it.

Her phone kept vibrating in her front pants pocket and she knew AJ was trying to get in touch with her. When she tried to roll so she could reach her pocket, the zip ties were so tight she could hardly move her arms. She wiggled her fingers every few minutes to stave off the numbness creeping in.

He'll find me. He'll figure it out, I know he will, she thought.

"You can't kill me. I know you can't. We're like one," Dani said, looking deep into his eyes.

Stalker walked toward her, the Glock still pointed at her head. Pulling out one of the chairs at the table he motioned with the gun for her to sit. He pulled her arms through the outer wooden frame and the middle section of the back of the chair where he zip tied them together. He then secured her ankles to the front legs of the chair.

Once he had her secure he looked around, taking in

the decor. He got a twinge when he saw the color scheme of her couch, the way everything in the house appeared so clean and orderly.

"I'll bet it looks a lot like yours, doesn't it?"

He did not reply, letting the slight nod of his head answer her.

Looking by the front door he saw the suitcase and walked toward the door, standing over it. The car pulling to the curb outside caught his attention.

"Going somewhere?" Stalker asked, looking over at her.

He saw her eyes dart to the front window and he went to the kitchen and grabbed the long, thin white towel from the stove handle. Setting the gun down on the table he moved behind her chair. Holding each end of the towel, he rolled it into a long, thick single-strand before he flopped it over her head. Pulling back, the towel went into her mouth as he tied off the two ends behind her head.

The man walked in front of the house looking back over his shoulder at the black car backed into the driveway. Stalker saw the man stop, his eyes got wide and he turned toward the car.

Grabbing the Glock, Stalker ran to the front door, slinging open the screen door.

The noise startled the man, stopping him in his tracks. He looked back, then at the car, and back at the gun.

Stalker could hear Bethany screaming in the trunk. Pointing the Glock at the man, stone faced and dead still, he waited. He had no problem shooting the man right there if he took another step toward the car.

Stalker recognized the man from previous recons at the house. Believing the man would follow orders Stalker pointed and waived the Glock toward the door. He backed into the house as the man followed. With another wave of the gun the man closed the front door.

CHAPTER SEVENTY-SEVEN

———◆———

"I'm almost back in town," AJ said to the detective secretary. "I need you to start the process to begin pinging Bethany's phone. I don't have time to explain. Tell Allison to get geared up and be in her car ready to meet me when I figure out where we're going."

"AJ ..."

"Not now. I need the location. *Please?*"

AJ hung up and worked his way through his contacts, searching for Dani's phone number. He pushed it and heard the ringing. Five rings later he heard her voicemail message come on. He didn't wait...he hung up.

AJ found Chad's number in contacts. He hung up when he heard his voicemail message, too.

———

"PULL UP A CHAIR NEXT TO HERS, HAVE A SEAT," STALKER said to the man.

He watched as the man's shaking hands reached for the chair and put it next to Dani's. He saw their eyes meet holding each other's wide-eyed stare.

"What's your name?"

"What, who me?" Chad asked, surprised.

Stalker tilted his head and Chad read the message...

stupid question.

"Chad. Chad Miller."

"Well, Chad, I'm sorry you got dragged into this."

"I've been in it from the start—I was at the accident."

Stalker's eyebrows scrunched together and he tilted his head again. He did not have the time to delve into the statement, although it did have him intrigued.

Stalker handed Chad two zip ties, directing him to put one on each wrist and pull them tight. Stalker slid behind Chad, quietly shifting the Glock to his left hand. Reaching under his shirt he unlatched his knife and guided it out of the sheath.

"Put your arms through the back of the chair like hers."

Chad looked at Dani's arms. He started with only putting his left hand back.

Stalker saw Chad's shoulders tense up, his right hand still in the same spot. In one swift move Stalker drove the knife into Chad's thigh and pulled it out before the screams started.

"Get your arm through the back of the chair, *now*. Next time I'll shoot you."

Reeling from the pain Chad moved slowly until the muzzle touched the back of his head. His arms shot through the openings where Stalker zip tied them together in seconds.

Stalker wiped his knife clean on the back of Chad's shirt and set his weapons down and untied the towel.

"Are you okay?" Dani blurted out looking at Chad. Before he could answer, her wide-open eyes with pinprick pupils darted upward.

"Why'd you have to stab him? He didn't do anything."

"Chad, you going to do what you're told now?"

Chad nodded his head. The look on Stalker's face told Dani, "That's why."

Dani stared at him shaking her head, her eyebrows low, her nostrils flared, and her lips compressed together.

"Chad, this is my twin brother, David, who's gone off the deep end."

Stalker grinned at Dani's anger.

"Where do you keep your duct tape?"

"What? Duct tape?" Dani paused having to think for a second.

"Top drawer on the right of the workbench in the garage."

Stalker made his way to the garage where he retrieved the duct tape from the drawer. When he turned to leave he looked back towards the workbench. He stopped, slowly nodding when he noticed the different brands of tools in each slot on the pegboard, none of them Stanley tools like before.

Smart move, he thought.

He walked back through the house, made sure neither had moved, and took the duct tape with him. He ripped off a six-inch piece, popped the trunk, and slapped it on Bethany's mouth. Grabbing handfuls of hair he slammed her head down a couple of time, wanting to take some of the fight out of her.

"Now we can't have you drawing any undue attention out here, can we?" Stalker asked as he checked her hands.

Before he left her he grabbed her cell and threw it on the front passenger seat.

CHAPTER SEVENTY-EIGHT

——— ◦ ———

When AJ saw Dani's name on the screen for the incoming call he breathed a sigh of relief.

"Dani, you guys need to get out of here," he said in a quasi-authoritative voice.

"I'm sorry, Dani's tied up right now, she can't come to the phone, Detective."

AJ hesitated, not expecting to hear his voice.

"David."

"He doesn't exist anymore."

"So is Michael Wilson your legal name now?"

"No, it's Todd Wilson. I had it changed once I became an adult. I used my middle name along with my mother's maiden name. You can call me Stalker."

"I'd rather call you David or Todd, or even Michael."

"I'd rather you not. Since I hold all the cards ..."

"Stalker it is."

"Learn anything in Madera?"

"How'd you know I went to Madera?"

"It's amazing what people tell you if you attach a title to your name, like Dr. Wilson."

"Nothing I didn't already know. Except for Suzi."

"I really liked her. Maybe in another life. Before you waste time asking, she could ID me. I had more work to do before today."

AJ got an intense pain in his chest, a definite feeling of impending doom.

"I really like you, Detective, but make no mistake about it, I'll kill you along with everyone else here if I have to."

"Wait, wait, wait. Nobody needs to die today."

"I wish I could agree…unfortunately you're wrong."

"Didn't violate my trust in you, did you?"

"You mean your girlfriend? Yes, I must admit I did."

AJ became nauseous, closely followed by dizziness. His foot slid off the accelerator.

"I want you to know, Detective, I really felt bad when I saw the two of you together. None of this is aimed at you, I respect you."

"Stalker, we're engaged. If you really respect me then you won't go through with this," AJ said, punching the accelerator again.

Silence filled the phone. For the first time AJ felt he had him on his heels because the good in him might be paying attention.

Fifteen seconds later Stalker broke the silence with, "I'm sorry, I really am." Beep, beep, beep.

AJ approached the Taylor Road exit, receiving a text from the detective secretary letting him know the location of Bethany's phone. She also let him know Allison was already on her way.

Allison called his cell less than a minute later.

"AJ, shouldn't we call in SWAT, see if they can negotiate with this guy?"

"Allison, I hear you, really I do. This is not about me disobeying policy. If you don't want to be part of this, I understand. You have your whole career in front of you."

"AJ, I'm not worried about my fricking career."

"You and Doc were the ones telling me this guy is on a mission. I just got off the phone with him. He's hell-bent on completing this mission today, right now. I might be able to save a life or two. Surrounding the place seals all of their fates."

Silence.

"I'm almost there, don't go in without me."

"Allison, he's never killed anyone I know of with a gun. But it doesn't mean he won't have one."

STALKER GRABBED HIS WEAPONS, RAN OUTSIDE, STARTED his car and almost burned rubber getting out of the driveway. He parked across the street two houses down to the left, deciding it would be quicker to leave the keys in the ignition and sprinted back to Dani's.

Stalker propped Dani's chair onto the back legs to drag her to the living room, facing the front window. He repeated the process with Chad.

His final preparation involved pushing the button for the garage door, pushing it a second time, then one last time, stopping the door with a thirty inch gap between the bottom and the cement floor.

He walked through the garage door into the laundry room, leaving the lights off while he waited.

CHAPTER SEVENTY-NINE

AJ approached from the east and parked on the wrong side of the street several houses from Dani's. He wanted Allison approaching from the west so she could have access to the gate on the side of the house.

From behind a tree AJ could see through the front window. He saw Dani and Chad sitting in chairs in the middle of the living room facing the window. When Allison approached on foot AJ signaled for her to go around back.

He made his way up to the front door, locking the screen into the open position. Kneeling at the doorframe, AJ turned the knob and pushed open the door.

"Detective, I presume you are not alone."

"You know we don't work that way."

"How long before the SWAT team gets here?"

"Didn't call them. I want this thing to end as peaceful as we can. I trusted what you said. Relationships are built on trust."

"I agree. I trusted someone would come looking for me—she never did. I trusted my social worker would find my sister who also lived—she never did. I trusted the system would not subject a young boy to such monstrous foster parents—the system failed, several times. My life shattered just like the windshield."

"Stalker, the CHP officer who would have tied all of this together died at your family's accident scene. CHP unintentionally dropped the ball when they closed the case the next day. I'm telling you, nobody else had any other information you were alive."

The squeak from the sliding glass door opening off the kitchen drew his attention. AJ saw the muzzle flash come from the laundry room and heard the glass shatter almost simultaneously with Allison's groan.

AJ bolted inside to get past Dani in her chair so he could return fire to cover Allison. AJ fired two rounds as he moved.

At the last second Stalker lowered the muzzle aimed at Chad's head and intentionally shot him in the back on the right, followed by a shot at Dani who screamed.

He's not even shooting at me, AJ thought.

AJ shot a quick volley of six rounds where he last saw the muzzle flash.

He heard the door leading into the garage squeak and seconds later heard at least three shots out front. AJ figured Allison had worked her way back and engaged him. He moved up to Dani and Chad. Instantly AJ knew David shot them both. Dani's seemed superficial, Chad's wasn't. His head had slumped forward and it looked like he had a through-and-through shot in his right lung area.

AJ ran through the laundry room and when he opened the garage door AJ saw the trail of blood and knew he hit David. He saw what looked like a bloody slide mark on the garage floor up to the door. AJ pushed the opener on the wall twice, the blood on the driveway coming into focus as the door ascended.

AJ presumed the tires he heard squealing were David fleeing the area, but he had to find Allison first. He started yelling her name and heard her respond from the backyard. AJ ran to check on her and discovered a shard of glass stuck in her left eye. She said she dropped down behind the doorframe for cover and waited. AJ guided Allison inside to the kitchen.

AJ called it in to dispatch, first asking for ambulances, then requesting they put out a BOL on David's car.

"Where's Bethany?" AJ asked Dani.

"Bethany. I don't know Bethany. I never saw anyone else. Hurry please, Chad needs help."

AJ assured her ambulances were coming and he started calling Bethany's name while he checked the other parts of the house.

"Oh my God, Detective Conti, he took some duct tape outside," Dani said.

"I'm sorry, I'm sorry. In all of the gunfire and us being shot, I forgot Chad whispered to me earlier he heard someone yelling from inside the trunk of the black car."

With her one eye covered Allison said, "Go, go."

AJ ran outside and cut across the lawn towards his car. He almost reached the sidewalk when he saw the flat tires.

David's last three shots, he thought.

AJ ran back to get Allison's keys and told her to call dispatch so they could start pinging Bethany's phone again, the same one they did earlier.

"I'll be going where I think he might be headed. Tell them to let me know as fast as they can."

CHAPTER EIGHTY

The odds, or so AJ believed, were David's house or Bethany's. Something inside told him David had no reason to take her to his house, he had every reason to take her to hers. A house should be a person's castle, their sanctuary from evil. He had already proven he could get into hers, and considering the bad things AJ presumed likely happened to David in foster homes, it seemed like the place he would try to finish things.

AJ drove east towards Geer Road following his instincts while he waited to hear from dispatch. His phone rang and when he saw Bethany's name on the screen he pulled over to answer.

"Detective, is the other officer injured?" Stalker asked. "I only intended to shoot through the glass as a distraction."

AJ could not believe what he heard. Stalker shot his sister, he shot the man who saved her, and he had AJ's fiancé held hostage. Yet, the good inside of him seemed worried about having hurt one of the officers.

"She is a detective. And yes, she got a shard of glass in her eye."

"Please tell her I'm sorry."

"Where's Bethany. I want to talk to her."

"I'm sorry. Not right now."

"David, I'm not calling you Stalker anymore. You have a good side to you. I'm not trying to minimize what happened to you, I'm only saying, you aren't a typical killer and you have the capability for empathy. You care about a lot of things. I'm asking you to care about mine and Bethany's future."

The silence lasted for nearly thirty seconds.

"Detective, I have been thinking about this for many years. I can't stop now."

"You can, I know you. You have a strong sense of right versus wrong. You can do the right thing here."

"We'll call you back." Beep, beep, beep.

AJ felt almost certain they were headed to Bethany's, so he headed north toward Hughson. He was passing through the Keyes Road intersection when the phone rang again.

Yes, she's okay, AJ thought as he answered it.

"AJ…my dear AJ," the fear in her tone palpable.

Hearing Bethany's voice AJ's heart started pounding.

David listened, he thought.

"Bethany, I'm headed your way. I know you are at your house, right?"

"AJ," her voice softened with a resoluteness to it.

"I love you…I'll always love you. You'll be okay, I'm—" Whoosh, a faint sound of the rush of air. Flop. The phone remained on but muffled.

"Bethany! Are you there? Bethany?"

BEEP, BEEP, BEEP. The phone went dead.

"*No,* you can't," AJ screamed.

The police radio came alive and Brenda spoke to him. She had always been like a rock, never tension in her voice. This time her voice quivered, eerily similar to Bethany's as she told AJ what he already knew…Bethany was in her own home. AJ punched the accelerator, taking the car to its max.

Rounding the last corner AJ saw the car in the driveway with the driver's door and the trunk open.

AJ heard Brenda say backup would arrive in one to two minutes…an eternity for AJ to wait. He couldn't.

AJ sprinted as fast as he could, his Glock in his hand, praying for the opportunity.

He paused to listen at the front door left ajar. Silence, so loud it almost took his breath away.

AJ entered…wanting, needing something…movement, noise, screaming, gunfire. He needed something. Nothing seemed out of place, except for the blood trail AJ hoped came from his earlier rounds to David. The throbbing of his heart pounded in his ears.

He moved to the hallway, a fatal funnel in its own right. AJ didn't care, he needed to get to her. The spare rooms were clear, the open door at the end of the hall lured him closer.

The bloody handprint on the open door to the master bedroom appeared like a seductive mistress, inviting him in.

Maybe she fought back. Please be alive?

AJ knew he should not go in but knowledge alone would not hold him back.

The quick look around the doorframe made his knees buckle. AJ's peripheral vision departed, overtaken by a whiteness surrounding David. His lifeless body lying on the bed, holding his Bowie knife stuck deep in his heart. His dead staring eyes aligned on the doorway. The writing in blood on the wall above him meant for AJ.

I'm sorry, Detective.
She chose my path.
My purgatory, thanks to foster care.
She took my opportunity of a good life from me.

I have now returned the favor.
Stalker

The whiteness cleared and AJ scanned the room. He saw her foot on the opposite side of the bed. AJ rushed to her, the shock of her blood everywhere stopping him. His legs were like weights.

He fell to her side, taking her outstretched hand, praying for a pulse that didn't exist. Her eyes were fixed open and her chest remained still.

In his head AJ could hear her. *"I thought you were going to save me."*

AJ gently lifted her head into his lap, tears flowing down his cheeks.

CHAPTER EIGHTY-ONE

A J sat in the darkness of his house, thankful everyone finally had left. Their hearts were in the right place, wanting to make sure he would be okay...whatever that meant. Exhaustion from crying had set in hours ago.

Seeing Allison had been good for him. Hearing her say she would be fine along with hearing the prognosis about no vision problems helped him relax knowing her career would not be over. The best part though, he got to switch roles for a brief time.

Comforting her about Bethany's death not being her fault took AJ away from having the very same feeling. Hearing himself tell Allison how Bethany wanted nothing to do with taking precautions, refusing to let her life be dictated by a zealot, helped AJ to rationalize a horrific outcome, even if only in some small way.

Seth and Teri made sure AJ had everything he needed, with Teri becoming the *keeper of the key* on who could get through his front door. Before they left AJ asked Seth to get him the hospital room numbers for Dani and Chad, telling Seth he would probably want to see them in a few days. Truthfully he longed to see them alive right then.

AJ arrived at the hospital on autopilot, having no recollection of how he got there. Despite being beyond visitor hours he had no expectation of being turned away. His guns were in evidence lockup, but he still had his badge. Spoken to in the right way, nurses do not refuse a badge through the door.

When AJ walked in the semi-private room he saw the lights turned off to the left, the curtain back against the wall exposing a made bed. To his right the area was lit, the curtain pulled partially around the bed. AJ heard a nurse's voice tell someone she would be back shortly to check on Chad's vital signs.

When the nurse came around the end of the bed she pulled the curtain back. AJ held up his badge. She winked and kept going, leaving the room.

Dani looked up from the chair next to Chad's bed. Her eyes began to fill with tears as she ran over to AJ, hugging him tightly. Somewhere inside of him, AJ knew what she needed to hear. Holding her, tears rolling down his cheeks, he had to reach very deep inside to help her.

AJ stepped away from her, his hands on her shoulders.

"Please, whatever you do, do not ask yourself 'why me.' Bethany would be thrilled you both lived. She would love knowing you have the opportunity for long and productive lives together. She wouldn't want it any other way. Please, honor her, do not allow yourself to wonder."

Dani nodded her head, hugging AJ again.

"Can I ask you something?"

AJ tilted his head and slightly raised his eyebrows as he nodded.

"Why did you risk your…I mean, Tom Sullivan, the tools, the DA, everything?"

AJ paused, softly cupping her hand in his.

"Sometimes doing the proper thing doesn't fit nicely

inside the confines of a statute, or even a standard operating procedure. It's about integrity, about doing the appropriate thing over what is expected. Right is always right."

Tears began to form in the corners of her eyes. She squeezed his hand, and hugged him, tightly. Her way of thanking him as the tears freely rolled down her cheeks.

AJ appreciated finding out Chad's surgery went well, comforted by the knowledge he would make a full recovery. Dani had already been released, the graze wound to her left arm bandaged. They sat together for several hours, often going long periods of time without a word, most of it with her holding AJ's hand while resting her head on his shoulder.

AJ's heart had been shattered, yet somewhere in the mess left behind, it ached for Dani. Her twin brother had been lost to her years before, and in the same day he returned to her life, only to leave it again for good.

"You know, David loved you."

"What?" she said, her shoulders moving away from him as she looked him straight in the eyes.

"He went from a bad situation to a worse one, over and over. He did not have the help you had to get through it all. He wanted you to suffer certainly, still, when it came down to it, he lightly wounded you. His love for you meant he could not kill you."

She stared for some time, and turned to look at Chad. When she looked back at him, AJ could tell she understood. David might not have been able to kill her, but he did want her to suffer, so he tried to kill Chad. Knowing Chad would fully recover, AJ hoped that somewhere inside of her, she could hold on to the belief her twin brother possessed a special tenderness for her…even if others could never see it.

When AJ walked in his house at three in the morning he turned on nearly every light he could. His body wanted sleep, yet his mind recalled what happens after critical incidents like these. AJ was not ready to face the demonic aftershock of nightmares he knew would come.

He opened a bottle of Bethany's favorite wine, grabbed two glasses, and went out onto the back porch. Staring at the moon, AJ toasted her for her strength and courage. With tears running down his cheeks he toasted her for making him a better person.

I miss you, Bethany. I'll always love you.

THE END